"A slow-building, delicious romance wrapped in a mystery that unfolds with tantalizing clues to keep you guessing! I am a fan of Jennifer Deibel, and I think you will be too!"

Erica Vetsch, author of the Thorndike & Swann Regency Mysteries

Praise for *The Lady of Galway Manor*

"Deibel beautifully recreates Galway's sights and sounds."

BookPage starred review

"Deibel deftly weaves fascinating details about Irish history and culture into the plot of her latest sweetly romantic love story, with an underscoring of the importance of compassion and faith in our lives that could not be more timely."

Booklist

"A gem of a novel set in the Emerald Isle, *The Lady of Galway Manor* immerses you in a world of differing loyalties, histories, and expectations in 1920s Ireland. Well done!"

Laura Frantz, Christy Award–winning author of *A Heart Adrift*

Praise for *A Dance in Donegal*

"Deibel's exemplarily executed debut is a touching tale of love and forgiveness that also beautifully captures the warmth and magic of 1920s Ireland. The author's flair for vivid characterization is especially striking in Moira, whose realistic struggles with her faith give her memorable depth and relatability."

"Deibel's descriptions of Ireland's landscape, enticing cuisine, sonorous language, and vibrant culture converge to form a spectacular background for the story."

"God's redemptive love is the highlight of this debut work. Fans of historical Christian romances in the vein of Kristi Ann Hunter and Jen Turano will want to keep an eye on Deibel."

"Jennifer Deibel's debut is rich in atmosphere, family mystery, and sweet romance. A gem!"

"With an authenticity born of having lived in Ireland herself, the author deftly paints a lush landscape, colorful customs, and memorable characters with personal journeys of their own. Certain to appeal to fans of historical romance, this impressive debut marks Jennifer Deibel as an author to watch."

The
MAID *of*
BALLYMACOOL

Books by Jennifer Deibel

A Dance in Donegal
The Lady of Galway Manor
The Maid of Ballymacool

The

MAID *of*
BALLYMACOOL

A NOVEL

JENNIFER DEIBEL

Revell

a division of Baker Publishing Group
Grand Rapids, Michigan

© 2023 by Jennifer Deibel

Published by Revell
a division of Baker Publishing Group
PO Box 6287, Grand Rapids, MI 49516-6287
www.revellbooks.com

Printed in the United States of America

Library of Congress Cataloging-in-Publication Data
Names: Deibel, Jennifer, 1978– author.
Title: The maid of Ballymacool / Jennifer Deibel.
Description: Grand Rapids, Michigan : Revell, a division of Baker Publishing Group, [2023]
Identifiers: LCCN 2022020830 | ISBN 9780800742713 (casebound) | ISBN 9780800741747 (paperback) | ISBN 9781493439768 (ebook)
Subjects: LCGFT: Novels.
Classification: LCC PS3604.E3478 M35 2023 | DDC 813/.6—dc23
LC record available at https://lccn.loc.gov/2022020830

This is a work of historical reconstruction; the appearances of certain historical figures are therefore inevitable. All other characters, however, are products of the author's imagination, and any resemblance to actual persons, living or dead, is coincidental.

Published in association with Books & Such Literary Management, www.booksand such.com.

Baker Publishing Group publications use paper produced from sustainable forestry practices and post-consumer waste whenever possible.

23 24 25 26 27 28 29   7 6 5 4 3 2 1

For my Heavenly Father—
may these words point to Your Name and Your Renown

For my parents, Jerry and Bonnie Martin—
thank you for giving me a firm foundation of
faith, family, and identity rooted in Christ

For the soul who feels unseen—
may you find in these pages the reality that
you're more seen, more known, and more
treasured than you could have ever dreamed

1

The slap had hit its mark, leaving a burning outline Brianna was certain showed perfectly on her cheek. Despite the sting, she refused to press her hand against it. She wouldn't give Mistress Magee the satisfaction. As the woman continued to rail about Brianna's endless list of short-comings, Brianna plotted out the route for her afternoon treasure hunt. She'd never call it thus to Mistress Magee. No, to that woman it was a *daily constitutional*—a phrase that always conjured images of outhouses and pig slop rather than the walk of a proper lady. Not that it mattered much. Maureen Magee, headmistress of Ballymacool House and Boarding School for Girls, saw to it that Brianna was reminded of the depths of her station daily. Nothing befitting a lady befitted Brianna. But that didn't bother her. Not really. All she needed were her walks in the woods, her treasures, and the good Lord. A friend wouldn't hurt though. Not that Magee would ever allow it.

"Do you hear me, girl?" The headmistress's strident voice pierced Brianna's thoughts.

She swallowed a sigh. "Yes, marm."

"Then you know what you're to do?" The severe lines on the woman's face hardened with judgment, serving to further age her. "Well, child? Do you?" Mistress Magee straightened her posture, cupped her fingers together at her waist, and waited, impatience flashing in her steely eyes.

Child? Brianna was twenty, yet Mistress Magee perpetually treated her like she was still a snot-nosed five-year-old. "Aye, miss." At a spark of indignation from her guardian, Brianna corrected herself. "Yes, marm." In truth, Brianna had heard nothing of what the woman had instructed, but she didn't need to. Mistress Magee piled on the same litany of extra chores any time Brianna deigned to show her humanity. Today's egregious error? Not having the morning's porridge pot scrubbed and shining prior to the students finishing breakfast. Never mind that Brianna had been kept busy clearing dishes, wiping spills, and the like. That mattered not. All that mattered were Mistress Magee's everchanging whims and Brianna's inability to meet them.

"Very well." Mistress Magee punctuated her thought with a sharp nod. "You know what's expected. See that you carry it out. Forthwith." She turned to leave, paused, then peered over her shoulder at Brianna, waiting.

"Yes, marm." Brianna swiped a sponge from the table and plunged it into a basin of water, then knelt and began scrubbing the massive copper pot.

Mistress Magee nodded again, a quiet "*humph*" escaping her lips before she swept from the hot, stuffy kitchen.

Once alone, Brianna plopped back onto her heels, finally

allowing the deep sigh she'd been holding in to press out, releasing with it all the tension Mistress Magee's presence always cultivated. Tempted to let bitterness take root, she closed her eyes and imagined she was sitting at the base of her tree. She could almost feel the coolness of the damp earth seeping through her skirt, the gentle breeze tickling her skin, cooling the ache that still pulsed on her cheek from Mistress Magee's strike. Whispering a prayer for strength and endurance, she retrieved the sponge and resumed scrubbing.

As she worked the filth from the pot, her anger lightened and lifted away. A plunking sound and a gentle splash shook Brianna from her thoughts. Another leak? A quick glance at the ceiling revealed nothing. Peering into the pot, panic jolted her. She grasped at her neck and chest. *My pendant!* She plunged her hand into the murky water, ignoring the sludge collecting at the bottom, and worked until her fingers found what they sought. She curled them around the chain, then sloshed her prize a bit to clear the muck away and pulled it out of the water.

She wiped it as gently and as quickly as she could with her apron and then inspected it closely. All appeared to be intact—as intact as it had ever been, anyway. Clearly only a broken piece of a larger pendant, its edges worn by time, it was bordered with double lines accented with several fleurs de lis. Within the borders lay three stamped flowers. Brianna ran her thumb over the flowers, imagining her mother had once done the same. It was all she had that connected her to her family and long-forgotten past. She'd been left with it around her neck, even as a small infant, Mistress Magee had told her long ago. Before her hatred of Brianna had fully set in.

She clasped her hand around the shard and then opened it again to view the back of the trinket. Letters that seemed to have been hastily carved by hand stretched across the surface. Only part of a word. The *c*, *o*, and *n* were clearly visible. Another letter, or part of one, was slashed in half by the broken edge. How many hours had she spent daydreaming about what those letters might spell? What they might mean? But there was no time for that now. If she was to have any hope of a walk in the woods today, she must hasten in finishing her tasks.

She worked the chain through her fingers until they reached the ends and refastened the clasp. The battered chain often came open and fell from her neck. And it had done so even more of late. Slipping it over her head, Brianna tucked the pendant into the bodice of her dress, praying it would stay. She needed a new chain. Since she did not receive any wages for her labors at the house—she was "earning her keep," according to Mistress Magee—the only way to procure one would be if she happened across one on one of her walks. But she knew better than to hope for such good fortune. Her years in the Ballymacool woods had taught her that treasure never reveals itself to the greedy, but rather the grateful. And so, as she plunged her hands into the now-cool water, she ran through her list of all that for which she was grateful.

The library was dark and quiet—just how Michael preferred it. The fire that had been laid down that morning was now nothing more than an orange glow. The curtains were drawn, shadowing the room in the blissful gray of an indoor dusk. For any other household, that might seem odd at this time of day, but not for Castle Wray. Michael snorted at the name for the house situated in the heart of the Castlewray Estate. Although a grand five-bay, two-story stone house, it was not quite what he would consider a castle. And after a long morning of managing the sprawling property—one of the few ascendency estates still in operation—a quiet afternoon with a good book was just what he needed.

Filling his lungs with the beloved musty scent of old books, stale tobacco, and a turf fire, he sauntered across the room to his favorite shelf. W. B. Yeats, George Moore, George William Russell, and others lined up like old friends ready to welcome Michael back into the folds of their confidence. Few things stirred Michael's heart and refreshed his spirit like an inspiring read, much to his mother's dismay. Other things more befitting a man of his age and station did so as well, though not to the same degree as words on the page. A bracing ride on his trusty steed, Cara, a rousing game of cards, or a well-brewed cup of tea or pint of ale all served to bolster his spirits after a trying day. But given his druthers, Michael would choose the quiet library—or a tree-canopied forest—and a familiar tome every time.

No sooner had he removed his book of choice from its spot than his parents spun into the room. His mother, equal parts the portrait of decorum and yet all a dither, fanned herself briefly before patting her hair and setting her shoulders, returning to the proper state of an ascendancy class lady of Letterkenny. Michael's father, tall and stoic as ever, clasped his hands behind his back and rocked forward and back on his toes once before settling his gaze on Michael.

"Good day, son," he greeted him. His words wished him

well, but his tone implied something else altogether. *Wasting the day away reading again, I see?* is what Michael imagined his father truly meant to say. Michael absently wondered why his father went through the expense of having such an expansive library if it was so wasteful to use it.

Michael set the book on a nearby table. "Father. Mother." He closed the distance between them and placed a brief kiss on his mother's cheek, having to bend at the waist to reach her face. She pressed into the kiss, but then rubbed her fingers where his dark mustache and beard had tickled her.

His father cleared his throat and glanced at his wife, who summoned the maid. With a flick of Mrs. Wray's wrist, the maid scurried to the tall windows and tied back the curtains. Michael flinched at the bright afternoon sun and breech of his solitude. Opening the drapes felt like inviting the whole of the estate to gawk at the family's daily goings-on. At *his* goings-on. Michael would always choose to be out among the people, preferring the company of the down-to-earth farmers to the pompous showboats of high society. With rumblings of trouble brewing again in Germany, the men his father rubbed elbows with would be insufferable as the group passed around their self-proclaimed vast knowledge of world events and warfare. But there were times it just seemed easier to hide away from it all. And that had been his aim for today.

Gesturing to a settee in front of the fireplace, his father crossed the room and placed his hand on the thick wooden mantelpiece. "I've a job for you, Michael."

Michael sank onto the seat. "Oh?" It wasn't unusual for his father to give him tasks. It was, however, unusual for the job description to come with such a fuss and formality.

"Indeed." His father swiped at a speck of something on the mantel that wasn't really there, brushed his fingers together, and turned to face Michael and his mother. "It's your cousin. Adeline."

Michael fought to hide the wince that naturally contorted his face at the sound of his cousin's name. A fourteen-year-old spoiled brat, who seemed to have placed Michael on a pedestal. Whether it was childish infatuation or idolization of him and his stable home life, he didn't know. But he did know that Adeline succeeded in bringing utter chaos wherever she went. Managing to keep his composure, he responded, "What about Adeline?"

"It seems she's having some trouble settling in over at Ballymacool." His father paced slowly in front of the dying fire.

Michael swallowed a guffaw. "Settling in? Father, 'tis been nearly a year!"

Ignoring the comment, Father continued. "The other girls have been . . . less than welcoming."

Next to Michael, his mother *tsked*. "You know how young girls can be," she added, wagging her head.

I know how she *can be.* He blinked the thought away before it could escape his mouth.

"Adeline just needs some guidance," his mother added. "And a strong presence to deter any further . . ." She circled her hand in the air and studied the carpet beneath them as though searching for just the right word.

"Incidents," his father finished for her.

"Incidents?"

Mother sighed. "'Twould seem the girl has been somewhat . . . antagonistic . . . toward the other students."

"Truth is"—Father cleared his throat—"she's put somewhat of a target on her back and needs a watchful eye."

Michael rose and absently twisted the whiskers of his mustache. "I see." Though he didn't really. What had this to do with him? "What of Uncle Thomas? Can he not intercede?"

His father snatched the copy of Russell's *Awakening* from the table where Michael had left it a few moments ago and shoved the book on a shelf. The wrong shelf. "You know very well Thomas has his hands full with all the nonsense going on down there. Being so close to Dublin has increased the troubles on his estate a hundredfold compared to ours. It's the whole reason Adeline was sent to Ballymacool rather than Kylemore to begin with. I must continue with the duties of running Castlewray Estate, and your mother has her society engagements to keep up. So, it falls to you."

Michael tugged the book from its misplacement and settled it in its rightful spot. *And what am I to know of the problems of a young girl?* He dismissed the thought as soon as it materialized. He knew full well any problems dear old Adeline was having were of her own making and not of the emotional variety. She didn't need a confidant. She needed a bodyguard. Since Adeline was Thomas's only child, she truly had no one to fill this purpose. Heaven forbid Father step away from his haughty circle of cigar-smoking pseudogentry to fulfill a true family obligation.

Gripping the bookshelf, Michael squeezed his eyes shut and whispered a silent prayer of forgiveness for having such a callous attitude toward his father. "Very well," he said on a sigh. He scratched at his beard and his mother winced. She hated that he refused to keep the clean-shaven face of a proper society man. The corner of his mouth turned up slightly, taking pleasure in the small rebellion. "When do I leave?"

"Directly."

Michael's jaw fell slack. "So soon? Is the situation so dire?"

"Not dire, but it requires expediency." His father's tone left no room for argument. "And you're to be there at least a fortnight. Perhaps longer."

Michael coughed. "*Stay* there? Father, Ballymacool 'tis only fifteen miles west. I can easily travel back and forth each day."

"You could, but you won't. Adeline needs someone there 'round the clock. And you're the man."

"Ballymacool House has some lovely cottages on their grounds for visiting family members and the like," Mother added. "They've got one already prepared for you, as they agree this is the best course of action."

Michael tried to ignore the fact that such plans would've taken quite some time to make. But since he couldn't stomach another debate, he chose to concede. "Very well."

"Aidan has your horse ready to go and your effects as well. Godspeed, son."

A puff of air blew from Michael's lips before he could stop it. At least his father had had the courtesy to allow Michael to use Cara instead of the blasted motorcar. He'd never trust those contraptions. At length, he shook his head, then accepted his father's outstretched hand and shook it. He ran his fingers through his thick hair and down the back of his neck before hugging his mother. "Good day, Mother. Father. I'll send word if I've need of anything."

2

Astride Cara not fifteen minutes later, Michael stared out at the waters of the North Atlantic. He loved this spot in front of Castle Wray. He watched as the frigid waters of the River Swilly widened and emptied into the sea after snaking through the city—the county, really. How often as a lad had he envisioned pirates or Vikings silently floating on the current, ready for adventure? He'd longed to join them for a life of excitement. He thought of his current quest while turning his mount to the west. *Not quite the adventure I had in mind.* He'd follow the river all the way to Ballymacool, though once he arrived, the waters would have narrowed significantly more than here at the foot of the powerful waterway.

The mid-September sun hung suspended in a mist-shrouded sky, scattering golden filtered rays like candlelight through gauze. The afternoon air held a refreshing chill, and the quaint spread of emerald hills and the glistening river snaking through the countryside bolstered his spirit. At a comfortable pace for both man and steed, the journey would take just over an hour.

A light breeze played with the ends of his hair that spilled out from beneath his flatcap and rested at the nape of his neck. He lifted his face to the sky, once again grateful for the hour of solitude to enjoy the natural world before plunging into the altogether unnatural world of Adeline and her incessant fawning over Michael.

Filling his lungs, he urged Cara onward, all the while steeling himself for what lie ahead.

The journey passed uneventfully, though it took longer than Michael had budgeted. Every manner of farmer and shepherd wanted to say hello and discuss the weather. Every conversation had been much the same as the one before, but Michael loved it. There was something so authentic about his encounters with folk in the real world, outside of his ever-tightening ascendency class circles. The interactions stirred something within him. Something he'd tried to stuff down but found increasingly difficult to keep at bay. An inexplicable pull to more. Like a leaf swept into the river's current, his spirit seemed powerless against this call to a different life—nae, to a purposeful life.

After he arrived at Ballymacool House and Boarding School for Girls, Michael slid out of the saddle and offered a fresh apple to his mount. The house loomed before them, towering a full three stories, every line and angle severe as shards of glass. Pairs of windows gawked out over the front garden from both the first and second floors, and a wider rectangular window peered down from the third. What would typically be a charming gabled roof on a humble bungalow, on Ballymacool appeared to pierce the sky ominously, like the tips of swords, three across. Chimneys polluted the skyline above, and the complete absence of plant life in the ten yards surrounding the building added to the sterile atmosphere. Only Ballymacool Wood, stretching east and south of the estate, softened the scene. For a place overrun with the gentler sex, the whole atmosphere lacked the softness of a woman's touch.

The tall door creaked open, and Michael startled as a slender woman in a floor-length black dress appeared on the stoop.

Michael resisted the instinct to flinch at the sight of her. *Oh.*

Equally as severe as the building she occupied, the woman had hair pulled so tightly into a bun at the back of her head, Michael feared it would tug her backward.

"Mister Wray, I presume?" The coolness in her voice tensed the muscles in Michael's shoulders.

He forced a cordial smile onto his face and removed his hat. "Good day, Miss . . ." He approached her with his hand outstretched.

"Magee," she hissed, eyeing his hand before taking it for the briefest of moments. "Not a moment too soon. Though, I must say, we expected you earlier. This way, please." She spun on her heel and headed into the darkened interior, not looking to see whether Michael followed.

Sooner? How much earlier could I have come? Opting not to raise the woman's hackles any further, he rushed into the house behind her. "I do apologize fer the delay," he replied. "However, I'm here now and plan to stay as long as is needed."

Mistress Magee stopped in a doorway halfway down a short hall and faced Michael again. Her left brow cocked and something in her expression suggested she doubted if there were enough time left on earth to set things right. In truth, Michael shared the sentiment.

He followed her into a dimly lit room, modestly outfitted with a wall of bookshelves behind a large desk, a small fireplace on the eastern wall, and two of the windows he'd seen from the outside on the western one. Mistress Magee circled around behind the desk and gestured for Michael to sit in one of the chairs opposite her. He did as she bade.

"Now, Mister Wray." She lowered herself into her own seat and busied herself adjusting an already straightened stack of papers. She opened her mouth as if to continue, then closed it and let her attention shift to the window. Michael wondered if she was tempering her words, given his family's station . . . and that of Adeline's. The light filtering through the panes made her skin almost translucent.

"Your cousin has had a difficult time adjusting to the routine of Ballymacool House," she continued.

Michael lofted his eyebrows in mock surprise. "Ya don't say?" He worked to keep the sarcasm from lacing his voice.

"*Mmm.*" Mistress Magee turned her full attention back to him. "The other girls have been quite . . . agitated by her arrival. Adeline is . . . a unique young lady."

"Unique, indeed." Michael crossed his ankle over his knee. "And she's caused a bit of a rift, has she?"

"Oh!" Eyes wide, Mistress Magee patted the air. "I'm not saying the blame lies with her." She cleared her throat. "Not *solely* with her, at any rate. But the fact remains that the whole of Ballymacool House has been in upheaval, and

I simply can't abide that. This house runs on rules and decorum. Without those, well, we must restore order. And that is where I hope you may be of some assistance."

Michael scratched at his beard and studied the woman. He could see how a young girl could be intimidated by her . . . and how Adeline would immediately see her as a challenge to be conquered. "My father mentioned something about Adeline needin' protection?"

"From herself more than anything. But until she is more settled, we thought it best the other girls see a member of her family here to deter any further . . . mischief."

Michael could only imagine what sort of "mischief" Adeline could inspire from a gaggle of young ladies. Threat of personal violence was more like it. *A swift kick in the backside might do the girl some good.* He swallowed a chuckle. "Yes, o' course. I'm here to help however I can."

Magee nodded and stood. "If you'll come this way, I'll show you to your quarters."

Michael followed the woman out of the office and down the corridor toward the back of the house. The walls paneled in dark wood created a cave-like atmosphere, and the only sound to be heard was the clacking of Mistress Magee's sturdy bootheels on the polished wood floor. For a house full of girls, everything was oddly quiet. Perhaps they were at study.

They took a sharp right and escaped into the back garden. An expansive lawn flanked by gorse bushes and hawthorn trees stretched before them. Some low thatched shed buildings lined the eastern edge. A narrow slate walkway broke off to the south heading into the woods. At the tree line stood several whitewashed, single-story cottages. Mistress Magee stopped at the second one. She unlocked the door and held the key out to Michael.

"This is where you'll stay for the duration of your visit. You'll find everything you need. If you wish to take your meals with us, dinner is served promptly at six o'clock. Though, be advised, the teaching staff does not live on-site and therefore typically dine in their own homes." She side-stepped him, then added, "Is there anything else you need, Mister Wray?" Though her question hung in the air, the look on her face reflected her desire that he not say anything.

He peered into the open door. "No, thank you. I am grateful fer the hospitality."

She nodded gravely and clacked her way down the stone path that sliced through the lawn.

Michael slid the door closed behind him and squinted at the dark interior of the cottage. Though not a mansion by any means, it was more spacious than it had appeared from the outside. The main room consisted of a sitting area near the turf-burning fireplace to the right of the front door. To the left stood a small cast-iron stove, a rustic wooden table, and a kitchen press that held a small set of dishes, teapot, and the like. While nowhere near the standard of Castle Wray, the furnishings were in good repair, and the whole room had a very cozy and welcoming atmosphere—unlike the main house and his hostess.

A doorway off the back of the kitchen caught his attention. Further inspection revealed it to be the bedroom. Sliding his hands into his pockets, Michael circled the cottage interior once again, quite unsure what to do with himself. He checked his pocket watch. Five o'clock. A full hour until dinnertime. He'd no idea what Adeline's schedule was, and he wasn't of the mind to seek her out just yet. A small stack of books on the mantelpiece caught his attention. Just as he was about to lift the first one from its place, a knock sounded at the door.

Stifling a groan, Michael crossed the room once again to open the door.

A wiry-haired man with a hunched back and a twinkle in his eyes smiled up at Michael. "Afternoon, Mister Wray. I took the liberty of stabling yer horse an' bringing yer effects to ye."

Michael stepped aside to allow the man to enter. "Much obliged, Mister . . ."

"Bartholomew Murphy's me name. But folk here call me Batty." A wheezy chuckle squeezed from Batty's chest, and he shuffled past Michael, his arms laden with all he'd packed. In truth, Michael had forgotten all about Cara and his bags. He reached into his pocket and pulled out a one-pound coin and held it toward the old man.

"*Wheesht.*" Batty flapped his hand in the air. "There'll be none o' that from ye, Mister Wray. But t'anks all the same." He swiped his sleeve across his forehead. "This is what the mistress pays me fer." Another raspy laugh bubbled out of the man's lips.

Heat crept up Michael's neck to his cheeks. He nodded and slipped the coin back in his pocket. "Very well, then. I thank ya very much."

Batty hooked his thumb toward the door. "The stables are just round the corner after the last cottage. Ya wouldn't know it's there to just look, but it's there. Ye're welcome to grab yer trusty steed anytime ya like. If ye want her saddled and ready for ya, just let me or my stable hand, Pádhraig, know." Batty had already started shuffling toward the door. He yanked a flatcap out of his back trouser pocket and shoved it on his head. "Good day to ya, sir."

Michael smiled and nodded. "And to you, Batty. And thanks again."

Batty shut the door in his wake, and Michael grabbed his bags and dragged them into the bedroom. Before he could open one, there was another knock at the door.

Good grief, we don't get this many callers at Castle Wray! He smiled to himself and hurried to open the door.

"Afternoon, sir. Mistress Magee said I should bring you some tea." A pair of eyes the color of dark sea glass stared up at him from a porcelain face. Michael's breath hitched as he took in the sight of the housemaid. A shock of red hair cascaded over her shoulder in a simple plait. She shifted her feet under his gaze and cleared her throat. "Well, if you don't want it, that's fine." She turned on her heel, taking care not to spill the tray.

"*Fan!*" Michael's call came out far louder than he'd intended.

She turned back, one brow hiked high—in interest or annoyance, Michael wasn't sure. He was sure, however, that he liked it. "Forgive me," he said. "Please, come in. And thank you."

The woman brought the tray in with the ease of someone who'd carried far heavier-laden trays a million times. Placing the tea service on the table, she spoke over her shoulder, "She also wanted me to remind ya that dinner's at six o'clock sharp." She wiped her hands on her apron and stepped toward the door.

"Thank you. I'll be there." Michael studied the woman's face. She was beautiful, aye, but there was something about her, something he couldn't place, that absolutely captivated him. "And you are?" He reached out to shake her hand.

"Brianna!" Mistress Magee's shrill call shattered the air between them.

The woman startled. She looked from Michael to the open door and back. "Brianna Kelly," she mumbled before grabbing his outstretched hand, shaking it, and scurrying from the cottage, leaving the scent of fresh bread and tea in her wake.

3

Brianna resisted the urge to look over her shoulder. She sensed Mister Wray's hazel eyes watching her from beneath his thick auburn hair that had fallen over his forehead, and it took every ounce of willpower she possessed to not find out for sure. As she scurried down the path, her mouth tipped up in a smile. Handsome men at Ballymacool were few and far between, and it did her no good to entertain thoughts of them beyond her duties. But at least there'd be a nicer view around Ballymacool for a few days.

Rounding the corner, she swept into the kitchen and nearly crashed into Mistress Magee.

"It's about time, girl." The woman's lips pursed, accentuating the lines around them, reminding Brianna of the bellows of a concertina. "Did I not tell you no dillydallying?"

"Yes, marm— er, ya did, marm." She tightened the frayed ribbon at the end of her braid. "I came back as quickly as I was able. Mister Wray took his time in decidin' whet'er or not he wanted the tea."

Magee snorted and looked down her nose at Brianna. "I've

never known an ascendant-class man to be slow in accepting anything"—her face darkened—"whether it was offered or not."

Unease twisted in Brianna's gut, and she wasn't sure how to respond. She opted for the safest option. "Yes, marm."

The older woman seemed lost in thought for a moment. She fiddled with the button on her sleeve cuff before blinking and pulling her posture even straighter. "Now, we've a dinner to serve." She rattled off the endless list of tasks that needed doing, while behind her, Cook rubbed the bridge of her nose. Brianna often wondered how she felt about Magee's need to have her hand in every little detail when Cook seemed perfectly capable of managing her own kitchen.

Brianna wagged her head, careful to do so while her guardian's head was turned. *Funny how she says* we *when it's always just me and Cook actually doing the work.* But Brianna was well versed in her tasks, well accustomed to the routine of Ballymacool. The table had long been set, the drinks had chilled, and an extra spate of cutlery and dinnerware was stacked by the door ready and waiting for the odd spill or dropped utensil. At the other end of the house, the meager servants' table was also set. Brianna would take her own meal much later, dining either on the kitchen floor or in the dark quiet of her bedroom when everyone else had retired for the night.

When the clock chimed quarter to six, she washed her face and hands, straightened her hair, and swapped out her dirty apron for a clean one. Though Magee had her wash up only to keep up the appearances of a house of means with a full-service staff, Brianna was grateful for the daily set of fresh togs. Once ready, Brianna ascended the three steps, pushed through the swinging door, and made her way to the dining hall where she took her place in the shadowed corner—there to be of service when needed. Otherwise, she was to be neither seen nor heard.

At the stroke of six, a rhythm like a steady drumbeat echoed from the stairwell in the hall. Mistress Magee entered through the double doors at the front of the room and stood aside as the girls filed in. In the well-rehearsed ritual they followed three times a day, the residents of Ballymacool paraded in, stepping in time with one another as they found their spots at the tables that were arranged according to age group and residence hallway.

When all were in their positions, Mistress Magee wheeled around behind her chair at the center of the head table. She eyed the empty seat next to hers and paused, scowling at it before folding her hands in front of her. "Let us pray," she began.

A rustle filled the dining room as seventy-five girls matched the headmistress's stance. When silence returned, she continued, "For all these gifts Thou hast bestowed upon us, may the Lord make us eternally grateful. Amen."

"Amen," the girls echoed. Chairs scraped against the wood floor and serviettes fluttered in the air as the residents settled in for the evening meal. Brianna slid out from her corner and made quick work of bringing large platters over. One by one, she placed them in equal intervals down the center of every table. The leader of each—older students Magee had assigned to the job—stood ready to help plate the food once it arrived. Quiet conversations ensued as the food was passed to each person, the whole routine operating like a well-oiled, if time-consuming, machine.

Mistress Magee was watching from her standing perch at the top of the room, a smug little smile on her face, when the double doors swung open and Michael Wray's tall, sturdy frame filled the space, the golden glow of the lantern light illuminating his chestnut hair. The smile melted from Magee's face as all movement and conversation ceased, and one girl—Brianna couldn't be sure who—let a low, slow whistle escape her lips. Mistress Magee shot a glare in the direction of the sound before turning her attention back to their guest.

Returning to her shadowed corner, Brianna's lips tilted up in a smile. *How exciting. Dinner and a show.*

Michael swallowed hard and resisted the urge to tug on his collar. He met his hostess's glare, and she inclined her head in a slight, swift motion. If Michael hadn't been looking right at her, he would've missed it. He pasted a cordial smile on his face and made his way to the head of the table to take his place next to the woman, keenly aware that every eye in the room tracked his every move. At the edge of the room, a familiar profile caught his attention. He glanced toward it to see Adeline, mouth agape in a crooked smile of surprise, adjusting her hair and straightening her posture. Michael turned his attention back to his destination, but not before he caught a wink thrown at him from his cousin.

"Ladies," Mistress Magee said, "please welcome our guest—Mister Michael Wray. He's going to be staying with us for the foreseeable future." A few excited gasps sounded throughout the group, and Michael gave the headmistress a sidelong glance. Foreseeable future? What happened to a fortnight?

"Mister Wray is cousin to our very own Adeline FitzGerald," Magee added. Grumbles rippled through the sea of girls. The rising ire in his chest took Michael off guard. Did he not hold the same feelings of disdain for the girl? But hearing such jeers from so many rose a protective nature within Michael—taking him by utter surprise.

Magee tipped her nose up and patted the air with her palms, shushing the girls. "Now, now, ladies. I trust you'll show Mister Wray the respect we are so well known for here at Ballymacool. Make no mistake, should there be any further . . . issues . . . among you involving Adeline, you will now deal directly with Mister Wray."

Michael scanned the crowd and met his cousin's eyes once again. Now, she sat with perfect posture, a look of pride with a hint of defiance painted on her face. She held Michael's gaze for a beat before eyeing the crowd, almost daring any of them to strike first.

After a long, awkward silence, Adeline looked to him once more and said, "Welcome, cousin!"

Mistress Magee nodded and in unison, the crowd uttered, "*Céad mile fáilte.*"

Magee sniffed and said dryly, "Yes, you're very welcome, indeed. Now, shall we eat?" She lowered into her seat and Michael followed suit. "I believe I told you dinner is at six o'clock sharp, Mister Wray," she reprimanded him under her breath.

Michael, in the process of flapping his serviette open over his lap, froze. "Indeed, ya did. I beg yer pardon for my tardiness." Inwardly, he scoffed that arriving at 6:01 might incur such wrath. Was there no grace given? No deference toward a clock that might be off a hair or an unforeseen obstacle on the path to the dining room?

"See to it that it doesn't happen again," Magee spoke to her plate. "And if it does, you're to take your meal in your cottage rather than disrupt my schedule."

"O'course," Michael mumbled around a painfully dry bite of fish.

The mealtime routine dragged on and on, and Michael found the whole routine tedious. The food, leaving much to be desired, was served in stages, and the students set their utensils down between each bite. When the marathon finally finished, Mistress Magee dismissed the girls, who rose in unison, pivoted on their heels, and filed out. Except for one. Adeline. She stood in the back, hands clasped behind her, swaying her shoulders back and forth like a small child waiting for an ice cream cone. Michael inwardly grimaced.

A loud clattering reverberated around the room, drawing the headmistress's attention to the table where Brianna worked. "Careful, Brianna!" she hissed.

Brianna kept her head down and only nodded. "Sorry, marm."

Magee clucked her tongue like the girl had dropped the heavy platter on purpose, then turned her attention to Adeline. "Miss FitzGerald, come greet your cousin." Magee curled her fingers inward, beckoning the child.

Adeline pasted a sickly-sweet smile on her face and all but skipped over. "Greetings, Michael." She batted her eyes and craned her neck, extending her cheek upward.

Michael's stomach turned, but he couldn't very well not greet his cousin in front of his host. Never quite sure how a simple kiss on the cheek from a cousin would be perceived by the girl, Michael made quick work of it, brushing his cheek against hers.

"How fare my aunt and uncle?" Adeline asked, her voice annoyingly sweet.

"Very well, thank you," he replied.

"I wish I were there." Her gaze drifted to Michael's face and for a split second the guile was gone. In that impossibly brief moment, Michael almost pitied the girl. From the corner of his eye, he noticed Brianna looking their way. He glanced at her briefly. Her eyes were wide and a hint of a smile mixed with curiosity played on her lips before she dropped her head to refocus her attention on the dishes.

Adeline stepped toward him. "'Twas good of you to come."

Clearing his throat, Michael eased back a pace. "Aye, well, when one's family is in need of aid . . ." He let the rest of the sentence hang in the air for fear he might say something inflammatory to incite his cousin's lightning-fast temper.

"Very good." Mistress Magee took Adeline's elbow. "You're already late for vespers and it will be lights out soon. You and your cousin can catch up more tomorrow."

"Can't I stay up just a little longer, marm? I haven't seen my cousin in ever so long!" Adeline's whine grated on Michael's nerves. The girl petted Magee's arm with one hand before turning toward Michael, her expression begging him to intervene.

Michael looked away, but not before catching Adeline shoot him a pouting look then turn doe eyes back at the headmistress.

Mistress Magee drew her lips together and shook her head. "Rules are rules, Miss FitzGerald, and routine is routine. In this house, we abide by both. Now, off with you before I get cross."

Adeline poked her bottom lip out before turning slowly, shoulders slumped, and slinking toward the door.

Magee looked to Michael. "You've got your work cut out for you, Mister Wray." She gestured toward the door and they began to make their way to it. "We'll need you most during recreation times and at meals. All other time is your own, though it wouldn't hurt for you to make your presence known during classes from time to time."

"Very well." The pair stopped in the hallway near the back door.

"I'll have a daily schedule of Adeline's activities brought to your cottage this evening."

Michael nodded and opened the door. "Much obliged, Mistress Magee. G'night."

The cool night air revived Michael's spirits as he made his way back to his cottage. But instead of going inside, he passed it and continued on the slate path, in search of the stables. He found them right where Batty had said they'd be—nestled at the end of the line of cottages before the tree line. The thatched roof glowed in the moonlight, while golden lantern light flowed from the windows and door. Inhaling deeply, Michael relished the mixed scent of damp soil, fresh night air, hay, and livestock. The world was impossibly silent. How did he always forget how much quieter it was outside the Letterkenny city limits? Even at Castlewray, there was the constant rushing of the River Swilly and an ever-increasing cacophony of sounds emanating from the city. But out here the silence was almost palpable. And Michael loved it.

After a quick visit to check on Cara and introduce himself to Batty's assistant, Pádhraig, Michael meandered back to his cottage. Rummaging around the kitchen area rewarded Michael with all the accoutrements for a bracing bedtime cuppa. How long since he'd brewed his own cup of tea? Taking great pleasure in each step of the process, he sat down to enjoy the fruit of his labors. But before he could take the first sip, a knock sounded at the door.

Confound it all. Is there never a moment's peace at Ballymacool?

Michael opened the door, teacup still in hand. "Oh, hello, Batty," he greeted the older gentleman, surprised by the genuine smile he felt spreading on his face.

"Oh, great day in the marnin', I've interrupted yer *cuppa ouiche.*" Batty *tsked* and wagged his head. "I'm about to go take my nightly cuppa m'self! Beggin' yer pardon, sir, and I won't be keepin' ya, but the mistress wanted me to bring this to ye afore tomorrow." He handed a piece of stationery to Michael. "It's the daily routine for that cousin o' yorn."

"Nothing ta be sorry for, Batty. Thanks very much." He smiled down at the man again when something in the distance caught his eye. Brianna was crossing the expansive lawn, her arms laden with firewood. Michael's brow furrowed, and Batty followed his gaze.

Batty blew a low whistle. "That Brianna's a right hard worker, she is."

Michael tried to ignore the way the moonlight danced on her hair and resisted the urge to run out and help her carry the wood into the house. "Does she always work this late into the evenin'?" In the distance, the church bells tolled ten o'clock.

Batty bobbed his head. "Oh, aye. She'll be goin' strong another hour or two. An' she'll be up afore dawn. Never seen a kitchen maid kept so busy." Batty flapped his hand in the direction the girl had gone. "Anyhow, yer tea's gettin' cold, and we can't have that. Good night to ye, Mister Wray." Batty tipped his flatcap and shuffled around the corner and out of sight.

His tea all but forgotten, Michael absently muttered his thanks and continued staring at the garden as if Brianna still stood there.

As he slid the door closed, a gentle resistance stayed the progress, and a grinding noise pulled his attention downward. Kneeling, he tugged at the hint of a chain poking out from under the door. Pulling it free and taking care not to break the worn links, he lifted a necklace to the light. A shard of a pendant twinkled in the dim light. He ran his thumb over the fading design—three gillyflowers surrounded by a double-walled border accented by a fleurs de lis. He shot a glance to the darkness outside. Perhaps Batty dropped it when he left? Then again, Michael couldn't imagine the old man sporting such a piece.

He slid the door closed with a muted thud and leaned against it a beat, letting his mind meander through any possible options there could be for an owner. Wrapping his fingers around the shard, ignoring how the edges dug into his palm, he retreated back to his seat by the dying fire.

He sank into a chair and examined the piece once more. He slid the chain between his fingers when, to his dismay, it broke into three sections. The links had clearly been worn long before getting stuck under his door, otherwise it wouldn't have fallen free of someone's neck so easily, but he couldn't help the sinking weight of responsibility on his chest for his part in it actually falling apart. Further examination confirmed there was no repairing it. He dropped his hands to his lap and racked his brain for what to do next.

Logic dictated it must belong to someone at the boarding school, so discovering who that was shouldn't prove too difficult—he hoped. He yanked his handkerchief from the inside breast pocket of his waistcoat and gently wrapped the pendant and chains. He'd deliver it to Mistress Magee in the morning. Surely she'd know who it belonged to and would return it to the rightful owner.

Brianna stifled a groan as she lumbered up the stairs to her attic room. Weariness always wrapped itself around her like a chain mail blanket at each day's end, and this day was no exception. Even with the excitement of the new guest, her mind fogged and her bones ached with fatigue. Indeed, the change in routine probably added to her exhaustion.

She sank onto her bed and rubbed the back of her neck, rolling her head from side to side to try to quell the ache from another day of hard labor. A shaft of moonlight flooded in from the small window at the top of the western wall and pooled in a silvery puddle on the rough wooden floor, drawing Brianna like a magnet. She crossed the room, then stood on an old crate that creaked under her weight and peered out over the quiet, slumbering world.

Orange light glowed from one of the guest cottages below, but other than that, all was dark and quiet. It was in these moments when Brianna felt most at peace . . . and most alone. The depth of her solitude settled on her like the stocks of old, pinning her in place in view of all of society. Absently, her hand drifted to her chest to grasp her pendant—the final vestige of connection to her family. Her blood chilled, and her breath caught as her fingers grasped at nothing but cloth. Where was it?

She dipped her hand into the bodice of her dress, searching, to no avail. Undressing hastily, she shook out each article of clothing, dread winding a tighter noose around her with each one. Standing in the center of the room in her shift, shivers overcame her—both from the chill of the night and the reality of her loss. With one last burst of adrenaline-fueled desperation, she clawed through the pile of clothing on her floor. Had it fallen off as she cleaned the kitchen? It couldn't have. It would have shown itself when she swept the floor before heading to bed. Panic threatened to erupt, but she forced herself to steady her breath and slow her thoughts. She'd been myriad places other than just the kitchen throughout the course of the day. She would most likely find it in the dust of the woodshed or concealed amid the thick blades of grass in the courtyard or any of a countless number of other places.

No, she wouldn't panic. She refused. She couldn't deny her life at times held elements of magic—nae, whimsy—what with her treasure finds in the woods and such, but in reality, logic and reason always won out. She'd retrace every step in the morning, and she'd surely find her necklace somewhere along the well-worn paths she trod daily.

Lifting her gaze, she whispered a prayer for favor to the diamonds hanging in the darkened sky, imagining *Tiarna*

Dia sitting behind the bejeweled curtain, listening. The windowpane fogged beneath the weight of her breath, and she watched the circle of condensation slowly shrink. At length, she gingerly stepped off the crate and sank onto her bed, grateful for the release of sleep that would undoubtedly take her before her duvet fully covered her.

4

Brianna stretched her arms tall, matching the stance of the trembling Scots pine, poplar, birch, and hazel trees towering over her. Unbidden, a smile tipped her lips as the sunlight speckled her skin and the trees whispered their secrets in the morning breeze. Breakfast had unfolded blessedly without event, though her pendant never showed itself. She'd counted the minutes until she could partake of the weekly break Mistress Magee so magnanimously granted her. Seemingly endless hours yawned before her, though she knew she must return to campus midafternoon to begin working on the massive evening meal. *Don't think of that now*, she told herself.

She closed her eyes, spun three circles, and went in the direction she was facing when she stopped. Her smile widened when she realized she was heading toward Finnuala's home. It had been far too long since they'd visited with one another. Kicking off her shoes and tucking them at the base of a large poplar, she ignored the intense cold of the earth and continued toward the old woman's house. She never really had minded the cold. It was all she had known in many ways. The feel of the grass on her skin, the dirt in her toes, and even the twigs that poked her soles, grounded her, as though connecting her with some unseen source of energy. Nae, life. She welcomed the connection to nature and its Creator. It both soothed and fueled her, stoking the fires of her spirit to continue another week. As she strolled, she stooped here and there to pluck some small wildflowers to bring to Finnuala, taking care to avoid the tiny white ones. While a lovely breed, Brianna couldn't ignore the old wives' tale she'd heard about them—about how they carried evil wishes with them if brought into the house. She'd never wish to bring death or ill will upon Finnuala's house or anyone in it.

At a break in the trees, Brianna quickened her pace. Her friend's home came into view and Brianna's heart warmed at the sight of it. The humble cottage, with smoke curling from the chimney and the thatched roof glistening in the muted light, was both inviting and chaotic. The walls, which at one time had been whitewashed, were now chipped and aged, with the crumbled remains of the once-attached shed off to one side. A stack of turf sat drying in the traditional tented pile, and stones lined the base of the home all the way round. Though not untidy, everything about the scene seemed intentional, yet also haphazard—much like Finnuala herself. As though summoned by Brianna's thoughts, the older woman rounded the corner. Hunched over, carrying a basket on her back piled high with more peat, Finnuala's brown wool dress fell to just above her ankles, revealing tattered socks and worn shoes. Her hair was pulled back in her customary low bun, but unruly tendrils stood out in all directions around her face, which lit up at the sight of Brianna.

"*Mo chailín!*" She lowered the basket with shaky limbs before Brianna could get close enough to help. Then she stretched her arms out wide.

Brianna happily entered Finnuala's embrace, and though much smaller than Brianna, the woman managed to encompass her in warmth, acceptance . . . belonging. Brianna fought back the tears that unexpectedly burned her eyes. "Hiya, Finnuala."

The pair held the embrace for a long beat before Finnuala extended Brianna an arm's length away. "I've not seen ya in a donkey's years! C'mon an' I'll get you a cuppa." She spun round quickly, but Brianna thought she saw a glisten in her eyes.

"I know 'tis been a long time," Brianna said as she followed her into the small cottage. "I'll try not ta let so much time go by before I get back next."

Finnuala *tsked* and shuffled to the fire where a cast-iron kettle perpetually hung on a hook, ever ready to serve a guest. Though Brianna was fairly certain she was Finnuala's only guest. Ever. "She works ya too hard, that Magee."

Brianna fetched two teacups from the press and settled herself at the rough wooden table. "Can't be helped," she said, though she doubted her words were true. "We got three new boarders last month."

Another *tsk*. "Desperate," she hissed under her breath. "*Anois.*" Finnuala poured the tea with trembling hands.

Had they always done that?

"Anyway, ya didn't come here to talk about that woman . . . that place." She stared off in the distance for a long moment before shaking her head slightly and turning her attention back to Brianna. "Tell me, now, how are ya, *peata*?"

"Can't complain, now." She fell back against her chair.

Finnuala laughed and shook her head. "God bless that spirit o' yours." She reached forward and squeezed Brianna's hand before shuffling back over to stoke the fire. The woman never could sit still. "No news, then?"

Brianna absently reached up to her neck to clasp her pendant—a habit she'd had her whole life—as Mister Wray's face flashed across her mind. "'Twas a bit of drama last night. We've a new visitor staying fer . . . well, I don't quite know how long. The cousin o' one of our boarders. He seems to have Magee all afluster." Along with most of the girls, judging by the faces of the students when he'd walked into the dining hall. Her stomach twisted at the memory. Why did that bother her?

A rattly chuckle rumbled from Finnuala's chest as she continued dithering with the fire, now adding another briquette of turf. "That must've been a sight." She straightened and stared off as though imagining the scene.

You have no idea.

"Well, if there's to be drama, that brought by a flustering gentleman is the kind you want." She ambled now to the basin and wiped it mindlessly. "As long as things are well with ye, that's fine by me." She smiled over her shoulder at Brianna.

Reaching for her neck once more, Brianna grimaced. "Well, there is one thing."

"Hmm?" More wiping and scrubbing at decades-old stains.

"My pendant. 'Tis gone."

Finnuala spun around and pierced Brianna with her gaze. "*Ceard? An ceann ó do mhamaí?*"

Brianna's head dipped. "*Tá.* The one from my mam." *Well, supposedly from her.*

"Oh, peata." Finnuala was at her side in a flash, grabbing her hands. "Have ya no idea where it could be?"

The weight of her loss settled on Brianna's shoulders once again. "Not really, no. I've checked my chamber an' the kitchen. I'll scour the school grounds when I get back."

"*Tsk.* We'll make sure ya find it. Come now." She waved Brianna over to the fireplace. With rickety, shaky movements, Finnuala lowered herself to a kneeling position. Brianna winced as the woman's knees ground against the stone hearth. She reached up and pulled on Brianna's hand, tugging her down to join her. Brianna complied.

Finnuala made the sign of the cross and clasped her hands at her chest. "Oh, Lord Jesus, grant that we may find Brianna's pendant, which has been lost."

Brianna glanced at her friend from the side of her eye. She recognized the traditional prayer for the return of lost items. It was typically addressed to Saint Anthony, but Finnuala had addressed her petition directly to Christ Himself. The subtle but immense change warmed her. She focused her eyes on the glowing turf and agreed with Finnuala as she prayed.

"At least restore to Brianna peace and tranquility of mind, the loss of which has surely afflicted her even more than her material loss." She cracked an eye open and peeked over at Brianna. "Even though she's pretendin' it doesn't rattle her, I know better. In the name of the Father, Son, and Holy Spirit, Amen." She repeated the sign of the cross and then winked at Brianna.

The corner of Brianna's lips curled, even as tears stung her eyes. "Thank you, *mo chara.*"

Finnuala cleared her throat as she rose. "Anois. Let's see if I still have a bit o' cake in the tin, will I?"

Magee's cave-like office held no welcoming charm. Even with a fire in the grate, a chill swirled about the room, and Michael shivered as it tickled his spine. Blowing into his cupped hands and rubbing them together, he stepped to the window and admired the wooded border outside. Shame that the beauty lying just beyond the leaded panes couldn't find its way inside.

The clock chimed ten and Michael turned to eye the door. Where was the honorable headmistress? He suspected she delighted in making her guests wait—a sign of her ultimate control over every happening within her walls, no doubt. Just as he released a heavy sigh, the door creaked open.

"Mister Wray," she said, her stone-like face as welcoming as a burr in the boot. "Sorry to keep you waiting."

Stifling a sarcastic comment, Michael nodded, then took a seat as Magee crossed to her desk. "You're a very busy lady, to be sure. I appreciate ya making time to speak wi' me."

Absent shuffling of papers on her desk ensued. "Mmm," was her preoccupied reply. After a moment, she sat in the overlarge chair and gave him her full attention. "Now, what can I do for you? Problems already with Miss FitzGerald?"

"Oh goodness, no. Nothing like that. I've yet ta speak wi' her much, in truth." He shifted in his chair and removed a pouch from his pocket. "No, I wondered if ya might know who this belongs to?" He stretched his arm out and deposited the fabric in her hand.

Magee frowned as she unwrapped the linen. When the broken chain and pendant came into view, something Michael couldn't place flashed in her eyes before her typical stoic expression returned. Lifting it closer to her face, she examined it with great, or feigned, interest. Michael couldn't be sure which. After a long moment, the corners of her mouth turned down, and she shook her head. "I've not seen it before. How did you come by it?"

Michael studied her for a beat before responding. "It was stuck under the door to my chalet."

"Well, then it could belong to any number of people." Her gaze drifted to the window and back to Michael. "Any visitors we entertain stay in those cottages. Not to mention all the grounds help and the like. Though I doubt any of them would have such a trinket in their possession."

Michael's eyes narrowed briefly. "Yes, o'course." He stood and reached out to take the pendant back.

Mistress Magee recoiled her hands in a flash. "Leave it with me. It likely belongs to the last guest to stay in your lodging."

"Do ya get many overnight visitors?"

Rising slowly, she bore her gaze into his. "Enough that we need the chalets."

"I see." Buttoning his jacket, Michael turned to go. "Do let me know when ya discover the owner, aye?"

The woman's jaw tensed and she rounded the desk. "Of course. Good day, Mister Wray."

Michael nodded and strode into the hallway.

Everything about the encounter gnawed at him. But why? What could Mistress Magee stand to gain from hiding who the pendant belonged to—that is, if she did in fact know? But if she didn't know, why would she react in such a way upon seeing it?

A sudden clanging jolted Michael from his thoughts, and

a rumbling like a million hoofbeats pounded above him. He glanced at his pocket watch. Half past ten. Morning lessons were over and now the girls were to take to the outdoors for recreation.

We'll need you most during recreation times, Magee had said.

Inwardly groaning, he made his way to the back door, absently wondering if he could solve the Adeline problem without ever having to encounter her. Before he could step through the door, his vision went black as ice-cold fingers wrapped around his eyes.

A childish giggle set his skin crawling. "Guess who, cousin?"

He clenched his teeth and used his thumbs and forefingers to grasp Adeline's wrists and pull them from his face. "If ya wanted me to guess," he said, keeping his voice as dry as possible, as he turned to face her, "ya might have left off 'cousin.'"

Adeline stuck her bottom lip out so far it nearly reached Belfast. "Now, cousin. Don't be cruel." She blinked up at him through her lashes. If she was trying to be coy, it wasn't working. At all. *Deranged* was more the word that sprang to mind.

"I was being nothing o' the kind, Adeline." He stepped over the threshold and welcomed the fresh breeze. "'Tis recreation time, aye?"

Adeline huffed and brushed past him. "Yes. And I hate it."

Michael swung his hands in a small arc. "Which way?"

Her eyes widened. "Are you joining us today?" She bit her bottom lip.

"Aye." He cleared his throat and lifted his index finger. "As an observer only."

Delight sparkled in her eyes, and she grabbed his hand, yanking him in the direction of the woods and stables. "This way!"

When he pulled his hand free, she pouted again. When that drew no reaction, she straightened her posture, smoothed her hair, and slid her hand through the crook of his arm as if they were out for a stroll along High Street. "It's just down here."

They continued in uncomfortable silence along the path before turning and walking past Batty's stables. Michael could hear him whistling a jaunty tune and hammering something to the beat. He smiled in spite of the dread that had wrapped itself around his arm.

Just beyond the stables lay an open field. Dozens of girls milled about, some lazily kicking a rock around a circle, others sitting on the benches that lined the area, while yet another pushed a very young girl on a swing that hung from the branches of a nearby tree.

At the sight of her classmates, Adeline tilted her chin up and puffed her chest out.

The pair neared a few girls chatting with one another, and the group turned in unison and walked away from Michael and Adeline. As the cousins continued along the grassy area, the scene repeated itself over and over.

From behind the swing, a rhyming, sing-song taunt including Adeline's name drifted to them on the breeze. His cousin's shoulders fell briefly before she righted them again and regained her haughty posture.

"Now," he asked, "who do ya play with during this time?"

Adeline scoffed and shot him a look that seemed to ask, *Are you serious?*

"None of these infants are refined enough for my company."

Michael's eyebrows soared, and he looked at her from the side of his eyes. "Is that so?"

Adeline nodded. "Of course. You know how Father has

raised me. None of these, these . . . ruffians know what to do with someone of my cultured upbringing."

The effort it took not to roll his eyes exhausted Michael. "I see. So, what do ya do during this time?"

Adeline steered them toward the nearest bench, then lowered herself onto it. "This, mostly." She gazed off in the distance, and it was the most honest moment Michael had ever witnessed of Adeline.

"Right." He joined her, making sure to keep a wide distance between them.

Several minutes passed, and while Michael wouldn't necessarily say the time was enjoyable, it was probably the most tolerable encounter he'd ever had with his cousin. If she'd just stay quiet most of the time.

A tall, lanky girl with brown hair sauntered up to them, followed by another boarder who looked her opposite in every way. "So, ya had someone come to yer rescue, did ya?"

Adeline rolled her eyes and crossed her arms over her chest but said nothing.

"What is it?" replied the second girl. "Yer man shows up, and suddenly cat's got yer tongue? Until now it was all talk, talk, talk wi' ye."

"Yeah," the tall girl piped in again. "Too afraid to show your true colors to your heartthrob, is it?"

Michael's cheeks burned, and he was once again grateful for his beard.

Adeline shot to her feet. "Shut your mouth, Katie, or I'll shut it with this." She held up a balled fist.

Katie's friend pushed herself between them. "I'd like ta see ye try," she said. "You'll lose t'ree teeth before ya land the first punch."

The friend strained her neck to scowl in Adeline's face, and Michael bit the inside of his lip to keep from laughing at the sight.

"Now, now, ladies," he crooned, rising to his feet. "There's no need fer all o' that." He placed a hand on Adeline's shoulder and eased her back a step. "As your headmistress informed you at dinner yesterday evening, I'm Adeline's cousin, Michael Wray." He pivoted his gaze between the girls. "I don't know what's transpired among you lot in the past, but it ends now."

Katie and her friend scoffed and assumed identical stances with arms crossed and one hip jutted out.

Michael pinned Adeline with a look. "Right, Adeline? It's over."

Adeline refused to look at him, instead fixing a glare on the girls so fiery, it would set the turf in the grate of his chalet ablaze. "Of course, cousin," she said through gritted teeth, her tone conveying the opposite intention of her words.

Just as the two girls took a step toward Adeline, their attention was drawn to something behind Michael. They straightened their posture, and said, "Of course, sir. No trouble, sir." They curtsied in unison and about-faced, heading back out onto the field where a game of tip had started. When Katie looked back at them, Adeline punched her fist into the palm of her other hand, narrowed her eyes, and scrunched her face.

Over Michael's shoulder, someone *tsked*. He turned to find Mistress Magee's gaze had been boring into the back of his head. She shook her head slightly in disgust and headed back in the direction of the house.

He had his work cut out for him indeed.

5

As she left Finnuala's, Brianna smiled and patted her apron pocket. The dear woman had sent her off with her last piece of *cáca millis*. Even now, guilt niggled at Brianna for accepting such a generous offering, but how could she have refused? Although cake was a rare treat for the woman whose homestead looked like something from a hundred years ago, it would have insulted her deeply had Brianna not taken it. She was proud to have been able to provide her guest with not one, but two pieces of the sweet cake. Brianna wondered where Finnuala had gotten it from. Had she made it herself? She couldn't imagine what painstaking, patient work that would have taken, given the rustic state of her kitchen. But if she hadn't made it, that would mean she'd ventured a trip into town, which Finnuala avoided at all costs. She would never tell Brianna why she stayed away. When asked, the woman always said the same thing. "The past is best left in the past, *a thaisce*."

Finding her shoes right where'd she'd left them, Brianna stooped to put them on, but she stopped short and straightened to examine the position of the sun. It was past noon but still well before she needed to be back at the school. Though there were tasks she could complete were she to return early, the woods beckoned her and she heeded their call. Leaving her shoes in their place, she sprinted deeper into the trees, giggling like a schoolgirl. She darted around pines and wove between birches. She rounded a poplar like a maypole and skipped along a cleared path. No thought was given on where to go. She didn't stop to think about direction or destination. Instinctually, her feet knew where she needed to be. At last, winded and spent, she stopped and clutched her hands to her knees. Jagged breaths came in all-too-short puffs, and she grimaced against the struggle to regain her breathing. Eventually, the huffing slowed and the stitch in her side eased. She stretched tall and laced her fingers behind her head, letting the cool breeze revive her yet again. Then she saw it. Of course her feet would bring her here. It had been far too long since she'd come, and now that she was here, it felt nearly impossible to leave.

She approached the giant oak with gentle, reverent steps. Sliding her hand over its rough bark, she breathed in the familiar, earthy scent. Her tree. "Hello, old friend."

Its countless moss-draped branches reached tall and wide, hither and yon, twisting and curling and taking up every inch of heaven it could while bathing the forest floor in an emerald glow. Several large limbs—more the size of secondary trunks—stretched out and nearly to the ground, like arms welcoming her home. Sometimes Brianna would nestle in their crooks and dangle her feet or lounge on them while she watched the leaves shimmering in the breeze. But her favorite place was what she called *Her Spot*. Her Spot was the one place in the world that felt like it was made just for her. She lowered herself down into it, nestling between two roots that arched up through the surface of the soil before retreating once again to the dark depths of the earth. The contours fit her shape perfectly, creating a seat more comfortable than any grand lord's armchair. She released a contented sigh and rested her back against the trunk, happy to while away the last hours of her freedom listening to the conversations of the trees with the birds.

Her eyes drifted closed in satisfied bliss. Then they slid open again. Something wasn't right. She shifted her weight and adjusted her seat. No better. An unwelcome ridge wedged itself into the fleshy muscles of her backside, no matter how she sat. An errant twig or rock, perhaps. She rolled onto her knees and inspected the ground beneath her. Everything appeared the same as it always had. No. What was that? The start of a new root was beginning to arch its back up through the soil.

"Oh, my dear friend. Ya know how much I appreciate ya, but this just willna do." She knew she sounded silly but didn't really care. With no one around to listen, it mattered very little what she said, or to whom. She scratched at the new root, hoping to pluck it free and reclaim her seat, but it wouldn't budge. She tried to hook her finger underneath the obstruction, yet it was too thick. She scratched some of the topsoil away and tried again, only to find her efforts were in vain.

Just then, a gust of wind rushed through the woods, swirling around the tree. It kicked up leaves and dust and pulled at her hair before disappearing as quickly as it had come. With the debris cleared away, Brianna could see the intruder was not a root at all, but rather something buried at the base of the tree. Memories flashed in her mind of the other treasures she'd found near this place. It was how she'd discovered her tree to begin with.

While on a walk alone as a young girl, she'd found a thimble embedded in the bark of the tree's trunk. It had taken all afternoon, but she was finally able to wrest it free. And thus began her treasure hunts. She'd found all manner of spoils. She was sure most of it would be considered rubbish by any proper member of society—why else would it be out here?— but to her, it might as well have been the Crown Jewels. No matter, now. She'd exhausted her tree's treasures long ago, and her hunts yielded fewer and fewer finds of late. Surely there was nothing else?

But treasure or not, she couldn't leave this . . . this . . . whatever it was to ruin the one happy place that remained for her, the one place she felt she could truly and fully be herself—other than Finnuala's, of course. So she started to dig. First, she scratched at the dirt on either side of the thin, rounded top, taking care not to tear her nails lest cleaning the kitchen be too painful. But the more she dug, the more curious she became, so the more furiously she scratched. What had first appeared to be the top of a tree root now revealed itself to be quite thin indeed—nearly flat, but tall and wide. Though dark brown, it almost had the feel of some kind of metal, but she couldn't be sure.

The longer she worked, the wilder her imagination became. No matter how hard she tried to venture a guess, she simply couldn't surmise what had been hiding underneath her all these years. The wind picked up again, but this time it refused to die down. It was as if it joined her in her frenzied excitement. The light started to dim, and in the distance, bells tolled. Slowly, Brianna became conscious of her surroundings. And the clanging from the church tower grew louder in her ears. She gasped. That could not be the time?

She shot to her feet but couldn't bring herself to leave just yet. She was so close. She could fit the length of her hand, plus a little more, over the unearthed portion of the item. Surely it couldn't be much bigger than that. Gripping it, she pulled with all her might, but it wouldn't break free from the ground. She shifted her hands and shook and wiggled it alternately forward and back, then side to side. It finally started to loosen. She continued this until her breath was coming in short puffs, and sweat dripped down her forehead, slid the length of her nose, and dropped on the loosened dirt.

Releasing a cry of frustration, she stood and kicked it. It shifted with a clang, and she was finally able to free it. Terribly rusted and bent so badly on one end that it curled upward, she still had no idea what she held in her hands. Bringing it closer to her face clarified nothing. In the distance a new round of bells tolled.

"No! No, no, no, no. The dinner." Clutching her new find to her chest, she sprinted toward home, thankful she knew when to dart and where to turn in the waning light. Perhaps she wasn't as late as she feared. Or perhaps Mistress Magee wouldn't realize her tardiness. Tears blurred her vision and streamed down her face. There'd certainly be no more days off after this.

Bursting into the house, she made not for the kitchen but rather her room. Taking the stairs two at a time, she made it to the top floor with record speed. She thrust the door open, ripped up the loose floorboard, and tossed the rusted treasure inside, then replaced the board. She'd have to clean it up later and investigate what it could be. But now she had to make haste to the kitchen.

She rounded the corner, entering the kitchen, but she stopped short at the sight of Mistress Magee and the head housemaid, Mary. "I'm . . . so . . . terribly . . . sorry . . ." She gasped for air, releasing each word between puffs of labored breath. "I . . . was . . . delayed."

Mary backed away and fled, presumably to the safety of the servants' dining room.

"Delayed?" Magee roared. "A delay is five minutes. Or perhaps ten. But not"—she closed the distance between them—"three hours!"

"I do beg yer pardon, marm."

"You'll have to beg more than that after this little stunt." She circled Brianna like a falcon stalking its prey. "Look at the state of you. Disgraceful!" The dishes in the cupboard rattled with her shrill exclamation, and Brianna wondered if the whole house could hear.

For the first time, she realized what she must look like. Her hands were black with dirt, her dress and apron filthy. Her shoes—

"And where are your shoes?" Magee's voice rose another octave.

Brianna swiped at her cheeks, feeling the grit caked on both. She'd been so worried about making it back here she'd left her shoes at the base of the tree near Finnuala's.

Mistress Magee clapped her hands, jolting Brianna. "Answer me, girl!"

"I-I lost them." Not entirely true, though after such wind, they likely were lost.

"God only knows what you've been up to, Brianna Kelly. But you'd better believe I'll find out if you've done anything untoward."

Brianna gasped. "Marm, I would never—"

A stinging slap tore across Brianna's face. "I doubt that very much." The headmistress wiped her hands on the rag draped across the basin, as though she'd just handled dung. "At any rate, you can thank Mary for doing your job and helping Cook prepare the evening meal for everyone. And seeing as how your work here pays for your room and board, I'd say it's quite clear you have not earned your keep for today. I can't very well have you tarnishing our good name and wandering all over God's creation out there, so you will spend the rest of the night in your room. Without dinner."

Brianna stepped closer. "Mistress Magee . . ." But she knew there was no arguing. Nothing she could say would change the woman's mind. Not about this. Not about anything. She sighed. "Yes, marm."

"Now, get. And don't even think about being late for your morning duties. In fact, start them two hours earlier."

Brianna's jaw fell open, but she snapped it shut and left the kitchen.

Once back in her room, she washed her hands and face with the frigid water from the jug on her empty chest of drawers. The floor creaked and she had the fleeting thought to pull out her treasure and examine it, but there wasn't enough light, and she was simply too exhausted. Her stomach growled as the scents of the evening meal finally wafted up to her corner of the house.

Her eyes grew heavy, from fatigue or her tears, she wasn't sure. It didn't matter. There was nothing else for her to do except try to get some sleep. In her foolishness, not only had she put her livelihood in jeopardy but she'd also squandered her chance to search for her pendant. The more time that passed, the greater the likeliness it would be lost for good.

Sighing, she untied her apron to change for bed. As she removed it, one side sagged with a weight. Furrowing her brow, Brianna reached into the pocket. *Bless you, Finnuala.*

She pulled the piece of cake from the pocket. Though crumbled, it had somehow survived the evening's rigorous activities and was still wrapped in the scrap of cheesecloth Finnuala had put it in. Brianna changed in haste, then slid beneath the thin covers of her bed. She took a bite of the sweet treat and her eyes fluttered closed. It was even better than it had tasted this morning. She leaned back against the wall and enjoyed her feast, feeling every bit a queen. And when it was gone, her belly contentedly satisfied, she drifted off into a blissful sleep with a prayer of thanksgiving on her lips.

Maureen Magee unwound the coil of hair at the base of her neck and sighed at the release of tension. Her head throbbed at the end of every day, but she wore the pain as a badge of honor. A sign of her discipline and decorum. She scratched her scalp, loosening the strands and releasing more pressure from her too-tight styling, then she turned her attention to the mirror. Ignoring the blackened desilvering spots on the glass, she examined her reflection. Black hair hung to her navel. Once thick and full, it was now stringy with strands of silver beginning to invade. Her gaze drifted up to her face. Pale, dull lines creased around her mouth and nose and between her eyes. Gray circles hung beneath them.

She combed her fingers through her hair, wondering where her allure had gone. She'd never been the epitome of beauty, but she'd been fair enough. That is, until him.

Shaking her head to dislodge the unwanted memories, she reached into her pocket and pulled out the linen pouch Mister Wray had given her. Staring down at Brianna's pendant, the fleeting thought brushed through her mind that she should return it to the girl. But the idea vanished like a snuffed flame. Rewrapping it, she opened the side drawer to her vanity and hid the necklace in the back corner. That child didn't deserve it.

Didn't she know how lucky she was to even be allowed under this roof after what she did? What *they* had done? No. It was only by Maureen's good graces that Brianna stayed. She deserved to be a street urchin, but instead, Maureen provided her with a home, food, and good, steady work— even if the sight of the girl brought it all back. The insolent child had no idea how she tortured Maureen with her mere presence.

Maureen slammed the drawer shut and shot to her feet, jaw aching from her clenched teeth. Brianna would learn to be grateful for all she'd done for her. And it would start first thing in the morning.

6

rianna!" The shrill voice jolted Brianna awake. Some-one pounded on the door. "Brianna. Up this instant." Magee.

She stifled a groan and rubbed her eyes. "Yes, marm." Even after her blissful secret snack lulled her into a sweet sleep, waking now was torture. She rolled onto her back, every muscle protesting. Opening her eyes was nigh to impossible. She squeezed them shut, rubbed them again, and slowly lifted the lids. The world was nothing but a gray blur. Blinking a few more times cleared it some, and she stared at the wood-planked ceiling.

More pounding. "Brianna Kelly, I don't hear movement. Get up!" Pounding footsteps retreated down the stairs, and Brianna pushed herself up to a sitting position. It was still dark—though it always was when she woke. But somehow, this darkness was even . . . darker, with a chill that reached to her bones. Dressing in haste, she quickly plaited her hair and headed downstairs.

The kitchen was black, save for one lantern—electric

lights had not yet arrived in their corner of Donegal. Even with the single lantern, it was too dark. Brianna gasped and ran to the oven. No embers from yesterday's cooking glowed, and none in the fireplace grate either. Who would have let all the fires go out? Brianna always used the embers from the stove to start the next day's fires. On Magee's tight budget, one had to make use of every last ounce of everything.

"That's what happens when you shirk your responsibilities." Magee's voice slithered from a dark corner, and Brianna jumped, spinning toward it.

With slow, marked steps, Mistress Magee moved closer to Brianna. Her fingers dug into the sleeves of her folded arms. Shadows darkened her face, and Brianna got the sense it wasn't just from the lack of light in the room. "A mistake you won't make again, I trust," she said, her voice low.

"Marm, I am terribly sorry about yesterday. I assure ya, 'twasn't on purpose. I simply lost track o' time."

Magee snorted. "Your assurances mean very little to me. I guarantee you won't lose track of time today, because I have every moment from now until dusk accounted for. And you won't go to bed until every last task is completed."

"Yes, marm." Brianna kept her posture tall, eyes locked with Magee's, though she wanted to collapse in a heap and cry. All she'd thought about since waking was returning to bed.

"You'll start by serving breakfast."

"Of course." That was always her first task.

"The servants' breakfast."

Brianna blinked. While she prepared all the breakfast food—Cook didn't start her work until preparing the midday meal—Mary was in charge of the service in the servants' dining room.

"'Tis only fair. Mary did your work last night." Magee sniffed and raised her chin, her brows arching higher.

Brianna's shoulders fell. Though it pained her to admit it, the woman had a point. She made a mental note to apologize to Mary when she saw her. "Yes, marm."

"Now, get to it. The girls' routine will not be disrupted just because of your insubordination. If you're going to keep on schedule, you'd best get started." Magee quit the room and shut the door with an authoritative thud.

Lighting the fire in the grate was more arduous without the aid of the stove embers to kindle the turf. At last, the peat briquettes took, and she could turn her attention to breakfast. Already behind, she hurriedly prepared the porridge and whisked the eggs so she could scramble them last thing before serving. Mary and the rest of the household help needed to be served first so they could start their normal duties. Getting their breakfast to them late would put the whole house off routine. Brianna shuddered at the thought and what fresh spate of consequences Magee would heap on her for it.

She worked feverishly, yet everything seemed to take twice as long as usual. Finally there was enough ready to take to the servants' dining room. She loaded a tray with serving dishes and a large pot of tea. After wrestling the door open, she stepped into the hall. As she passed Magee's office, she heard, "Don't forget the dishes."

The table hadn't been set? Of course, it wouldn't have been. That was always the last thing Brianna did before retiring for the night. Mary would have done it, she was sure, so Magee must have instructed her not to. Brianna stood in the corridor looking from the kitchen door back to the direction of the dining room, torn on whether or not to deliver the food first or go back and bring the dishes and food all at one time. A stirring of footsteps overhead caught her attention. The girls were lining up and would be marching down the stairs any moment.

She scurried back to the kitchen, set down her tray, and loaded a second one with plates, cutlery, teacups, and serviettes. She propped the door open and then lifted the food and settled that tray into the crook of her right arm. Then, she carefully finagled the tray of dishes onto her left arm. The weight of them both nearly toppled her, but she steadied herself and made for the servants' quarters. Taking care to roll her feet smoothly from heel to toe so as not to jostle anything, she kept her gaze on the entryway at the end of the long corridor.

Suddenly, the back door slammed open, and Brianna was flung against the wall. By some miracle, she managed to hang on to the tray of dishes, but the food toppled onto the floor with a sickening splat.

"Oh, good gracious me. I beg your pardon." Mister Wray cupped her elbow with his hand and inclined his head to look at her face. "Are ya alright?"

She puffed at a strand of hair that had fallen over her face. "I'm fine." She puffed again, but instead of helping, it frayed the strands, some of which curled into her eye. She clamped them shut against the sting.

"Allow me." Tender fingers brushed the hair from her face, gently grazing her forehead and temple. Goose bumps prickled her skin at his touch. "There. Can you see now?"

Brianna blinked hard and forced herself to meet his gaze while heat crept up her cheeks. "Aye, thank you." She knelt down, setting the tray of dishes carefully on the floor, then started picking up the broken pieces of pottery.

"No, no, please let me." He knelt beside her and started scooping handfuls of porridge and eggs back onto the fallen tray. "'Tis my fault," he added. "I was rushing to not be late to breakfast and carelessly neglected to look where I was going."

Brianna opened her mouth to respond, but Magee flew around the corner and shrieked. "What have you done now, you *amadán*?"

Brianna blanched at the word. Being called a fool stung, but no more so than Magee's use of Irish. Irish Gaelic was only allowed in certain circumstances within the walls of Ballymacool. "As a center of decorum and propriety, we will speak only proper, civilized English," the headmistress had said when one of the boarders deigned to converse in her first language. Magee's slip into her native tongue belied just how furious she was.

"My apologies, marm," Brianna said. "'Twas an accident."

Magee's lips clamped into a thin line. She planted balled fists on her hips. "I'm growing quite weary of hearing that from you, Brianna. And to add insult to injury, you've forced Mister Wray to help you." She turned her attention to the man. "Please, sir, you mustn't help her. This is a problem of her own making."

Mister Wray stood, hands held in front of him, porridge dripping from his fingers. He studied the headmistress for a moment before responding. "I'm afraid you're mistaken. It was I who ran into Brianna in my haste to be on time for breakfast. Therefore, 'tis only right that I be responsible for cleaning this mess."

Fire flashed behind Magee's eyes, and she scowled at Brianna. She opened her mouth to retort but closed it again when she looked back at her guest. A guest who, Brianna noticed, somehow still managed to be blindingly handsome even while covered in porridge. Seemingly weighing how to respond to the man whose family practically ran this county, at length Magee blinked and a sickly-sweet smile slid across her face. It was the first time Brianna could ever remember seeing the woman smile. It did not suit her at all.

"As you wish, sir. However, the girl will never learn if someone is always swooping in to save her from her own foolishness."

A look of confusion flashed on Mister Wray's face, then he knelt once more and continued picking up the shattered serving dishes and splattered food. "Very good, Mistress. I've got things well in hand here. I do believe the girls will be arriving soon?"

As if on cue, the sound of rhythmic marching snaked down the stairwell, and Magee shot one more fiery glance at Brianna, turned, and left.

"Ya really don't have to, sir," Brianna said softly.

Mister Wray set the last shard on the tray and lifted it. "Aye, I do. Now, if you'll kindly direct me to the kitchen?"

Brianna retrieved the intact tray of dishes and inclined her head and started in the right direction.

He followed her in, set the aftermath on the counter next to the basin, and washed his hands. Brianna busied herself emptying the serving dishes of the spoiled food. When she grabbed a new pot to set more porridge on to boil, Mister Wray took it from her hands and filled it with water for her and set it on the stove. "What goes in here?"

Unable to form words, she pointed to a sack of dry porridge oats sitting next to the stove. He nodded, grabbed the scoop, and dumped a heaping portion into the pot. He looked back at Brianna, brows raised in question. When she failed to respond, he scooped another portion and held it over the pot. Brianna nodded. When he set the scoop down, she cleared her throat. He glanced over at her, then paused. "More?"

She nodded and held up her hand, five fingers splayed.

Mister Wray's jaw slackened. "Cúig?"

She chuckled and her voice returned. "Aye."

He shook his head and turned back to the stove. He added the final scoops, looked under the pot, examined the dials, and fiddled with one until flame burst out. As he stirred the pot, Brianna studied him. Never before had a man been in her kitchen, and if there had been, he certainly hadn't cooked. Mister Wray was wearing a knit jumper the color of the cream from Batty's cows. The sleeves were bunched up to his elbows, and the collar of a button-down shirt poked through the top. Brianna wondered why he didn't wear the suit so common to ascendancy class men. Then again, he also sported a beard, which she'd never seen on any gentleman. He stopped stirring and raked his fingers through his chestnut hair and turned to her.

Brianna quickly spun and began washing her hands, willing the bright red that was surely coloring her cheeks to fade.

"What now?" he asked.

Brianna's shoulders rose and fell with a deep breath. "Now we serve."

"Right," he said with a nod, picking up the tray with the food. "I'll take this one." He smiled and teasingly winked a steely hazel eye. Brianna bit back a grin.

"I'd say ya should," she said, laughter thickening her voice. "In fairness, ye're the one who put us in this bind." Goodness, she was bold.

Mister Wray's smile slowly widened. "Touché, madam." A baritone chuckle rattled his chest. Brianna warmed at the sound of it. He climbed the three steps into the hallway ahead of her, then turned to enter the main dining hall.

"Wait!" Brianna caught up to him. "Not there. This way."

Lines creased his forehead. Brianna brushed past him and headed toward the servants' dining room. When she entered, the rest of the staff were waiting for her. All of them. Mary's eyes widened when Mister Wray followed Brianna in, but she said nothing. Batty stood, took the tray from him, and greeted him while Brianna set the dishes around the table.

"Morning, everyone," she said. "I do apologize for the delay. We had a little mishap."

The group voiced their forgiveness, but all eyes bounced between Mister Wray and Brianna. All eyes except Pádhraig's. The stable hand was already tucking into his porridge and slurping his tea.

"Brianna's being too modest," Mister Wray said. "Any tardiness is completely my fault."

Mary pinned Brianna with a stare, intrigue lighting her eyes. Brianna responded with a playful look of reproval. "Speaking of tardiness," she said, "I've another breakfast to serve. And ye're expected elsewhere, Mister Wray."

"A very good day to ya all." He nodded to the group and stepped into the corridor.

"I'm much obliged to ya, sir," Brianna said, walking quickly back to the kitchen. She called over her shoulder, "Now, if ye'll excuse me."

Heavy footsteps closed in, and a gentle hand grasped her elbow. "Wait." Mister Wray tugged softly so she turned to face him. "I am sorry. Are ya sure you're alright?"

"Cousin—" Adeline stopped short when she rounded the corner and saw Mister Wray and Brianna together. She looked from him to Brianna and back, her features tight. Her gaze fell and rested on his hand on her arm. Brianna's stomach dropped and she pulled her arm free.

"Mistress Magee sent me to fetch you, Cousin Michael." She spoke to him, but she glared at Brianna.

Mister Wray took a half step toward the girl. "Thank you. I'll be there shortly." When Adeline set her stance and folded her arms across her chest, he extended his arm and pointed in the direction of the dining hall. "I said, I'll be there shortly. That is all."

Adeline huffed and stamped her foot. "Very well." She pinned Brianna with a final glare and stormed off.

Mister Wray sighed and tucked in the corner of his mouth. "I'm afraid all I do is apologize to ya. Once again, allow me to say I'm sorry." He stepped closer to her, but she stepped back.

"Don' mention it." She eased backward a bit more and then turned toward the kitchen. "Please, excuse me."

She hustled down the hall, feeling his stare boring into the back of her head.

7

When Michael entered the dining room, Adeline was at the head table whispering into Mistress Magee's ear. Magee fixed her eyes on Michael. Around the room, the rest of the girls were engaged in quiet conversation.

"Bridget, I'm hungry," a young voice sobbed softly.

Michael followed the direction of the complaint and found a small girl who couldn't have been more than seven or so. Bridget, who looked to be in her early teens and was clearly the head of that table, stroked the child's hair and crooned softly in her ear. He had no idea children so young attended Ballymacool. He had assumed it would be older girls from families similar to his and his uncle's. How did Magee care for such young ones? What sort of nurturing did they receive? He'd seen precious few adults around the school and suddenly wondered where they all were. Magee had said the teachers don't typically eat with the students, but what about all the other times? He decided he'd join Adeline for her lessons that day to find out.

Adeline had returned to her seat, so Michael headed toward Magee. Taking his place next to the headmistress, he uttered a half-hearted apology for his delay.

"You shouldn't encourage her, you know." Magee dabbed at her nose with her handkerchief.

Michael didn't respond, but merely raised his brows in question.

"Brianna's an impertinent, insolent child who shirks responsibility at every turn. Her added duties are the consequences for her unfortunate choices, and she needs to complete them on her own if she's ever to learn her lesson."

Michael scratched his beard while he thought over Magee's words. While Brianna was younger than Magee, to be sure, she was no child. "Mmm," he said in response. He reached for his serviette to place it on his lap, but it wasn't there. Nothing was there. No dishes were laid out, no cutlery or the like.

As if summoned by his thoughts, Brianna entered bearing a tray loaded with teetering dishes. A ripple of comments rolled through the girls. Things like, "at last" and "it's about time." Michael pursed his lips and worked his jaw back and forth.

Brianna approached the head table and began by putting a full place setting in front of Mistress Magee who stared straight ahead and said nothing. She did the same for Michael who turned and thanked her. When he turned back, Adeline was glaring at him, face pinched.

When the head table was set, she started with the girls' settings. No one thanked her or even acknowledged her presence. Anger burned in Michael's chest, and he stood.

"Right, ladies. We're going to do things a little differently today." The roomful of young faces turned to him, admiration and bewilderment glowing in their eyes. He rounded the table, counted out a stack of bowls and handed them to Bridget. "Take one for yerself and pass the stack to the next girl."

Bridget stared at him for a moment, confusion painted on her face.

"G'on, it'll be fun," Michael said.

Slowly, Bridget took a bowl for herself and set one in front of the young girl she'd been comforting, who now grinned and carefully lifted the stack of bowls and passed it to the girl on her right. Brianna, wide-eyed, took another stack and started to carry it to the next table, but Michael approached and reached for it. His hands rested on hers and he whispered, "We've got this well in hand. Go get the food. We'll be all set to go when ya come back." He took the dishes from her and headed for another table.

When he returned to his place, he surveyed the scene before him. Girls were smiling and turning to one another as they passed dishes. Giggles and grins lit the room, and satisfaction radiated from Michael's core.

"I do believe you are confused as to our pecking order here, Mister Wray," Magee said dryly when Michael returned to his seat.

Michael grinned and placed his serviette on his lap with a flourish, fully enjoying the fact that she could do very little for fear of offending him, his family, and their governance of this area. "On the contrary, I'm well aware."

As Brianna hurried back to the kitchen, she squeezed her fingers where Mister Wray's hand had been. They were alive with energy, and she could still feel the warmth from his touch. She scolded herself for her childishness. *He's only being kind*, she told herself over and over. *It means nothing.* Only it meant everything. It had been so long since she'd been shown any sort of kindness. The household staff were kind to her, sure, but she rarely had time to see or speak to them. And visits with Finnuala were few and far between. The experience of being shown any sort of compassion was so foreign, Brianna wasn't entirely sure what to do with it. She chose to attempt to ignore it and focus her energy on her duties.

Preparing the serving dishes for the boarders took much longer than it did for the servants. The girls sat at five long tables that held fifteen people each. Every table needed three dishes of each food, which was then served family style. She worked as quickly as she could and loaded them onto the rolling cart Magee miraculously allowed Brianna to use for this task. She suspected it had more to do with keeping the schedule than it did easing her burden, but she didn't care. She was grateful for it nonetheless.

When she rolled the cart into the dining hall, Mister Wray nodded. Confusion stopped Brianna short when three girls from each table rose. They each approached the cart, took dishes of porridge and eggs, and returned to their places. One even said, "Thank you." Breakfast was served in record time, and all that was left was to clear it when they finished. Brianna glanced at the head table. A funny sort of grin played on Mister Wray's face. Magee's expression, on the other hand, was hard as stone except for the fire that burned behind her eyes.

While the students ate, Brianna washed the pots and pans she'd cooked with and set out whatever Cook would need for lunch preparations. Then she headed outside to bring in more wood for the boiler and turf for the fireplace. As she crossed the lawn, her eyes searched the ground for sign of her pendant. Nothing. At the woodpile, she scoured the area, thinking perhaps it had gotten wedged between logs, but to no avail.

After delivering the wood and stoking the boiler fire, she turned her attention to the cottages. She refilled the turf baskets and swept the floors, then changed the linens and took stock of the pantry items needing to be replaced.

When she came to Mister Wray's cottage, she almost didn't go in. It felt like an invasion of his privacy, though she'd never had such notions with any other guest. It was almost as if they didn't exist. Or rather that she didn't. She was like a little fairy who granted all their wishes without ever being seen. And now that she had been, she didn't know what to do. Again, she considered skipping Mister Wray's chalet but thought better of it at the realization that doing so would likely ignite even more of Magee's wrath.

She knocked on the door, knowing full well he was still taking breakfast in the hall. Creaking the door open ever so slowly, she peeked inside. "Hallo?" No response. Entering, she slid the door closed and looked around. Everything was neat and tidy, with nothing out of place except for a book that rested open near the fireplace, the arm of the chair serving as a bookmark. A pair of wire spectacles lay atop the book. An image of Mister Wray's face with the glasses perched on his nose floated into Brianna's mind. She smiled at the thought, even as butterflies tickled her stomach.

She shook her head to dislodge the picture and scolded herself. She made quick work of replacing the turf and stoking the embers to ensure it would relight more easily in the afternoon. Not much needed to be done in the small kitchen area so her tasks there were finished quickly. She swept the floor, taking more care—nae, more *time*—than usual, fully aware she was stalling, avoiding having to go into his room. But, alas, there was nothing more to be done except the linens.

She entered the darkened room almost reverently. A light but heady scent of leather, musk, and men's aftershave greeted her, and she breathed it in deep. Releasing her breath, she changed the linens as quickly as she could, forcing herself not to think about them having been draped over a sleeping Mister Wray.

As she worked, she sang to distract herself from her wandering thoughts. She removed the dirty linens and piled them in a heap. She replaced them first with the one she tucked around the mattress, then the top linen, woolen blanket, and thick down duvet. She tugged and smoothed the fabric until no wrinkles remained, then fluffed the pillows and set them at the head of the bed, continuing her song throughout each step.

"You have a lovely voice."

Brianna screamed and threw the pillow in her hand at the intruder, hitting him square in the face. He crouched to dodge the projectile, and she raised her fists and took a fighting stance. "Don' come any closer, *a mhac*. Ye'll be sorry."

Mister Wray stood, brushed the hair from his eyes, and held his hands up in surrender. "I believe ya."

Brianna huffed as if she herself had been punched, and

she wagged her head. "Mister Wray, I beg your pardon. I'm terribly sorry."

"'Twas I who startled you from your duties, therefore, 'tis I who—once again—should apologize to you."

She looked away.

"Brianna?"

She turned to him again, face burning.

His eyes were on hers. "Ya did nothing wrong, alright?"

She didn't believe him but nodded.

"Now," he said slowly, bending to the side, "I'm goin' to pick up this pillow. Is that OK, or are ya still going to pummel me?" He gestured to her hands, which, to her dismay, were still raised and balled tightly in fists.

She dropped them to her sides. "I suppose ye'll live to fight another day."

"Perfect." He laughed and even through his beard she could see two deep dimples punctuating his smile.

Heaven help her, he was handsome. "If ye'll excuse me, I need to clear the breakfast." She crossed the room, snatched the pillow from him, placed it hastily on the bed, and fled the room with as much dignity as she could muster.

"If you'll wait a moment, I'm going back that way m'self."

She was already outside, relishing the brisk air on her flushed cheeks. He reappeared a second later and waggled his glasses between his fingers.

"Just needed to fetch these. I'm observing Adeline's lessons today." He gestured toward the main house.

Brianna was suddenly grateful for her myriad tasks to complete that morning. Wild horses couldn't drag her to morning lessons. She'd had to go in once when a student had snuck a flask of tea in and proceeded to spill it all over the floor. Master McDaid had insisted his instruction continue while she cleaned the mess. The few minutes she'd experienced under his tutelage were enough to send her back to her scullery duties with gratitude. Not only were his lessons dry and boring, but he berated the girls so severely. Brianna had wondered if the parents were aware of the treatment their children were receiving. Then again, she wondered how much they might care. Perhaps that's why they had sent them to Ballymacool.

She suddenly realized she hadn't responded to Mister Wray. "Ah, aren't you the lucky one?"

"I suppose that remains to be seen," he said. "At the moment I'm feeling quite lucky." He glanced at her, then cleared his throat.

Brianna's chest burned and she hoped her face wasn't flushed. Of course, he couldn't be speaking of her. How arrogant was she? "Indeed," was all she could muster in reply.

"What song was that you were singing?"

"Oh, that? Nothing, just an old tune I picked up along the way. '*An Cailín Rua.*'"

Mister Wray lifted an index finger. "Oh, aye. 'The Red-Haired Girl.' It's a classic."

Brianna fiddled with the end of her braid and suddenly realized how egotistical it must seem for her to sing such a song. He must think her to be quite puffed up, especially for a scullery maid.

Before she could embarrass herself any further, their arrival at the back door came to her rescue. "Well, good day, Mister Wray." She scurried inside and down the hall before he could engage her in any further conversation.

She fetched the rolling cart and made for the dining room.

When she arrived, her jaw once again fell slack. At the end of each table were neat stacks of dishes. Plates were together, with any scraps having been scraped into the top of the serving dish stack. All the cutlery had been gathered and placed on another platter. The only remaining task was for Brianna to load everything onto the cart and take it to the kitchen. It would save her at least half an hour.

She began at the first table while shaking her head in wonder. She whispered to herself, "What are ya doing to Ballymacool, Mister Wray?" And as she moved to the next table, she added, "Whatever it is, keep doing it."

8

Adeline's classroom was on the third floor. Mistress Magee had given Michael an informal tour of the building as she walked him to Master McDaid's room. The second floor, she'd said as they approached the landing, held the boarders' rooms. "Nothing for you to see there," she'd said. Michael would have to agree, except that he was curious what sort of condition the rooms were in. How many girls were in each one? What sort of bathing facilities did they have? When he'd first arrived, Ballymacool had appeared above par. The house, while cold and lacking flourish, seemed up to the quality even the wealthiest family could appreciate. But upon closer inspection, everything just looked a bit old, tired.

There were hints that it had once been a grand house with fine finishes. Now, however, the wood floors were scuffed and the carpets were faded. Paint peeled in places and some of the wallpaper bubbled. It was not enough to be readily noticeable, but upon closer inspection was apparent. Even the wardrobe of the staff was dated by several years, probably more. He almost felt as if he'd stepped back three decades in time.

Once at the third floor, Magee walked him down the long corridor to the last door on the left. She extended her hand and gestured for Michael to enter. He slid inside and the teacher crossed the room to meet him.

"Mister Wray, you're most welcome to my classroom." Master John McDaid was a round, squat man in black robes and an odd square fabric cap. Silver spectacles perched precariously at the end of his bulbous nose. The scent of boiled cabbage and roasted fish wafted from the folds of his robe As he held out his hand to Michael.

"Pleasure." He coughed as he returned the handshake.

"Master McDaid comes to us from Stranmor College outside of Belfast." Magee beamed.

Michael was familiar with Stranmor. It had been embroiled in controversy when he was in secondary school over its severe punishments and treatments of its pupils. "Oh?"

"Yes, that's right." Master McDaid rocked on his toes, clearly very impressed with himself. "Most educational institutions in this area are taught by nuns or members of the clergy. Not so here. These girls are getting the finest modern education." He punctuated his statement with a nod of superiority.

"Well said," replied Magee. "And yet we haven't lost the importance of the classical, social graces either."

"No, no, of course not."

Shuffling feet sounded outside the door, announcing the arrival of students. "Eh, Mister Wray, I've a seat prepared for you just there." McDaid pointed to the window at the far back corner of the musty room. There sat a hardback chair and a small table just big enough for a notepad. Michael took his place and crossed one leg over the other. Master

McDaid then bade farewell to the headmistress and strode to the door. His face transformed from an expression of genteel kindness to one of severity. "Enter," he barked.

The girls filed in in neat lines. If there were assigned seats, which Michael presumed there were, they were ordered such that each girl wound up at her own desk. Once everyone was in, they stood straight as soldiers and waited.

McDaid paraded to the front of the room as if he were the king himself. He turned, faced the group, and clasped his hands behind his back. "Class."

"Good morning, Master McDaid," they droned in unison. "Thank you for teaching us today."

"Sit," he commanded, and they did so. Each girl's posture was impeccable, with both feet flat on the floor, backs straight as an arrow, necks stretched long, and hands folded on the desktops.

Ruler in hand, Master McDaid began his lecture on past participles and dangling modifiers. As he spoke, he strolled up and down the rows. Michael noted how each girl tensed as he passed by. At one point when he was writing on the board, Adeline turned her head slightly and looked at Michael with one of her awful, sugary grins.

"Miss FitzGerald!"

She startled and spun to face forward again. Master McDaid stormed to her seat. "What is the rule about socializing in this class?"

Adeline swallowed hard. "At no time shall a student speak or pay heed to another unless directed to do so by the teacher." The words slipped past her lips, almost as if it were a mantra.

Michael's eyes widened and he shifted in his seat. Was this a normal occurrence in class?

"Exactly," McDaid snapped, then he rapped her knuckles with the ruler.

Michael flinched.

"Now," McDaid continued, walking back to the chalkboard where he'd recorded a sentence in sloppy handwriting, "tell me, Miss FitzGerald, where should this modifier be placed?"

When she answered incorrectly, he returned to her seat and rapped her knuckles three more times while the most putrid stream of demeaning names spewed from his lips.

Michael jumped to his feet. "Master McDaid, that is quite enough!"

The schoolteacher shot his attention to Michael, and something akin to fear flashed in his eyes before the smug arrogance returned. "Tell me, Mister Wray, have you been trained in the skills of education?"

Michael ground his teeth. He'd been blessed with the finest education available and had yet to experience anything like what he'd just witnessed.

"No, you have not," McDaid answered for him. "Therefore, I would not expect you to understand the nuances of such an undertaking. And until you do, I'd thank you not to disrupt the lesson." He slapped the ruler onto the palm of his hand, and the whole room flinched. He then strode to the front of the class.

Michael returned to his seat. Not because he'd been instructed to do so, but because he was deep in thought over what this trip was revealing about all that was going on right under his family's nose. Yet they had no idea. Ballymacool was believed to be one of the finest boarding schools in the county, if not the whole of Ireland. But what he was seeing stood in stark contrast to that. What good did Michael's position do if he turned a blind eye to such egregious behavior?

The way those considered of lower station were treated within these walls was appalling. Granted, Michael had not seen how Mistress Magee treated the rest of the service staff. Perhaps she was only vitriolic to Brianna. While still not permissible, Magee was from a generation that believed treating the help in such a manner was not only appropriate but expected. And maybe Master McDaid was the exception. There were several other teachers at the school. Surely they treated the pupils with more dignity. Michael decided to discuss the matter with his parents when his stint at Ballymacool was over.

He tried to recall what had been on the schedule Batty had given him the other day. He could remember some of the classes but not all. He would have to ask Adeline or just shadow her for the whole day. He had hoped to take Cara out for a ride—the poor steed likely grew restless. But that would have to wait, it seemed.

Movement caught his attention, and he realized he'd been staring out the window. In truth, he'd seen nothing, so lost in thought as he was. But now, his gaze was met with Brianna looking directly at him. He nodded slightly and offered a meager smile. She blinked, barely lifted her hand in a wave, and hurried off toward the shed.

Magee hadn't exaggerated when she said she had every moment of Brianna's day accounted for. On a normal day, Brianna was busy from at least five in the morning until close to midnight, with few to no breaks. She would eat her lunch standing over the basin before washing the midday dishes. Breakfast went uneaten or consisted of a few spoonfuls of cold porridge congealed at the bottom of the pan just before she washed it. Dinner was typically taken hurriedly after ten o'clock, before she did her final sweep of the kitchen and set the breakfast tables, and it was almost always cold.

Brianna had assumed Magee's threat had meant no meals or a few extra chores that were typically only done once or twice a year. Those were added to the list, of course. But so were a whole host of other tasks Brianna had never done before and didn't know existed. But now, as she removed cobwebs from the rafters of the shed—a truly futile task, especially in a thatched building—she realized the headmistress was capable of creating an endless list of things for her to do, whether they held any real value or not.

The rest of the day passed in an exhausting blur, and before Brianna knew it, dinner was over, the dishes were washed, and the clock chimed eight.

Magee swept into the kitchen. She ordered Brianna to take tea to Mister Wray's cottage and left the kitchen just as quickly as she'd arrived.

Brianna's head dropped back and she groaned. It wasn't the task of making a tea tray that vexed her. It was seeing their guest again. Entirely too much of this day had been occupied by Michael Wray. When he wasn't smashing into her or popping up unannounced, he'd occupied her thoughts and invaded her daydreams as she worked. Before his arrival, she envisioned herself lunching at Finnuala's or wandering her woods . . . or on the hardest days, being back with her family. In her daydreams, they were alive and together and happily laughing over tea or snuggled up reading a book. But she didn't let herself go there often. It was too painful. So she stuck to musings that were attainable. Not today. Today her thoughts were filled with the echo of Mister Wray's laughter and the image of his dimpled smile. The scent of his room lingered in her memory, unlocking desires she'd buried long ago. Having him here was dangerous. Oh, she'd never act on any impulse, and she knew better than to truly anticipate that he returned whatever these feelings were that he stirred in her.

No, he was dangerous because he awakened something far more treacherous in her. Something she couldn't afford to cultivate. Something deadlier than any poison or illness. Hope.

Michael couldn't help the smile that slid onto his face when he opened the door to find Brianna with a tray of tea service. And it wasn't because of the tea.

He stepped aside to grant her access to his sitting room. "Come in."

She entered and made her way to the table. "Mistress Magee—"

"Said you should bring me some tea?" He chuckled. "Ever have déjà vu?"

A brief but hesitant smile flashed on her face. He joined her near the table and started to pour the tea but stopped. He glanced at her, and when their eyes met, all the air seemed to vacate the room. What was it about this girl? There was something that drew him to her. She was beautiful, aye, but it was more than that. She seemed almost . . . familiar. He faced her fully and let his gaze trace her features as she took over setting out the service and pouring the tea. Porcelain cheeks spotted with freckles held stark contrast from the green eyes, clear as emeralds, that stared back at him. Her face was framed with a fiery red plait draped over one shoulder, except for a strand that fell over her eye.

Michael's heart pounded in his chest and he stepped closer. Brianna froze, one hand hovering over the teapot. After a beat, she met his gaze. A scant handbreadth separated them. He reached up to brush the hair out of her face.

Her eyes drifted closed and she stepped back.

He regarded her for another moment, chiding himself for likely making her feel uneasy. Or, God forbid, like he was wanting to take advantage of her. He slid his hands into his pockets.

"G'night, Mister Wray." She brushed past him and headed toward the door. But he couldn't let her go, not like this. He should at least try to explain.

"Brianna—"

She stilled but kept her back to him.

When words failed him, he sputtered, "Thanks for the tea."

She nodded once and hastened away.

Later, he tried to read but found he was merely staring at the page, not seeing or processing any words, but rather humming a tune. His tea long forgotten and the fire in the grate getting low, he shuffled to the kitchen and snuffed the lanterns to go to bed.

With the light gone, he could see clearly through the window, and there she was in the moonlight. Brianna, her back to the cottages, scrubbed the windows of the main house. Rather than give in to the temptation to watch her further, or run out and help her, he headed for sleep. As he went, he softly sang the last line of the song he'd been humming, "*Is bhi sceimh mhna na finne le mo chailín rua.*"

9

Brianna flopped onto her bed, exhaustion lacing through every fiber of her being. For days now Magee had run her ragged, waking her hours early and keeping her up long past her normal bedtime. She knew she couldn't keep this up or she'd be in the grave before her twenty-first birthday. But as taxing as it was, it had given her reason to avoid Mister Wray—a task that was becoming increasingly more difficult, for more reasons than one.

But today she'd seen him in heated discussion with Magee. And then magically tonight after dinner, the headmistress had told Brianna she could return to her normal duties and schedule. When a shadowed figure in the corner had cleared his throat, Magee had added, "And you may resume your customary constitutionals."

"And?" said the mystery man.

"And your weekly break," Magee had conceded through clenched teeth.

Brianna smiled in the darkness and whispered a prayer of thanks. Her hand drifted to grasp her necklace, only to remember it was gone. Over the past four days, her increased workload had taken her all over the grounds of Ballymacool House—even to some areas she had never been before—and still her pendant remained missing.

Magee had reinstated her morning off just in time. Tomorrow, after breakfast, she'd have one final search before resigning to the fact that it was lost for good.

Maureen rubbed her temples, a futile attempt to quell the throbbing ache that had taken up residence there. This ache was not a product of her hairstyle, but rather of her impudent charge and scullery maid.

Rising from her bed, she crossed the room and lit a lantern, keeping the flame as low as possible. She slid the vanity drawer open and searched the back corner for Brianna's pendant. She half expected it to be gone, but there it remained. She groped around until her fingers landed on what she truly sought. Pulling the small, framed photo from its hiding place, she held it up to the light. The grainy portrait of Richard Boyd stared back at her. Tracing the lines of his face with her finger, she allowed herself the rare indulgence of reliving her favorite moment with him.

"I must be brief," he'd whispered, his voice thick with longing. They stood together in the ornate study. Richard kissed her repeatedly, starting with her forehead, then moving to her cheeks and finally her mouth, where he lingered.

"How long must we wait to be together, my love?" She ran her fingertips along his lips, memorizing every curve and crease.

He gripped her hands and covered them in more kisses until Maureen's knees weakened. "Just a bit longer, my dear. We must be patient. And prudent."

Maureen slid her arms around his waist and laid her ear against his chest. The sound of his breathing and the beating of his heart soothed her. He held her close for a long, yet all-too-short moment, before releasing her and taking her hand.

When Maureen's fingers grazed his wedding ring, her heart dropped, and she stepped away from his embrace. But he pulled her close again and whispered in her ear. "You'll come to stay with us. Soon we'll need you even more, and I can convince Margaret to keep you on full-time."

Maureen wanted to beg him again to run away together. But it could never be. He was too well-known, his family too connected. If she wanted to be with him, she'd have to settle for his plan. A floorboard creaked in the hallway outside the study, and Maureen risked pulling him in for one more kiss. One deep enough to convey all that she could not say to him.

They'd broken the embrace, breathless, and he whispered, "Soon, my love. Soon." With a final squeeze of her hand, he'd breezed into the hallway. "Ah! There you are, my darling."

Maureen swiped at the rebellious tears sliding down her cheeks. Though she knew herself to be alone, she cast a glance around the dark room just to make sure. When she was certain, she brushed a kiss onto the photo before replacing it in the drawer, ensuring it was well hidden.

She returned to bed, and the unwanted memory that always accompanied the previous one threatened to resurface. Maureen fought to shove it back down and lock it up before it could do its damage, but it bullied itself into her mind just the same. This vision, though more than a score old, replayed just as vividly as the torrid one she'd just relived. The moment Richard had shattered her dreams and broken her heart with one simple phrase. "I've changed my mind."

Though a sordid affair was not what she had dreamed of as a child, that had mattered very little after the first time they kissed. She'd admired him for years and never dared hope he would share her feelings. But once their romance had begun, it progressed very quickly, with feelings deepening far swifter than Maureen was prepared for. She had fallen head over heels and would have done anything to stay with Richard—even if it meant living under the same roof with his wife, serving as nanny by day and lover by night.

But rather than finally being with the man she loved, she'd instead been relegated to the shelf. Rejected. He'd given no reason other than, "It wouldn't work." And without giving her a chance to reply, he'd left. That one conversation set into motion things that could never be undone. And Maureen wasn't even remotely close to being finished making Richard Boyd pay.

The following morning, astride Cara for the first time since his arrival a week ago, Michael resisted the urge to giggle like a juvenile as he snapped the reins, encouraging the steed to gallop. They'd circumnavigated the empty recreation field several times, but both man and beast were itching to fly. So Michael had guided them to the edge of Ballymacool Wood. A wide path cut through the trees with very few low-hanging branches to endanger them, so he'd released Cara to her good will.

As they careened around pines and birch trees, with the earthy scent of turf and moss enveloping them, the tension in Michael's shoulders began to ease. While he'd expected his stint at Ballymacool to vex him, he anticipated all the issues to stem from Adeline. Though his cousin had done plenty to contribute to his frustrations, more and more of them came from those who were supposed to be caring for the students under the tutelage of the school.

He tugged the reins and slid from the saddle after Cara trotted to a stop. He led her to a lush grassy patch while he enjoyed the solitude of the woods. How long since he'd enjoyed such a morning? Too long. He lowered himself to lounge against the base of a large Scots pine. He'd always loved the way the branches of that breed started farther up the trunk than most trees, and then how they stretched their branches into collective tufts of needles.

He leaned against the trunk, but his admiration was interrupted by a lump protruding into his lower back. He shifted and pulled the item from behind him. He frowned at what he held in his hand—a shoe. By the looks of it, a woman's shoe. He stood and searched for its mate. Several yards away, he spotted another shoe wedged at the base of a large rock. But before he could get to it, he was smacked over the head by something.

"Oy! What're ya like?" he screeched, rubbing his head. Clumps of dirt and turf tumbled down.

"Oy yerself there, lad!"

Michael turned to face a small woman with a basket strapped to her back. He hadn't heard her approach and had no idea whence she'd come.

"What've ya done wit' her?"

He looked around. "With who?"

She reached over her shoulder and produced a spate of turf, like an arrow from a quiver. She wagged it at him, gesturing to the shoe in his hand.

"That's her *bróg* ye've got." She stepped closer, now brandishing the peat briquette like a sword. "An' she wouldna gone far wi'out her *bróga*. So, I'll ask ye again, *cá bhfuil sí?*" Desperation laced her voice.

Michael stepped back and held up his hands. "*Níl a fhios agam.*" He hoped using their mother tongue would disarm the woman. "Forgive me, but I've no idea who you're referring to."

She *tsked* and rolled her eyes. "Ye're holdin' Brianna's shoe. What have ya done wit' her?"

The shoe fell from his hand. "Brianna? Brianna's missing?"

"She missin' fer me. She's not missin' if ya know where she is." She stepped closer still and slayed him with a threat reserved for Ireland's worst offenders.

Ignoring the insult, Michael's thoughts shifted to Brianna as concern for her safety settled heavy on his chest. If these were, in fact, Brianna's shoes, then where was she indeed?

"I believe there's been a misunderstanding." He spoke slowly, choosing to use their native language again. "I didn't take this from Brianna. I came out riding my horse"—he gestured to Cara—"and found this shoe laying at the base o' this tree. And the match is near that rock there."

The strange woman craned to see around him.

"Do ya have any idea why she might remove her shoes way out here?"

She looked at him like she thought him the biggest *amadán* in Donegal. "She always does that when she's out here. It's how she communes with Him." She inclined her head upward.

The corner of Michael's lips tipped up at the thought.

"But"—she held up a crooked finger—"she's never left without them. And she's not been out this way in days."

Michael peeked behind him, as if Brianna would be standing there to solve this mystery. She wasn't. "When was the last time ya saw her?"

The woman's eyes rolled back in her head as she thought. "'Bout four or five days."

Michael's head bobbed, relief making a tiny dent in his worry. "Well, I saw her this morning when she served breakfast. She was still doing the washing up when I left."

The woman's shoulders fell in relief. Then she uttered a strange, guttural growl, as if acquiescing to a request she didn't want to follow. Turning toward the muted daylight at the far edge of the woods, she waved him forward. "C'mon, then."

He looked around to see if he was being set up as the butt of some kind of prank or jest. But no one was there.

"Are ya comin' or not?" she called over her shoulder.

Michael gave Cara the command to stay and jogged after the strange woman. He followed her into a run-down chalet and blinked as his vision adjusted to the dim interior. Though aged, everything inside was neat and tidy, which he found surprising.

"Sit down and have yerself a cuppa before ya go." She shuffled to the fireplace and lifted a kettle from a hook. "I don't have any cake, so this will have to do."

"*Go raibh maith agat, a . . .*" He winced. "Beggin' yer pardon, but I don't believe I caught your name."

"Finnuala."

"Finnuala," Michael repeated. Then he extended his hand. She eyed it for a moment, then accepted and shook it.

"Michael." He smiled. "Michael Wray."

Finnuala stilled, a twinkle sparkling in her eye. "Wray? As in Castlewray Estate?"

"That's right." He nodded. "I'm at Ballymacool House for a bit, lookin' after my cousin."

She stepped back and regarded him again and muttered something. Michael wasn't sure, but it sounded like, "flustering man."

He took a sip of tea and let his eyes drift closed as the warm, soothing liquid trailed down to his stomach. Finnuala's chuckle brought him back to reality.

"*Go maith*, eh?"

"Aye," he said after another sip. "Very good."

They sat in silence, enjoying their small repast until Michael asked, "So, how do ya know Brianna?"

Finnuala's gaze drifted far away and her eyes became glassy. "We go way back. I've known her since she was a wee one scamperin' around the woods."

Michael smiled at the image. He waited, but when Finnuala didn't offer any more of the story, he finished the last of his tea and stood. "Thank you, again, for the tea. It was just what the doctor ordered."

Finnuala took their cups and set them in the basin. "Always is," she said, chuckling. She shuffled past him and opened the door.

She placed a knotted hand on his arm as he passed through. When he stopped, she waited until he met her gaze. "Take care, now."

Michael's brow knitted for a beat. It was a typical parting sentiment, but her tone seemed to hold more weight somehow, and he got the distinct feeling she had laid more meaning behind it than met the eye. "I will."

He stooped through the door and squinted at the daylight outside. Finnuala shuffled out behind him, stopping near the tented pile of turf about halfway between her chalet and the tree line. Michael smiled to himself at the tradition of a multistaged farewell.

"*Slán abhaile*," she said.

"Slán."

He turned at the forest edge and waved. She lifted a shaky hand and lowered it. He knew she'd watch until he could no longer be seen.

Cara was right where Michael had left her, and so were Brianna's shoes. He stuffed them into his saddlebag, hopped up into the saddle, and urged her back to Ballymacool House.

10

As Michael and Cara wound their way back through the woods, movement in the distance caught Michael's attention. He tugged the reins to halt the horse, then slid off the saddle and craned to see around a large poplar.

There was Brianna, barefoot, arms reached to the sky. She didn't move or talk, but stayed perfectly still, head back. Sunlight trickled down in dappled streams and pooled at her feet. Michael couldn't help but wonder if God Himself was visiting her. He wouldn't be surprised.

Much as he wanted to talk with her, he couldn't bring himself to interrupt her communion. But just as he tried to remount his steed, Cara whinnied loudly in protest, not wanting to leave the patch of clover she'd found. Michael winced.

Brianna's hands dropped and she faced him, mouth agape. "Mister Wray?"

Michael had thought about ducking behind a tree, but it was too late now. He'd been caught. "Hi there."

She strode over and stopped in front of him. "Did ya"—
she looked around, brows drawn together—"did ya follow
me here?"

Michael waved his hands in front of him. "No, no, nothing like that." She cocked a brow at him so he hurried to
continue. "I decided to go for a ride after breakfast. Cara
has been pinned up in that stable since I arrived, an' we both
were a bit antsy for some fresh air."

Brianna sent a puff of air through her nose and nodded
as if to say, *I know what you mean.*

"Anyway," he continued, "while I was out here, I found
these." He reached into his saddlebag and produced Brianna's shoes.

Her mouth fell open. "*There* they are!" She took the shoes
and slid them onto her feet. "Thank you. I've been havin'
to wear a borrowed pair from Mary, and her feet are much
smaller than mine."

"Not at all." He smiled. "In fact, I think I met a friend of
yours. Finnuala?"

Brianna grimaced. "She didn't hurt ya, did she?"

Michael laughed as he pictured the old woman jumping
up on his back and pummeling him. "No, she didn't. She
threatened to though. She can wield a mean turf briquette."
He rubbed the spot on his head where she'd hit him.

Her brows soared. "Oh, ya must tell." Brianna stepped
over and sat down on a large boulder. She gestured for him
to join her on the smaller one next to it.

He did, feeling quite foolish when his knees reached almost up to his chin with his feet flat on the ground.

Brianna tried to hide a chuckle behind her hand.

Michael stretched his legs out long and crossed them at

the ankles, then he regaled her with the tale of the brave and noble Finnuala and her quiver of peat.

By the end of his story, Brianna was laughing so hard tears ran down her cheeks. She wrapped her arms around her stomach, doubling over. Michael watched, relishing the sight of Brianna laughing with abandon. This was the first time he'd heard her laugh—or seen her really, truly smile, for that matter—and he wanted more of it.

When her laughter died down, she wiped her eyes and sighed. "Oh heavens, Batty an' Mary are gonna love that one." She clamped her lips together, and her shoulders started to shake. Before long, a guffaw burst out as she was sent into another spate of laughter.

Eventually, Michael found it impossible not to join in, contagious as hilarity is and all. So the pair of them sat there in the woods cackling like they'd just escaped the asylum. He felt every bit a cabbage, but he didn't care. Let the world think him an eejit. He'd endure far worse insults if it meant making Brianna Kelly laugh again.

"Alright," he said when things died down. "Now 'tis your turn."

She recoiled in confusion. "My turn? For what?"

"What were *you* doin' out here?"

"Oh." Her chin lowered. She picked at an errant snag in her apron and shrugged. After a lengthy moment of silence, she said, "'Tis the only place I'm truly free."

How does one respond to that? They sat in comfortable silence until a gust of breeze rattled through the woods.

"Listen," Brianna whispered.

"What?"

"Just listen. Close your eyes an' be still."

He gave her a sidelong glance, but she wasn't paying any attention to him. Her face was tilted up to the canopy, her eyes shut, a funny little smile tickled the corners of her lips. His gaze lingered there overlong until she said, "Hear it?"

"Umm . . ." He let his eyes drift closed, turned his face upward, and waited. At first there was nothing. He was tempted to forget it all and just pretend he heard something, because he felt a bit ridiculous. But then it happened.

It started softly at first and then grew to resemble the rushing roar of water. He opened his eyes and gazed upward. The branches of the trees swayed, and the leaves trembling in the breeze were like the reflection of candlelight dancing on silver. The rushing died down to a whisper before crescendoing again with gusto. Some of the branches bumped together, clacking and creaking while the carpet of dried foliage on the ground sprang to life, swirling and whirling with a million crackles and crunches. A symphony was unfolding before him.

"They're tellin' each other their secrets." Brianna's voice was soft and reverent. "And if ya listen closely, you can understand them."

Michael turned to her, but she said no more. He watched her for a moment in wonder, then turned away to offer the space the moment demanded.

When the wind died down and the whispering of the trees stopped, she spoke again. "I've been comin' here since I was a girl. Some of my earliest memories are from right here."

Michael shifted to sit on the ground and rested against the stone. "No wonder ya love it so much."

"Mmm." He sensed she was nodding. "That's how Finnuala found me. I was out here playing and dancing, an' suddenly there she was. I couldn't have been older than maybe four or so. I can't remember now."

He craned his neck to see her face. "Oh, did your parents bring you out here often?"

Brianna's expression darkened as her gaze drifted to the forest floor. When she spoke, sadness laced her voice. "No. I'm an orphan."

He shifted now to face her fully. "Goodness, I am so very sorry. I had no idea."

Brianna shrugged and a sad smile tugged at her lips. "Don't fret, sir. How could you have known?"

Michael plucked a strand of grass from a crack in the rock. "So, you've been at Ballymacool . . ."

"My whole life, yep."

"I confess, it surprises me to hear Mistress Magee would bring you here, but I'm glad for it. Do she and Finnuala get on well?"

Her forehead crinkled and she looked at him like he had three heads. "I don't believe they've ever met."

"Really? What did she do when Finnuala appeared that day?"

Brianna flapped her hand. "Oh, she wasna out here. I was alone."

Michael's mouth gaped. "At four?" His voice cracked. "You were out here, alone, when ya were four years old?"

Brianna shrugged, unfazed by the notion. "Oh, aye. Well, I had probably been out here when I was younger than that, but I was four when I met Finnuala."

Michael stood and raked his fingers through his hair and scratched at his beard. "Unbelievable," he said through gritted teeth. "To let a child, not even old enough to make her own cuppa, out in the woods alone? Unthinkable."

"Is it so unusual?" Bewilderment etched on Brianna's face.

Angry pressure built in Michael's chest until he thought he might explode. Then he looked on Brianna again and softened. "Never mind. What matters now is that ye're safe. And happy . . . well, safe."

Her eyes searched his for a moment, then her gaze drifted, and he could tell she was somewhere far away.

He broke the silence that had settled between them. "Well, I'd better start headin' back. I need to check in with Adeline."

Brianna looked to the sun. "I'll come too. I don't want to be late again, though I still have plenty o' time. I have some things I want to do."

Michael nodded and finally managed to cajole Cara from the clover patch, which was now merely . . . a patch. Michael and Brianna had walked a few paces, with Cara trailing reluctantly behind them, when Brianna suddenly stopped.

"Wait!" She spun on her heel and sprinted back to a large, sprawling oak tree.

When she returned, she held up a pair of shoes. "Can't forget these. Mary would never forgive me."

Michael stooped and picked up a twig that resembled a brick of peat. "What've ya done wit' her?" He put on his best shaky old woman voice, which sent Brianna into another fit of laughter.

They were still chuckling when they reached the edge of the woods. "Thank ya again, Mister Wray." She laid her hand on his arm.

The whole world stilled at her touch. "Please, call me Michael." He cringed at how gravelly his voice sounded.

Her gaze met his and held for a long moment.

"Well, well, well, what do we have here?"

Michael's and Brianna's heads turned in unison. Adeline stood on the path where it forked toward the barn and recreation field. Her lip curled.

"Adeline," Michael said, "I was just coming to see you."

"Mm-hmm, sure looks that way." Adeline crossed her arms and stomped up to Brianna. She growled something under her breath so that Michael couldn't hear.

"Enough," he said. "Come, cousin, we need to talk."

Adeline kept her eyes glued to Brianna. "Yes, yes, we do." Then she sidled up to Michael, hooked her arm around his elbow, and tugged him in the direction of the stables.

Michael looked over his shoulder and mouthed a silent plea. "Help me."

She laughed again and clamped a hand over her mouth.

Adeline was saying something, but all Michael could hear was Brianna's laughter echoing in his ears.

Brianna practically glided up the stairs to her room. She never would have imagined that her time in the woods could get any more refreshing and restoring, and yet it had. Sharing such laughter and stories with someone like Mister Wray—nae, with Michael—had enriched the entire experience beyond what she would have ever thought possible. And such depth of laughter had lifted a weight she hadn't realized had settled on her chest.

Once in her chamber, she looked out the window onto the world below. Rounding the corner from the stables was

Adeline, with Michael in tow. Her arm was still wrapped around his, and he was a good half a pace behind her with a look of absolute resignation on his face. Brianna chuckled again. Then she remembered why she'd come up here.

Being at her tree again had reminded her of the . . . well, whatever it was she'd uncovered last time she was there. Kneeling down, she removed the loose floorboard and set it aside. She pulled out a tattered box filled with all the treasures she'd found over the years. The chain to a pocket watch. A rusted tin cup. A mangled twist of Bríd's Cross made out of rushes. The thimble. She smiled at each one, as though revisiting old friends. Once she'd gone through all her old trinkets, she turned her attention to her new one.

She reached into the opening in the floor and groped until she came upon it and pulled it out. She examined it for the first time in bright daylight. One end was bent up so much that it almost curled in and touched the flat area near the center. She thumped it and the telltale clang confirmed it was some sort of metal. Probably tin. She held it at arm's length and studied it. It seemed to have been an oval shape at one point, and the edges appeared slightly scalloped, though that could just be more distortion from being buried.

She scratched at the rust, but other than a light dust that fell in her lap, none of it would come off. She turned it over, but no distinguishing marks were there. She took the edge of her apron and rubbed vigorously, but all she got for her efforts was an orange stain on her apron that she'd have to clean later and a sore finger from scrubbing. In the distance, the clock chimed four.

Och! Go luath? Already? What was it about this warped hunk of metal that seemed to warp time? If Brianna wasn't careful, she'd end up with another week of round-the-clock duty. She returned all her treasures to their hiding place and stood. She hastily splashed water on her face from the wash jug and basin and replaited her hair before going downstairs to help Cook start preparations for the evening meal.

11

The next morning, as Michael was preparing to leave the cottage, someone knocked at the door. His smile faltered a bit when he opened it to find Batty standing there. "Oh, it's you." He kicked himself for the flatness in his voice.

"Ah," Batty said, "me wife says the same thing. Or she did, God rest her soul."

Michael laughed and grimaced. "Sorry, I thought ya were . . . someone else."

"Oh, yer parents aren't here yet, lad."

Michael blinked. "Pardon?"

"We're expectin' yer folks, but they're not here yet. They sent word it won't be 'til this afternoon."

"Oh, right." Michael shook his head. Leave it to Father to plan a visit without sending word to him first. Another reminder that the world revolves around Edward Wray's whims. "Thanks."

"Ye're welcome, but that's not why I'm here. Mistress

Magee wants to see ya before *bricfeasta*." He tipped his cap and turned to go.

"Thanks, Batty," Michael called after him as he slid the door shut. *Magee? Hmm.* He looked down at his clothes. The wool jumper, button-down, and casual trousers wouldn't do today. He strode to the press in his room and peered inside. He fingered through the items hanging there until he found what he was looking for. Removing the fine three-piece wool suit that his parents had insisted be packed, Michael muttered, "Never thought I'd be glad to see you." He made quick work of changing and headed for Magee's office.

Once again, he found himself alone while he waited for the headmistress. This time, rather than sitting or gazing out the window, he took the liberty of perusing the shelves of books lining the wall behind her desk. She had several thick tomes of one kind or another, none of which interested Michael in the slightest. One shelf housed a row of educational manuals and textbooks. He ran his finger along their spines and was about to move to the next shelf when a thin book caught his eye. He tilted his head to read the spine. *Ballymacool House: A Complete History.* No author was listed.

He tugged the book until it slid free from its place wedged between two massively thick books about grammar of the English language. The cover was plain, black with white text stating the title. A short table of contents followed the title page, and the title of chapter 3 caught his eye. "The Boyds of Ballymacool."

He flipped to the page and began to read. A lineage of the Boyd family ensued until finally it stated that the Boyds had bought the lands of Ballymacool in 1783 and built a "palatial mansion" on the grounds. Michael tried to envision what this place had been like as a family home. Was it warmer? More welcoming? He fanned through the rest of the chapter, but before he could skim any farther, the door closed with a thud.

"Make yourself right at home, why don't you, Mister Wray." Mistress Magee circled the desk, snatched the book from his hand, and waited for him to take his place on the other side of the desk.

"Ah, good morning, Mistress Magee." Michael smiled and waited for her reply. When none came, he added, "Batty said you wanted to see me?" He sauntered around the desk, stood as straight and tall as he could muster, and looked Magee in the eye, waiting for her to speak.

"Have a seat, please, Mister Wray." She sank into the oversized chair behind her desk and deposited *Ballymacool House: A Complete History* into one of the drawers.

"I prefer to stand, thank you," Michael said, clasping his hands in front of him.

The lines on Magee's face deepened, but she said only, "Very well. It has come to my attention that you are spending time in the company of my scullery maid."

Michael let no reaction register on his face, but he couldn't believe what he was hearing. For goodness' sake! He'd helped Brianna clean up the mess he had caused, and then just happened to run into her while on a ride in the woods. He would hardly define that as keeping the company of the girl. "Is that so?"

She folded her hands on the desktop. "Yes, and I simply cannot abide it. Brianna is needed here. She has far too much work to do to be galivanting with the likes of . . . well, that is, it is simply improper."

"Mistress Magee," Michael said while adjusting the cuffs of his jacket sleeves, "I can assure you, nothing improper has transpired."

Magee's forehead creased. "So you say. Nevertheless, I cannot have Brianna distracted from her tasks here."

"Begging your pardon, mistress, but the one time I happened to run into Miss Kelly was on her day off. I hardly find it fair that you expect her to while away her hours here when you've granted her leave."

Her gaze narrowed. "It's Brianna to you, Mister Wray. You know very well her station does not afford her such formalities. What my staff does with their leave time is none of your concern."

"It is when their leave time involves accusations against me." He kept his voice even, his face stoic. "And it seems to me, the way you treat your staff—Miss Kelly, in particular—leaves quite a bit to be desired."

Magee slowly rose to her feet, pressing the tips of her fingers on the desktop. "I have given you a lot of leeway, Mister Wray, out of respect for your family and all you—er, they—have done for the parish. But you are here to assist with the problems involving your cousin. Nothing more. I must insist you keep your interactions with this institution to just that."

His eyes widened. "Leeway?"

"Yes." Her voice rose even more. "You must agree you've overstepped by quite a degree. What with your interfering during our mealtimes and disrupting lessons and tolerating unruly behavior from your cousin on the recreation field. Enough is simply enough, sir, and I must put my foot down."

At his sides, Michael's fingers curled into tight fists and

uncurled, buying him a moment to regain his composure. "You are right, headmistress. My family has done quite a bit for this parish and will continue to do so. And ya would do well to remember the influence we hold in this area." Michael hated using his family's station to manipulate any situation, but in this case, it was necessary. The only thing Magee responded to was fear. And while he wasn't entirely sure what exactly it was she was so afraid of, the longer he was at Ballymacool, the more he got the sense that its headmistress was hiding something. "And not that I have to explain myself to you, but since ya seem to have misinterpreted just about everything that has transpired since my arrival, I will enlighten ya."

He crossed to the door and placed his hand on the knob. "What you call my 'interference' in the dining hall put your precious routine back on schedule. During the lessons, I stepped in when Master McDaid was physically harming a student. And as far as Miss Kelly, I happened to bump into her on my way back in from a long ride on my horse. But, by all means, make sure I don't cause any more trouble. See to it I am informed the moment my parents arrive this afternoon."

Michael's parents arrived just as the midday meal was finishing, timing that perturbed Magee greatly. "Could they not have waited half an hour more?" Michael had heard her mutter to Batty as he tended to the motorcar. She still held her serviette in her hand, which she stuffed in the pocket of her skirts.

"Hello, Mother." Michael kissed both of her cheeks and embraced her once she alighted from the vehicle.

She scrunched her nose and rubbed where his beard had tickled. "Hello, dear. It's quite the bumpy drive, isn't it? And so dusty." She brushed her sleeves and skirts absently.

"Funny. I've never had that problem with Cara." He flashed a teasing grin at his mother, and she swatted his arm playfully.

Michael's father came around the front bumper, his face fixed in his usual dour expression of superiority. "You've got to change with the times, lad, or you'll be swept away into history with the past."

"Hello, Father." Michael couldn't keep the dryness from his voice. It wasn't that Michael resisted progress. He just didn't see the point in a rickety motorcar for a journey just as easily taken by steed. And why would you want to miss the solitude and . . . well, it was a losing argument. With Edward Wray, anyway. Michael bit his tongue and shook his father's hand.

His father just nodded and muttered a cold, "Son."

"We do hope Michael's been of assistance to you with Adeline," his mother said to Mistress Magee, who'd quietly stood behind the family as they reunited.

Magee flashed a sidelong glance at Michael, then replied, "We're making progress."

His mother clasped her hands in front of her. "Oh, good. Now, may we see the cottage?"

"Of course." Magee gestured to the door. "Right this way. How long will you be staying with us? Shall I have our maid prepare one of the other cottages for you?"

Michael's stomach dropped. He hadn't expected his parents to stay. He loved them very much, but without the usual social engagements and management duties that filled their calendar at Castlewray, they would be bored to death. And he'd be the one to bear the brunt of their boredom.

"That won't be necessary." His father straightened his cravat. "We'll only be a couple of hours."

Michael breathed a sigh of relief.

As they passed through the main house and headed toward the back lawn, Master McDaid hurried down the stairs in a huff. "Mistress Magee, I have need of you posthaste."

Magee's gaze pivoted between the Wrays and the agitated instructor. "Very well, McDaid. I'll come directly after I see our guests settled."

"You must come now," he hissed. "It's urgent!"

Magee puffed an annoyed sigh. "Very well." She stepped toward the kitchen. "Brianna! Come show our guests to Mister Wray's cottage."

Michael stifled an eye roll. "Mistress, I'm well familiar with the way."

"Nonsense." Magee flapped her hand as Brianna appeared in the doorway. "A good hostess always escorts her guests." With that she scurried to the stairs, and she and Master McDaid ascended them, their flustered chatter echoing in the hall.

"Right this way, if you please." Brianna extended her arm toward the chalets.

His parents brushed past without a word. Michael floated her an apologetic look and shook his head. "Thanks, Brianna."

She offered a brief smile and nodded. When they reached Michael's cottage, Brianna opened the door and showed his parents to the sitting area. The fire was already going full bore, and Michael invited his parents to settle in around it.

"Shall I bring tea?" Brianna asked.

"Splendid idea," his mother said. "Thank you."

Michael slid a chair from the table over to join his parents, who occupied the two wingback ones flanking the fireplace. They filled him in about all the goings-on at the estate, and they chatted about the weather and Adeline. Before long, Brianna returned with the tea.

She deftly poured a cup and brought it to his mother, who thanked her. As Brianna was serving his father, his mother asked, "Eh, Brianna, is it?"

Brianna nodded.

"Did you work on the McGonigle Estate in the past?"

"No, marm, I'm afraid not."

"For the Mansfields at Oak Park, then?"

Brianna shook her head. "I've been at Ballymacool my whole life."

His mother's brows knitted together, and she tipped her head slightly to the side. "Truly? Are you certain?"

A soft chuckle fluttered from Brianna's lips. "Yes, marm, very certain. May I ask why?"

His mother *tsked*. "It's nothing. Just that you seem very familiar to me. Have we met before?"

Brianna thought for a long moment before shaking her head.

"Well, never mind. You must have one of those faces." His mother smiled and sipped her tea.

Michael continued watching Brianna as she finished with the tea and left. Odd that his mother would have the same thought as he had. One of the things that had drawn him to Brianna was the strange sense that he'd seen her before. But after his time here, and talking with her, he still couldn't place where they would have crossed paths in the past.

"Michael, are you listening to me?" His father's voice shattered Michael's thoughts.

"Hmm? Oh, yes, Father. Carry on."

The rest of the afternoon passed more slowly than Michael would have liked. And there was never a good opportunity for him to divulge all he'd discovered here—McDaid's mistreatment of the students, as well as Magee's shadiness and ill treatment of Brianna and possibly the rest of the staff. The truth was he simply didn't have enough information for them to do much of anything. He'd have to visit the matter once his duties with Adeline were complete.

At last, just before dinner, his parents took their leave.

12

Brianna hurried to the kitchen, the frigid October morning prickling her skin awake with each step. The days since Michael had first run into her in the woods a week ago had been like a dream. Magee had been just as abrasive with her as always, and the workload was the same—or more arduous—but it didn't bother Brianna in the slightest. Looking forward to her weekly leave time had refreshed her spirit more than usual. She pretended that bumping into Michael several times since then hadn't played a big role in the change. He'd smiled at her the few times they'd passed one another in the corridor and seemed genuinely pleased to see her when she delivered his nightly tea tray. Magee probably assumed he either thought himself above preparing his own or was completely inept at it. Then there was the next time she walked to the woods and back on her daily constitutional. They'd crossed paths as she was returning to the house and he was just heading out for a ride on Cara. Their conversation had been brief but enough to quicken her heart. Not that they'd spoken of anything terribly intimate. The changing of the leaves, the perpetual dryness of Cook's fish, things of that nature.

Near the door to the kitchen, Brianna gathered up an armload of turf briquettes and passed through the threshold. Stepping inside, she headed to the fireplace to deposit her burden, but her foot caught on something. Her knees buckled and she crumpled to the floor, the peat tumbling from her arms. Brianna rubbed her shin and squinted in the dark. Not much could be seen, but something seemed amiss. She groped the area around her until her hands found what had tripped her—one of the large copper pots by the feel of it. Odd.

Slowly climbing to her feet, she reached for the hurricane lamp always kept on the counter near the door. Lighting it and winding the flame as high as it would go, she let her eyes adjust. She gasped and her heart dropped. Dishes were shattered all over the floor, pots and pans were strewn about, and the bags of flour and oats were tattered, their contents covering everything like a dusting of snow. Water dripped from the grate in the fireplace and Brianna's apron strings dangled from the oven door, which sat ajar.

"*Céard sa diabhal?*" she whispered to the chaos. What on earth had happened? With marked steps, she walked the periphery of the room. Not a single thing remained in its original place. Who would have done this? How had no one heard the racket? She grabbed a rag and started swiping the mess into her hand. She stopped short. A message was scrawled out in the flour and oats on her main workbench. *Ballymacool sees all. And you're next.*

Brianna spun around as though the perpetrator was standing behind her. But nothing was there, save the disarray.

Pressing the palms of her hands to her head, she turned in a slow circle, racking her brain for any clue as to who could have done this—and why.

"Brianna!" Magee's voice shattered the silence, drifting in from the hallway. "Before you start the porridge"—Magee's voice trailed off as she scurried through the door and noticed the mess. "What in the heavens?"

In a flash, Magee closed the distance between them and landed a hearty slap across Brianna's cheek. "What have you done? You imbecile! What were you thinking?"

Brianna rubbed the burning spot on her cheek. "'Twasn't me, marm. I don't know who it was. But not me." She worked her jaw, hoping to ease the aching that had set in.

Magee dragged a finger through the mess caking the countertop, then brushed her hands together while her eyes surveyed the damage. Her head wagged slowly from side to side as she rounded the workbench. When her gaze fell on the message, she stopped and pointed a long, bony finger in Brianna's direction. "What have you done?" she growled through gritted teeth. "What have you done?" She grabbed Brianna's shoulder and shook her violently. "You've done something, I know it! What? What is it?"

Brianna squeezed her eyes shut and tried to brace herself against Magee's flailing. Finally, she thrust her arms up, breaking the woman's grasp on her. Brianna rubbed the back of her arms where the woman's fingers had dug into her skin and backed away from Magee. "I've no idea what it means, marm. No idea 'tall. I've done nothing improper or worthy of such scorn."

Magee snorted and smoothed her hair back, as though it took great effort to settle her rage. "Well, you had to have done something, girl. Why else would someone have done this? Written that?" She practically spat the last word.

"Truly, marm, I've no idea." She shook her head. "I'm just as perplexed as you."

Magee scoffed. "Now you've really got your work cut out for you, girl. You've got to get this, this . . . *praiseach* cleaned up. And there's breakfast to prepare. So you'd best get going."

Brianna gaped at the headmistress, but quickly steadied her composure. "All due respect, marm, 'twould take days to fully set this to rights."

"Well then, *déan deifir!*"

"I-I will, miss. But . . . it just isn't possible to fully clean it today, let alone before breakfast." She scanned the kitchen and her gaze fell upon a few untouched loaves of bread tucked in a corner. She sighed in relief. "Since we've no oats left for porridge, allow me to fetch some eggs from the henhouse an' make scrambled eggs an' toast for the girls. I'm sure they'll be delighted."

Magee's hands balled at her sides. "Brianna!" The outburst jolted her. Magee took a deep breath, and when she spoke again, her voice was unnervingly calm, almost sickly-sweet. "Yes, that will be fine." She paused with a long blink. "But make no mistake, this mess will get taken care of. And until it does, you will not eat, you will not sleep, you will not take a moment off."

Brianna's head slowly dipped forward. "Yes, marm."

Suddenly, the side door burst open. "Is everything alright?" Michael entered the room, breathless. "I heard shouting." When he noticed the disarray, he gasped and hastened farther into the room. "What happened?"

"Ask Brianna," Magee said through gritted teeth.

When he looked at her, Brianna shrugged so slightly, she wasn't sure anyone would have been able to see it. Michael's face softened, and his eyes met hers. They seemed to be asking, "Are you okay?"

Magee's sudden and strident clap startled both of them. "I believe you have work to do." Her stare bored into Brianna before she headed toward the hallway. She stopped at the top of the steps.

Michael's face darkened and he stepped closer to Magee, who blinked rapidly a few times and softened her stance a mite. "You remember what I said, girl?" Magee said, glaring in Brianna's direction.

"Yes, marm."

When Magee had gone, Michael moved to Brianna's side. "Are you alright?" he asked.

Brianna fought the stinging behind her eyes. Why must his kindness undo her so?

He stepped closer still, his eyes searching hers. He winced and lifted his hand as though he was going to touch her face. Brianna's breath stilled. But he merely gestured to her cheek and lowered his hand. "Does she do that often? Hit you?"

Brianna's hand absently drifted toward the sore spot just below her eye, which still burned. "'Tis nothing."

Michael studied her for a long beat, his jaw working back and forth. "Hmm."

"Truly," she said, keeping her gaze on the floor, not trusting herself to meet his. "'Tis fine. If you'll excuse me, I'm far behind schedule preparing breakfast."

"How can I help?"

A laugh slipped from Brianna's lips but not a joyful one.

"Ya don't need to do anything, Mister Wray." She hoped using his formal name would bring her feelings toward him to heel. "I just need to get started."

He pinned her with a look that communicated his disbelief. "Brianna. Let me help." He laid his hand on her arm. "Please."

Fighting the electricity shooting up from his touch, she nodded and pointed to the corner. "The bread." The words eked out shakily, so she cleared her throat. "It needs to be sliced so it can be toasted."

He smiled. "Perfect. Now, where would I find a knife?"

Brianna looked to the stand where the knives usually stood, but it was toppled over and empty. "Well, typically they're there. But your guess is as good as mine."

He chuckled. "Indeed. I'll find one. You do what ya need to do."

Brianna stooped and tugged the apron strings dangling from the oven door. Pulling it free, she held up the blackened fabric. "I need to go gather the eggs from the hens. But first, it seems I must fetch my other apron." When she looked at Michael, his eyes were so wide and there was such a perplexed look on his face, she couldn't help the laughter that rumbled up into her chest and bubbled out of her mouth.

He nodded. "Aye, I believe ya do." He flicked his wrist toward the door. "G'on. I'll start on the bread."

She started up the stairs to the hallway and called over her shoulder. "Thanks."

"*Cinnte*," Michael said and Brianna smiled at his use of Irish.

Her smile faded when she reached her bedchamber door. A rugged square of paper had been nailed to it. *You deserve far worse than a wrecked kitchen. Watch yourself or you'll be next.*

With shaky fingers, Brianna ripped the note from the nail and studied it, for once wishing the headmistress hadn't insisted she learn to read. The script was unfamiliar. She so rarely saw handwritten words, though, so she likely wouldn't have recognized anyone's penmanship. Shivers crept up the back of her neck, along with the eerie feeling she was being watched. Though her room was the only one at the top of the stairs, and the landing was small, she couldn't shake the sensation. Hesitantly, she pushed the door open and scanned her room before entering. When all seemed in order, she hurried in, snatched her apron from the nail on the wall, shoved the note in its pocket, and scurried down the stairs.

Michael had just finished slicing the last heel of bread when Brianna returned. She held her apron in a pouch, which sagged under the weight of the eggs she carried. The red mark had mostly faded, leaving her cheeks looking paler than usual. He swiped a small basket from the floor and carried it to her. "*An bhfuil tú ceart go leor?*" he asked as she gently dumped the eggs into the basket. She looked truly vexed—in a way he'd never seen as a result of Maureen Magee.

"I'm fine, thank you." She busied herself cracking and preparing the eggs, then she prepped the pan where Michael would toast the bread.

They continued their tasks in silence for a few moments, all the while Michael stole glimpses of her as he worked. She chewed her lip and would pause and stare off in deep thought. A couple of times she slid her hand into the pocket of her apron and fiddled with whatever was inside. When she rested her hands on the workbench, shoulders hunched with a sigh, he could remain quiet no longer.

He stepped to her side and asked again, "Are ya sure ye're alright?"

Her head remained low, her voice quiet. "I'm fine."

Placing a gentle hand on her shoulder, he turned her to face him. "Brianna, what's wrong?" A shock of hair fell across her forehead, and he resisted the urge to brush it from her face.

"I don't want to burden ya with my troubles." She turned and scraped the cooked eggs into a few of the serving dishes that had survived the tirade of the night before. "Besides, it's likely just a prankster."

Michael layered the finished toast on a platter. "It must be some prank to drain the color from your face as it has, and to vex ya so." He loaded the dishes onto a large tray. When Brianna reached to pick it up, he laid his hand over hers. "I'd like to help, if I can."

She stilled, her gaze fixed on their hands, but she didn't pull away. When she finally lifted her face and looked at him, her eyes shone with unshed tears.

She slid her hand from underneath his, reached into the pocket of her apron, and pulled out a crumpled piece of paper. He took it from her and read it. His brows pulled together.

"Have ya any idea who it could be? What they could mean?"

Brianna shook her head and tucked a strand of hair behind her ear. "Not at all. That's the strangest part of it." She rested against the counter and crossed her arms. "I mean, I'm no stranger to teasing. Often the boarders feel the need to remind me o' their elevated position and make jokes at my expense. But they've never done an'thing as . . . menacing as these notes seem."

Michael's face scrunched. "Notes? There've been more?"

"Tá, one was scratched into the oats and flour here on the workbench this morning. Its sentiment much the same as that one." She gestured to the note in his hand. "Both allude to some wrongdoing on my part, but I've done no such thing."

"I should think not." Michael's head bobbed. "Everything I've seen from ya since I arrived has been nothing but proper and polite."

A hint of color returned to her cheeks as she smiled. "Thank you."

"I'd like to help ya get to the bottom of this," he said. "If that's alright with you?"

"That's very kind of ya, but I'm really not sure what good it would do." She lifted the tray of toast and eggs. "Now, if ye'll excuse me, the girls will be waiting for their breakfast."

"O'course." Michael slipped past her, climbed the three steps, and opened the door to the hall. "And I'll keep my eyes and ears open. I'll let ya know if I learn anything that might be of any use."

She thanked him and disappeared around the corner.

13

Breakfast had gone blessedly smoothly. The girls felt the meal of eggs and toast was a veritable feast compared to the bland porridge they ate every other morning. So they had taken extra care not to drop a single morsel, making cleanup minimal and easy. Cleanup of the dining room, anyway. Brianna now stood in the disastrous kitchen and surveyed the damage more fully in the daylight. She combed her fingers through her hair, fastened it in a tighter plait than usual, and wound it into a knot at the base of her neck.

Starting in the southwest corner of the room, she began wiping the counters free of the fine flour and scattered oats. She focused on one area, making sure to get into every nook and cranny to avoid attracting any critters or encourage any molding. Two hours later, that corner of the room shone, except for the floor, which she would save for last. No point in sweeping when cleaning the rest of the surfaces would undoubtedly drop more dirt and dust, requiring her to clean it again.

The door from the hallway creaked open and Michael descended the stairs. He'd pushed up the sleeves of his cable-knit wool jumper to reveal his corded forearms, giving him the casual air of a working man. He surveyed the room and smiled, revealing his bearded dimples yet again and allowing his impeccable teeth to peek through and belie his station. "Makin' progress, I see?"

Brianna puffed a sigh and pressed her hands to the small of her back. "Slowly but surely, it'll get there. One o' these days."

"I was looking for Mistress Magee," he told her. "Batty said he thought she might be in here?" As he stepped off the bottom stair, he slipped on a rag and staggered forward. Reaching out to grab the counter, his hand slapped onto a pile of flour, which puffed out forcefully, landing directly in Brianna's eyes.

"Good gracious me, I'm terribly sorry," he said. And with her eyes closed, Brianna felt his presence draw nearer.

"Never mind. It's fine. I'm fine." She tried to open her eyes, only to have to clamp them shut again from the stabbing pain. She rubbed feverishly at them.

A warm hand pressed onto her shoulder. "No, no, don't rub at it. That'll make it worse. Here." Brianna flinched slightly as the coarse edge of a towel brushed her face, but it was soiled and only sent another dusting of flour into her eye, adding to the already searing pain.

"Thank you, I'm fine. Truly." She waved her hand, but her palm swatted his cheek. "Oh *muise*! I'm so sorry!" She tried once more to open her eyes but couldn't. She lifted her hands again to try to clear it, but Michael softly caught her wrists.

"Hold still." His voice was deep. Soothing, yet unsettling

in the most wonderful way. "Hold still," he repeated, the tenor of his voice reverberating in her chest. "Let me see." She felt him draw even closer. So close his toes brushed hers. She rocked back, off-balance, and reached out to steady herself, grasping onto his jumper. Warm, tender hands cupped both of her cheeks.

His breaths fell softly on her face, sending her heart thudding in her ears, but she kept her hands pressed against his chest to hold herself still. He brushed the excess dust from her lids. "Ah, here we go." His finger tenderly swiped the corner of her eye. "There. Better?"

Brianna squinted up at him. The lines of his face blurred. She blinked a few more times and tried again. Gradually his features came into view. A scant handbreadth separated them, and the reality of his nearness stole her breath away.

"Better?" he asked again, barely above a whisper. His eyes were locked on hers, but dropped briefly to her lips, then back up again.

She nodded, only now realizing he still cupped one of her cheeks with his hand. Just as she opened her mouth to thank him, the side door flew open.

"Cousin Michael, Mistress Magee said—"Adeline stopped midskip, mouth agape. Michael and Brianna flinched and pushed away from each other, cold air rushing between them, quelling the rising heat of the moment. Brianna bumped into the center workbench, sending a pot clattering to the floor.

"Well"—Adeline twisted up her face and approached Brianna—"I see you're bent on tarnishing our good family name with your . . . your filthiness. And never mind the state of your kitchen. You keep your workplace as clean as your personal life, it would seem."

"I . . . we . . ." Brianna stammered.

"Oh, you are quite the little who—"

"Adeline." Michael's voice was firm and low, and it commanded the girl's attention. "There'll be no more of that talk out of ya. 'Twas nothing like that, not that it's any of your concern. Miss Kelly was hurt and needed aid."

Adeline scowled at Brianna. "I bet she was."

"Enough!" Both girls startled at Michael's shout. "What did ya need, Adeline?"

She looked between Brianna and Michael a few times and then started to pout. At a stern look from Michael, she straightened her posture. "Mistress Magee sent me to fetch you. It's recreation time."

He tugged his pocket watch from his trousers, checked the time, and sighed. "So it is." He instructed the girl to wait outside for him, then turned to Brianna. "So, ye're alright, then?"

"Aye. Thank you again, for all yer help."

She watched as he followed after his cousin. Once out of sight, Brianna finally released a full breath and sank back against the counter. She laid a hand to her chest, willing her heart to slow its pounding, then touched her cheek where Michael had rested his hand.

He had been right in what he said to Adeline. Brianna was hurt and needed aid. Just not in the way he thought. Though he had no business doing so—ascendancy class people rarely even noticed her, let alone treated her with dignity and respect—Michael heaped kindness upon kindness on her. On everyone he met, from what Brianna had seen. But one kindness at a time, he was stitching up the wounded parts of her heart. And if she wasn't careful, he'd mend the whole thing only for it to be torn open—irreparably, she feared—when the stark truth of the disparity between them finally jolted her back to her senses.

Maureen paced behind her desk, hands massaging the knotted muscles in her shoulders. Surely the disaster in the kitchen had nothing to do with her. Did it?

Ballymacool sees all. And you're next. She could picture the scrawling on the dusty countertop as clearly as if she was staring at it even now. Did someone know? Sinking into the high-backed chair, she ground her elbows onto the desktop and lowered her head into her hands. Images of Richard floated into her mind, but she shook them free. No one else had known about their trysts. Had they? Even if they did, why bring things up now with cowardly veiled threats under the guise of anonymity?

The whole affair had been so long ago. A lifetime, really. But even now, all these years later, Richard Boyd was still managing to destroy her life. Hot coals of anger kindled within her. Not yet a raging fire, but a slow, simmering sort of burn. The kind that lures one to its comforting warmth only to scald them when they get too close. Would she never be free of him, of his sway over her? It was bad enough to have spent all this time pining over him—over what could never have been to begin with. But now, without the benefit of his love to protect her, his arms to shield her, she was left exposed to the fiery darts that now flew mercilessly in her direction.

Setting her jaw, she blinked hard. She'd shed far too many

tears on account of Richard Boyd. She wasn't going to shed another one. Ever. Besides, why was she to assume the mystery aggressor was targeting her? Surely if she was the one in their sights, they would have hit something else, somewhere else. It made no sense. Yes, the whole of Ballymacool House was under her purview, but the kitchen was not truly her domain. No.

The kitchen belonged to Cook. At least, it should. But Maureen always had to tend to the details Cook unfailingly left undone. And then there was Brianna. Maureen slowly rose to her feet. Of course. It had to be directed at that girl. Who knows what that urchin was capable of? After all, the apple doesn't ever fall too far from the tree. And truly, how closely did Maureen watch her? So long as Brianna performed her duties and completed her chores, she was left very much to her own devices. Maureen had far more pressing matters to attend to each day than watch Brianna Kelly scrub the floors. But with so much unsupervised time, she would be able to engage in all manner of lascivious activities. And if she carried any of her family traits, it was entirely possible that she'd done some horrible thing to bring these threats upon herself and this house.

Maureen smoothed her hands down the sides of her hair, then tugged her dress to straighten the fabric. She wouldn't let a scullery maid from a line of heartless unsavories tear down all she'd worked to build.

She'd keep the girl on an even tighter leash, making sure an extra set of eyes were on her as often as possible. And she'd see that her own memories and heartache stayed hidden away, impossible for anyone else to uncover.

Movement outside the window caught her attention. In

the distance, a train of girls marched south to the trail that would take them to the recreation field. At the sight of Michael Wray walking behind his cousin, an idea bloomed. The corner of Maureen's mouth slid up as she congratulated herself for her brilliant scheme that would both ease her of the burden of Adeline's petulant ways and provide additional supervision for Brianna.

A low chuckle rattled in her chest. It was simply too good. And she couldn't wait to implement it.

14

Brianna ignored the bark digging into her skin as she scooped up an armload of wood for the kitchen fireplace. While they used turf for the other fireplaces around the property, Cook preferred the stiffer heat of wood in the large, roaring hearth over which she kept a pot of water hanging. She also used it for other things, including warming the room, though Brianna thought it was never needed for that purpose. Once preparations for both the midday and evening meals were in full swing, Brianna and Cook were always glistening with perspiration—both from their exertion and from the heat that radiated from the cooking itself.

Now Brianna had been sent to fetch the wood while Cook visited the cool room to procure the day's meat, so that's what she did. As she was returning, a whisper drifted from the open door to the kitchen. It was so soft, Brianna almost dismissed it as the breeze. But she stopped short at the sight—she was certain she'd closed the door when she left to keep Cook's precious heat contained. Perhaps when Cook returned, her hands had been too full to shut it properly.

Brianna crossed the threshold, then narrowed her gaze. Adeline was hunched down in the corner near where Brianna had been cleaning earlier. The girl was whispering to . . . to her hands?

"Can I help you find something, Miss FitzGerald?"

The girl jumped to her feet and thrust her arms behind her back. Her eyes were wide, and her mouth bobbed open and closed for a moment before her proper posture returned. "I doubt you could, given the unkempt manner in which you keep your kitchen." She tilted her chin up and added a haughty sniff for good measure.

Brianna shook her head and a sarcastic laugh puffed from her lips. Rather than reply, she shuffled to the fireplace and dropped the wood into the cast-iron bucket by the hearth.

"There ya are." Michael's voice filled the room. "What are ya doing in here, Adeline?"

Brianna stood, brushing wood dust from her arms and torso. "Mister Wray," she greeted him.

"Oh, hello, Brianna." His gaze bounced to his cousin and back. "Is she . . . is she helpin' ya?" Disbelief colored his voice. Behind Michael, Cook entered the room and stopped short. Michael didn't seem to notice her.

The corners of Brianna's mouth tugged downward, and she shook her head. But before Michael could ask her anything else, Adeline yelped. Whatever she was holding fell to the floor and she sucked on the side of her finger. On the ground, a mouse scurried toward the door. Brianna's mouth gaped open, and Michael snagged it by the tail, held it aloft, and cocked a brow at Adeline. Her cheeks flushed.

"And what was your plan for this fella?" Michael's voice was firm.

130

Adeline blanched for a split second before pinning Brianna with a glare. "Just finishing what I started."

Michael's eyes narrowed and he pursed his lips. He took a step toward his cousin when Cook's voice broke in.

"Well now, I didna know it was visitin' hours in *mo chistin*." Annoyance lined Cook's round face as she surveyed the scene, her thick Donegal brogue hanging in the air.

"Beggin' your pardon." Michael crossed the room and took his cousin by the elbow, his other hand still holding the mouse. "We were just leaving."

"Ow!" Adeline winced and squirmed against Michael's grasp, but he held fast and all but dragged her from the room. Brianna could hear a heated discussion outside the door but could not make out what was being said. As their conversation trailed off into the courtyard, Brianna tried to reconcile what she'd just heard. Why on earth would Adeline hold such a grudge against her? That could make life quite a bit more difficult indeed. Turning to place more wood on the fire, she comforted herself with the fact that at least she didn't have to spend that much time around the girl. As long as they could keep her out of the blasted kitchen.

Back in his cottage, Michael paced in front of Adeline. "So ya admit to it?"

Adeline puffed her chest and crossed her arms. "Aye."

Michael's eyes widened. "The mess in the kitchen, the note on Brianna's door, the whole lot?" He ticked off each item on a finger as he spoke.

She nodded proudly.

"What could have possessed ya to do such a thing?" He fought to keep his tone below a shout. "You are a guest here and this is how ya treat your hosts?"

"A guest?" Adeline clucked her tongue. "So Father doesn't pay a tuition for me?" The smug grin on her face made it all the more difficult for Michael to keep his composure. He turned and gripped the mantel of his fireplace. "I was under the impression that these people were under our employ," she continued in her cloying tone.

Michael spun to face her and held up an index finger. "Don't."

Adeline's face became the portrait of feigned innocence. "Don't what?" She stood from the wingback chair and clasped her hands demurely in front of her. "That girl deserved what she got. All I did was remind her what happens when one strays beyond one's station."

Michael stopped pacing and faced her directly. "That's where you are sorely mistaken, Adeline. We were not blessed with our position in the community in order to lord it over others. On the contrary. We must use our authority to stand up for those who cannot do so for themselves."

Adeline scoffed.

"Balk if you wish, but until ya understand that our position is a weighty one that carries with it the responsibility of ensuring justice for all those under our care, ye'll continue to miss the mark and purpose the Lord has given ya." He waited until she looked him in the eye. "And ye'll continue to be miserable because you're not living the life you were intended to live."

Silence filled the room and Adeline's gaze drifted to the floor. Michael wondered if he was actually beginning to get through to her when a knock sounded. The spell of the moment broke, and his cousin's trademark countenance settled back into place.

Wagging his head, he opened the door.

Batty stood on the stoop. "Hello there, Mister Wray. Mistress Magee is askin' for ye."

When it rains, it pours. "Thanks, Batty. Adeline, ye'd best go get yourself ready for lunch."

"Eh, beggin' yer pardon, but she'd like to see the both o' ye." Batty shrugged and started to scurry off to his next destination. "She's in her office," he called over his shoulder.

Michael sighed. "Very well. Let's go. I was going to have to seek her out so you can let her know what ya did anyway."

Adeline blanched. "Michael, no. Can't you just punish me?"

"Oh, I will. But Mistress Magee needs to know what ye've done. And I'd wager whatever she has in mind for ya will strike deeper than anything I could come up with."

The girl pursed her lips and shot him a look that if it were possible would've been fatal for sure.

In her office, Magee paced behind her desk, hands clasped at her back, a look of smug satisfaction on her face. She reminded Michael of Sherlock Holmes—no, some other cut-rate brand of investigator—itching to reveal his findings.

She stopped centered behind her desk, faced Michael and Adeline, and gestured for them to sit. They complied. "I suppose you're wondering why I asked you here today," she said.

Michael bit his lip to keep from laughing. *Sherlock Holmes,
indeed*. When he was certain he could speak without guffaw,
he replied, "I am. However, before ya begin, there is something you should know."

"Oh?" A single brow arched.

"Actually, 'tis Adeline who has something she needs to
say. Adeline." Both he and Magee turned their attention to
the girl.

She crossed her arms and clamped her lips together.

"Adeline," Michael repeated. She shook her head.

Magee hissed an exasperated sigh. "Let's hear it, child.
I've a schedule to keep."

Adeline rolled her eyes but straightened in her chair and
mumbled something unintelligible.

"Speak up," Magee commanded.

"I . . . I was the one who caused the chaos in the kitchen."

Mistress Magee flattened her palms on the desktop and
leaned forward. "Excuse me?"

Adeline dropped her hands to her lap. "It was me," she
said. "I created the mess in the kitchen." Michael nodded for
her to continue. "I was trying . . . I was trying to teach that
scullery maid a lesson, and I guess I went too far."

Michael cleared his throat.

"I'm sorry." Adeline practically choked on the words, and
Michael wondered if this was the first time she'd ever apolo-
gized in her life.

"I see," the headmistress said and lowered herself into her
chair. She eyed Adeline for a long moment before turning
her attention to Michael. "And what do you propose we do
about this? She cannot go unpunished."

Michael shook his head. "Absolutely not, and I wouldn't

dream of it. In fact, I brought her to you to ensure she has a way to make things right."

Magee's eyes lit up and something Michael couldn't place flashed across her face before her typical stoic facade returned. "Make things right, you say?" She leaned back in her chair and drummed her fingers on her lower lip. "I might have just the thing. Adeline, over the past months, you've been given just about every sort of consequence we have here at Ballymacool."

Michael's brows soared and he looked at his cousin out of the corner of his eye. She sat still and straight, an almost daring look on her face. But when he looked at her more fully, uncertainty billowed like a cloud behind her eyes.

Magee continued, "Despite that, not much has improved in terms of your behavior. Thus, your cousin was summoned. Now, I believe it best for you to experience more ... natural consequences of your actions."

Adeline shifted nervously in her seat but remained quiet. When she didn't respond, Mistress Magee rose and rounded the desk. She stretched to her full height and looked down her nose at the girl. "I had intended on having you work for Master Boyle as an aid of sorts—"

"What?" Adeline shot to her feet, hands pressed in fists against her hips.

Magee lifted a silent finger, some unnamed delight dancing in her eyes. Michael wondered if Adeline noticed it too.

"But with this new information coming to light, I think it more befitting that you help clean the kitchen and set it to rights," she said. "And then you will carry on and report to Cook daily to help in the kitchen for at least the next month."

Adeline's jaw fell open. "That's not fair! I'm the daughter of one of the highest families in Dublin County, if not the entirety of Ireland." She stamped her foot. "I won't stoop so low as to do the work of a mere kitchen maid. I won't!"

"You will." Magee's voice remained cool. "Or you will no longer be welcome at Ballymacool House. I'm well aware of your family's station, young lady, but you are still a student within my charge, and I'll not have you wreaking havoc on my house."

A smile tickled the corners of Michael's mouth, but he kept his face solemn. Despite his misgivings about Maureen Magee, she'd come up with a fair and just punishment for his cousin.

"And to ensure you fulfill your duties properly"—the head-mistress returned to her place behind the desk and sat down—"your cousin will supervise you."

"What?" Michael and Adeline asked in unison.

Magee shrugged. "You've proven yourself to be untrust-worthy, Adeline. Mister Wray was brought here to see that you behave in the expected manner, and he will continue to do just that as you work out your punishment." Adeline pouted and slunk back into her seat.

Michael's thoughts spun in dizzying circles. He stood and walked to the window, welcoming the cold that radiated from the glass. Another month at Ballymacool? He'd been away from Castlewray for weeks already. And while in many ways it was a welcome respite from the ever-tightening noose of his family's position in a rapidly changing world, he couldn't very well stay away forever. Could he? Father did seem to have things well in hand. At least, he hadn't said otherwise when he'd visited.

Michael raked his fingers through his hair and stared at the woods beyond the house. What he wouldn't give to ride Cara deep into the heart of the trees and listen to their secrets as he'd done that day with Brianna. Brianna. This new twist meant another month away from home, but it also meant another month with her. In her kitchen, working near her, getting to know her better. And making sure Adeline couldn't do anything else to hurt her.

"'Tis a fair consequence, Adeline," Michael said at length. "And ye'd do well to understand that yer actions affect far more than just yerself and the target of yer venom."

"Fine." Adeline sighed, but Michael heard her mumble under her breath. "Not that I have any choice in the matter." Her arms crossed once again.

Magee didn't seem to have heard her little addition, or if she did, she was ignoring it while she scribbled something on a sheet of paper.

"Cook isn't terribly partial to having people in her kitchen," she said, holding the paper out to Michael.

"So I've seen." He took the paper and skimmed the directions Magee had scrawled out.

"Give this to her and tell her I've sent you." She clasped her hands at her waist. When no one moved, she gestured to the door. "It's almost lunchtime. You'd best get going so as not to hold things up."

15

Brianna was chopping potatoes to make roast spuds for the midday meal when Michael and Adeline descended the steps and presented Cook with a slip of paper. A hushed but animated discussion took place before Cook tossed her hands in the air and stormed to the back of the room.

"That woman's got no right disruptin' my kitchen," she muttered as she passed Brianna.

Michael cleared his throat, pulling Brianna's attention toward him—the very thing she was trying to avoid doing.

"Sorry to disrupt your working. I know lunch is soon, but Adeline needs to tell ya something," he said, urging his cousin forward.

Adeline stumbled toward Brianna. Disdain practically dripped from her eyes as she looked her over. "I was the one who made a mess of things in here. Sorry."

Brianna coughed as though she'd been tossed a heavy sack of potatoes. Unsure what to do with the revelation, she sputtered, "Oh, well . . . I believe 'tis Cook or Mistress Magee ya owe the apology to, then."

"She's already made her apologies to them, actually." Michael stepped closer. "But 'tis you who deserves the lion's share of them, Brianna." He bumped his elbow on Adeline's.

Adeline sighed deeply and shifted her feet. "I did it because I was cross with you."

Brianna cocked her head. "Me? What for?"

"Because you've been sticking your nose where it doesn't belong!" she shouted. Michael silently laid a hand on her shoulder, and she rolled her lips together and huffed through her nose. When she spoke again, her voice held the chill of forced calm. "My cousin was sent here for me and you were taking up all his time and attention."

Brianna blinked hard and absently wiped her hands on her apron. What on earth was the girl talking about? Yes, they'd run into each other in the woods a couple times, but it was happenstance. She'd never sought him out—would have never thought to. Never even dreamed of it. When she opened her mouth to respond, Michael raised a hand, staying her reply. Which was good, because she still had no words.

"I've already spoken with Adeline about her misunderstanding of the situation so ya needn't say anything else."

Brianna nodded.

"And she sees now the depth of her folly." He gave Adeline a sidelong glance.

Brianna doubted that highly but kept that thought to herself. "I see. Well, thank ya."

"Are ye goin' to help get the food ready or stand here yappin' awee all day?" Cook pushed her way through the group and shoved an apron at Adeline.

Michael must have read the question that undoubtedly showed on Brianna's face and said, "Mistress Magee and I thought it would be good for Adeline to help clean up her mess, and then spend some time working in the kitchen to gain a deeper appreciation for all the hard work ye ladies do down here."

Adeline rolled her eyes as she struggled to tie the apron around her waist. Brianna forced her face to remain stoic, but inside her stomach dropped. Apparently there would be no keeping Adeline out of the kitchen, after all.

"Where would you like her to start, Brianna?" Michael asked.

"She needs to clean up her *praiseach* first," Cook called over her shoulder as she stirred a large pot. "Give her the broom." She flapped her hand in the direction of a small closet on the north wall.

Michael fetched the broom and handed it to his cousin. "What shall I do?" he asked.

Cook grabbed a stool from the corner and slammed it at the end of one of the counters. "Ye'll sit here and make sure the *cailín* doesna mess anything else up." She scrunched her face and gave a grumpy nod. "I'll not have a man attempting to cook in my kitchen, even if he is some high-fallutin' ascendant." She continued muttering under her breath in Irish, and Brianna couldn't help but chuckle.

Returning to her potatoes, Brianna fought to keep her eyes on her work. No matter how hard she tried, she couldn't stop her gaze from flitting up to Michael and back every now and then. As she tossed the spuds in melted goose fat on a large tray, she realized that Adeline was doing some muttering of her own.

"This dumb thing is broken. It's not doing anything."
Adeline grunted in frustration, and though Brianna's back
was to her, she could hear the pout in the girl's voice.

Brianna glanced over her shoulder. Adeline was stabbing
at the ground with the broom's bristles. She went back and
forth with herself on whether or not she should say anything.
She didn't wish to raise the girl's hackles any higher than
they already were, and yet if the kitchen was to ever be put
to rights, she had to learn how to clean it properly. She had
probably never swept anything before and just needed to be
taught.

"You're meant to drag it," she said, testing the waters.

Adeline stopped and gaped at Brianna, perspiration already dotting her forehead. "What?"

"The broom." Brianna pointed to it. "Ya need to sort of
brush it along the ground. Like this." She took it and dem-
onstrated how to hold the handle at an angle and sweep the
bristles along the floor. "Now you try."

Adeline swiped the broom from Brianna's hands. She
gripped the top end of the handle and tugged. "Ugh! It still
won't work."

Her whining tone grated on Brianna's nerves, but she remained patient. "Spread your hands apart more, like this."
She repositioned the girl's grip and showed her how to stand
to get better leverage. "Okay, try again."

Adeline attempted a couple more sweeps and successfully
gathered a small pile of flour, oats, and dirt. "Well, that is
much easier." She dropped her gaze. "Thank you," she said,
barely above a whisper.

"Don't mention it." Brianna turned back to the counter
and found Michael smiling at her, brows raised in surprise.

"Wow," he mouthed and flashed a quick thumbs-up.

Brianna grinned and turned away so the warmth creeping up her cheeks wouldn't show.

The next hour passed surprisingly quickly as Brianna and Cook put the finishing touches on the main dishes and Adeline finally finished sweeping the floor. She'd done a fairly good job of it—particularly for someone who'd never done it before, not to mention she had very little interest in it even now. Brianna showed her where to discard the swept piles, and then Cook sent her to clean up and march in with the rest of the girls.

"If it's alright with ya, Cook, I'll stay here," Michael said. "I can help bring the food to the dining room."

"Makes no never mind to me," she replied. "Servin' and cleanin's Brianna's job. I'm off now until time to start supper. Just don't cook anythin' and ye'll do fine by me." A twinkle flashed in the woman's eye, and if Brianna didn't know any better, she'd think Cook was flirting with Michael. Never mind that she was old enough to be his grandmother.

"Go raibh maith agat," Michael replied.

Cook waved a dismissive hand at him, but not before Brianna caught the hint of a smile that played on the woman's face. "*Slán leat.*"

"Slán," Michael and Brianna muttered in unison.

Awkward silence filled the room in her wake, and the pair stood staring at anything but one another until the rhythmic marching began overhead.

"Do ya mind?" Michael asked.

Brianna looked at him, eyes questioning.

He gestured to the serving dishes. "May I assist with bringing the food in?"

"Oh, no, I don't mind at all, though ya needn't feel duty bound." In truth, it elated her. She was finding there was very little she didn't want Michael around for, and that was a dangerous thing. If she didn't get ahold of and manage her own expectations regarding Michael Wray, she was headed for a real heartbreak. She knew it and yet could not help this growing affinity for him.

Michael wheeled the cart over and began setting dishes on it. "Not duty bound, no." He took a bowl of the freshly roasted potatoes from Brianna. "But I do feel a distinct sense of . . . responsibility. While I cannot say for certain why, I can say that I've learned that 'tis always best when I listen to those niggling little thoughts that won't leave me alone. There's almost always an important reason that plays out in the end."

Brianna shook her head.

"Does that trouble ya?"

She waved her hands front of her. "No, no. On the contrary, I relate to it."

"Oh? How so?"

"I often will have a person or situation that won't leave my mind, no matter what I do." She hung her dirty apron on the hook and put on her serving one. "And I've found that if I use those as reminders to pray for that person, I learn later that there was a reason for it. An illness, an accident, an important item that had been misplaced and needed finding. That sort o' thing."

Michael hoisted the cart and carried it up the three steps to the hallway as if it were a cloud, his corded forearms flexing. Brianna averted her eyes, wondering how the life of an ascendency class man would garner such physical strength. She tried to shake the thought free.

"I thought I was the only one."

Brianna's gaze flew to meet his. Good heavens, she hadn't spoken her thought aloud, had she? "Only one?"

"That used those nagging intuitions as a call to prayer." He paused, seemingly lost in thought for a beat. "Makes one wonder how else He might be workin' that we would never see or think about."

Brianna could only nod. Her world had been so small for so long, it was hard to believe there was a whole civilization outside the walls of Ballymacool. She'd felt so alone and unseen under the cruel weight of Magee's rule that it never dawned on her that God might connect the world in such an intimate yet intangible way. Perhaps that's why the Good Book speaks of faith as being a mystery. Brianna realized that at any given moment, she might be connected to countless others in faith through prayer, perhaps even united in their requests. And that was a great comfort to her tired and lonesome heart.

16

As Brianna climbed the stairs to her room late that night, she shook her head, marveling at the latest turn of events. Glancing down at the basket Cook had given her, she smiled to herself. Once Michael and Adeline had left, Cook had asked her if she'd found any new treasures. It shouldn't have surprised Brianna—the woman seemed harsh but had always been at least distantly kind to her. And she'd always asked about Brianna's finds in the woods, sometimes sharing in a chuckle or even at times a moment of amazement at what she'd found.

When Brianna had told her about the mangled piece of metal she'd discovered a couple weeks ago, she found herself unable to answer Cook's questions about it.

"It's too rusted and dirty to tell and I've no way to clean it. Water and a rag did very little," Brianna had said, unable to keep the disappointment from lacing her voice. Cook had insisted she take a jar of metal polish, scrubbing pads, and a fresh cloth.

"Ye aren't gonna keep me wonderin' about what it is,"

Cook said. "We have to take life's excitements where we can get 'em, right?" She'd smiled and poked Brianna's side with her elbow. The fleeting thought passed through Brianna's mind that perhaps she wasn't quite as alone as she'd always believed. But then Adeline arrived to wash dishes and the idea had vanished as quickly as it had appeared, keeping it from taking root in her heart.

Once in her room, she dug the rusted hunk of metal from its hiding place and buried it at the bottom of the basket. She'd take it to the woods tomorrow and try to clean it up. It was the only place that offered any semblance of true privacy.

The next morning a slate sky hung low, blanketing the land and casting a silvery pall as far as the eye could see. Brianna's heart sank at the thought of being cooped up indoors on her day off. But so far, the ground remained dry and the air was still, so a sliver of hope remained that she could venture out to her sanctuary after breakfast.

When she arrived at the kitchen, Michael was already there, fussing with the kettle over the fire.

"Mornin'." He smiled up at her, perspiration glistening on his forehead.

"Ye're here early."

He shrugged. "I wasn't certain when you and Cook got started in the mornings and wanted to be sure I was here when Adeline arrived."

"Ah," Brianna said, removing her apron from the hook. "Well, Cook doesn't come until preparations for the midday meal." Michael was still hunched over the fireplace. "What—watcha doing?"

"Well"—his voice was strained as he reached gingerly over the flames—"I thought I'd prepare a pot of tea, but I can't seem to fetch the kettle." He swatted at the hook but quickly pulled his hand back, shaking it.

Brianna chuckled and joined him at the hearth. He finally straightened, still shaking his hand, which was wrapped in a towel. She pulled her brows together. "Did ya burn yourself?"

"Hmm? Oh, no. The rod on the hook was far too hot, so I wrapped my hand to try and pull it closer."

Brianna smushed her lips with her fingertips, attempting to suppress her laughter. Keeping her gaze on his hand, she reached to the side of the hearth and produced a long iron rod with a small crook on the end. She extended it, hooked it onto the rod where the kettle hung, and rotated it until the kettle hung outside the flames. Then, using the same rod, she lifted the kettle free and set it on the countertop.

Michael watched with a blank expression. "Well, that was much easier, indeed." The bare spots of cheeks above his beard pinkened, and Brianna could no longer hold back her laughter. She fetched a plain teapot from a shelf and set it next to the kettle. "The tea's in that canister over there." She pointed to a shelf behind Michael.

As he made the tea, Brianna set to work on the porridge. When Michael placed a steaming cup next to her, she regarded it for a long moment. She couldn't remember the last time anyone had made her a cup of tea.

"Milk an' sugar?" The question jolted her from her thoughts.

"Oh, er, just a wee splash of milk, please."

Michael sidled up next to her, then poured in the milk. "Sláinte." He clinked his cup to hers.

A timid smile tipped the corners of Brianna's lips. "Sláinte. Go raibh maith agat."

Michael took a hearty gulp, winced, and then released a satisfied sigh after swallowing. "Ye're welcome. Best way to start the day." He met her gaze and paused.

Brianna's breath caught and she managed a small sip. "Indeed."

Suddenly the door to the hallway opened and a bleary-eyed Adeline appeared, hair disheveled. She ran her hands down her face and groaned. "I can't believe you're up this early every day."

"Aye, well, needs must." Brianna shrugged. She directed Adeline to a crate of eggs and showed her how to crack and dump them into the awaiting bowl. "When ye're finished, whip them up with this whisk, then I'll cook them."

After another groan and a warning look from Michael, the girl started cracking.

Brianna couldn't believe how much faster the preparations went with three of them doing the work.

When the church bells tolled in the distance, Michael checked his pocket watch. "You'd best go up and get ready to march down with the others, Adeline."

She nodded and made her way up the stairs while yawning and scratching her head.

Michael watched her, shaking his head. "That child."

"Do ya think the work is helping?" Brianna asked.

Michael shrugged, still staring at the door. "Who knows? She's always been . . . difficult."

"Oh?"

"Mmm." Michael returned to the kettle and successfully removed it from the hook. "Always has been, but it's gotten worse in the last few years."

Brianna fetched her and Michael's cups and set them near the teapot. "I wonder why that is."

He filled their cups. "I think the unrest around Dublin has been a big part of it. Many people view us on par with the British landlords, even though there are none of those in Ireland anymore. But many folk down there see the ascendancy class as a continued threat, so there's been some retaliation against Adeline's father . . . her whole family, really. And I don't think she knows how to deal with it and the fear that it brought her."

"I see." Brianna had been sheltered from much of the political unrest that had plagued Ireland most of her life, just by the sheer fact that she never got out into the real world. Though she had heard Magee mutter things against the ascendancy class over the years. Brianna had never paid it much mind but could imagine if she had a family and felt they were threatened in any way, that would cause her unease as well. "Perhaps Adeline just needs reassurance . . . and enforced boundaries."

Michael regarded her for a long, uncomfortable moment before taking a swig of his fresh tea. "Perhaps." He dropped his gaze and studied the contents of his cup a little too hard.

Unsure what to do with herself, Brianna took her own drink and went to sit on a stool in the far corner. After several awkward minutes of silence, footfalls sounded overhead. Michael drained the rest of his drink. "Let's get the food to the dining room."

The pair worked in tandem to get the trays and cart up the steps in what was becoming a well-choreographed routine. Once back in the kitchen, Michael took their teacups and set them in the basin. "I'd best be off. What's on your docket for the rest of the day? It's your day off, yes?"

Brianna blinked, surprised he remembered. "'Tis, yes." She shifted on the stool. "I'm goin' to go out into the woods."

Michael chuckled as he crossed to the coatrack by the door. "I should've known." He tugged a flatcap over his hair and Brianna had to force herself not to stare. She'd never seen him don a hat before, and that coupled with his woolen jumper gave him an all-too-approachable look. "Enjoy." He tipped the brim and disappeared into the diffused morning light.

Brianna spent a few more minutes tidying up the breakfast dishes, making a stack of items in the basin for Adeline to wash later, then headed upstairs. She gathered her basket, changed her apron, and wrapped a shawl around her shoulders. The weather still seemed mild enough to venture outdoors, and she was not going to lose the opportunity to get away.

Entering the woods, the distinct scent of moss, bark, and damp enveloped her, and Brianna released a deep sigh of contentment. The leaves had almost all changed, and the contrast of the vibrant reds, yellows, and oranges against the still-dark evergreens was utterly stunning. A sunset-toned carpet stretched out before her on the forest floor, and she hurried to Her Spot. But she stopped short at the turnoff to Finnuala's.

It'd seemed ages since her last visit, and she decided to call on her friend first. When she knocked on the door, there was no answer. Smoke lazily curled from the chimney and lantern light glowed orange in the window, so she couldn't be far. Brianna looked around, but the front of the property was empty. She rounded the corner to the back. "Finnuala? *Cá bhfuil tú?*"

The woman's raspy voice drifted from the tree line. The tune of "Molly Malone" danced in the breeze. Brianna smiled and called out to her friend once more. Finnuala's eyes squinted, then widened when she recognized her visitor. "Brianna, *a stoir!*"

The pair embraced and Brianna kept her arm around the old woman's shoulders as they made their way to the house. "Cupán tae?" Finnuala asked.

"*I gconaí.*"

"I know ya always want the cuppa. I shouldn't have even asked." They laughed and headed inside.

With the tea prepared and the women settled at the table with a small plate of nearly stale biscuits between them, they enjoyed their repast in the peaceful silence of old friends. While refilling their cups, Finnuala asked, "So, how're ye farin', dearie?"

Brianna sighed and sat back in her chair. "Oh, fine, I suppose."

"Any luck on the pendant?"

Brianna's chin dipped and she shook her head.

"*Tsk.*" Finnuala sucked in a sharp breath and added, "It'll come, I know it."

Brianna pulled her lips into a thin line. She didn't share Finnuala's faith in that matter but didn't have the energy to argue.

"And last we spoke, there was a certain gentleman who'd

come to Ballymacool." A smile filled her voice, and she took the teapot and shuffled to the basin. "I met the man an', I must say, I can see why he caused such a stir." A playful chuckle bubbled from her lips.

"Aye, I agree," Brianna said. "He's still there. Still . . . stirring." She explained about Adeline's antics and how both she and her cousin were to be in Brianna's kitchen almost all day every day.

"Is that what's got ye so restless then, love?" Finnuala asked, pinning Brianna with her stare.

Brianna shifted under the woman's gaze and shrugged. "I suppose so." The truth of it was, somehow Michael's presence had awoken in her a desire she had buried a long time ago. A sense that she was meant for something more—something meaningful. She'd accepted long before that she was bound for a life of meaningless servitude. That was her lot in life. But now she couldn't deny that she still wanted more.

Finnuala cocked her head and raised her brows. "What aren't ya sayin', *a chailín*?"

Brianna sighed and crossed to the fire. She stirred it, letting herself get lost in the mesmerizing flames and breathing in the earthy aroma of the peat.

A tender, warm hand slid up her back. "Brianna, what is it? I know there's more than what ye're sayin'."

"What's the point?" Brianna muttered, still staring into the blaze. At length, she turned her attention to Finnuala. "Have ya ever felt like ye were meant to do something—*be* something—other than what ya are?"

Finnuala lifted her gaze to the ceiling in thought. "I suppose I have."

"I used to feel that way. Ya remember when I was a girl, all the dreams I had?"

"Oh, aye." Finnuala chuckled and cupped Brianna's cheek briefly. "Ya had such big plans to change—nae, take over—the world."

Brianna shook her head and chuckled through her nose. "That I did." She returned to her seat and absently ran her finger over the rim of her cup. "But somewhere along the way, I just . . ."

"Settled," Finnuala finished for her.

Brianna blanched. "Not settled. Realized."

"Realized what, exactly?"

"That I'll never be more than a scullery maid. And I was wasting precious energy hoping to be anything more."

Finnuala lowered herself into the seat across from Brianna and took her hand. "Oh, child. Yer purpose in this world has precious little to do with what job ya hold. It's to do wi' the way ya impact the people around ye."

Brianna dropped her chin.

"'Tis true, a stoir. God has put ya where ye are for a reason. There's no 'just' when it comes to the identity of His *páistí*. If He's kept ya where ya are, that means He's not done using ya there."

"I guess."

"Child, there's more to yer story than ye could ever know. And there's things the good Laird has for ye to do that no one else can."

Brianna scoffed. "*Is sea*, no one can wash a dish like me."

Finnuala sighed and scratched at her chin. Finally, she rose, rounded the table, and lowered herself in front of Brianna and waited until she met her gaze. "Brianna Kelly, don' let anyone tell ya that who ya are doesn't matter. Everything ya do, shows His glory to the world. At least, it can if ye'll let it. You are a daughter of the King, and it's high time ya treat yerself as such."

"How would I do that?" Visions of fancy robes and demanding breakfast in bed flitted across her mind's eye. That would never do.

"By followin' His example. He washed the feet o' others, He befriended the unfriendable, and He never lost sight o' the purpose laid afore Him by the Father. *Our* Father."

With shaky arms, Finnuala braced herself on the table and tried to stand. Brianna gripped her elbows and helped her up. Once again, Finnuala cupped Brianna's cheeks and looked into her eyes. "Ya were meant for greatness in this world, a stoir. Even if yer station never changes." She leaned forward and brushed a tender kiss to Brianna's forehead. "Now, ya best be off afore ya waste your whole day wi' this auld woman."

Brianna smiled in spite of herself and fought against the burning in her eyes. "Thank you, Finnuala."

Finnuala nodded, then extended her hand. Brianna took it and rose to her feet.

"Slán abhaile, a stoir," Finnuala said.

"Slán." Brianna smiled and pushed the door open, but a gust of wind ripped the knob from her hand, and the door slammed against the outside wall.

"Oy. If my bones are tellin' the truth, there's a storm a brewin'," Finnuala said. "Ye get yerself home safe."

Brianna stepped over the threshold and grabbed the door. "I will. Thanks, Finnuala."

Finnuala winked and Brianna slid the door closed, then headed back to the woods.

17

Brianna made her way toward her favorite spot in the woods, pulling her shawl tighter against the chill as she mulled over what Finnuala had said. At face value, it seemed like surface platitudes—just something one says to make another feel better. And yet, something about it resonated deep in her soul. Perhaps her friend was right. But what purpose could the Lord possibly have for her in the life He'd allowed her to lead? A rootless, lonesome existence of servitude.

The wind picked up and the branches above her clacked angrily. "What've you to be so cross about?" she spoke to the trees. As though they'd heard her, things quieted once again. At last, she reached Her Spot.

Settling onto her knees, she pulled the mystery metal from the bottom of Cook's basket. She examined it again, trying to see if she'd missed any clues the last time she looked it over. Then, remembering Cook's directions, Brianna took the dry scrubbing pad and worked it over the surface. Ignoring the orange dust that sprinkled down her lap, she continued scrubbing. The layer of rust was much thicker than she'd anticipated, and she was so grateful for Cook's instructions. While Brianna had polished plenty of silver in her day, she'd never attempted to restore something so badly rusted. In fact, she'd never dealt with anything rusted, and she'd have wasted loads of the polish trying to buff away the rust rather than polishing the metal itself.

Eventually, the thick layer gave way and Brianna could see the tarnished metal surface peeking through. She wetted the scrubber and worked vigorously until it was ready for the polish. Slowly but surely, the platter revealed itself. It had been fine silver at one point in its existence. 'Twas a shame it had been lost for so long. It was bent beyond repair and would never serve its intended purpose again. Yet it still held a hint of its original beauty.

Something was etched in the center, but the dimming light made it difficult to make out. Overhead, the trees resumed their angry dance and thunder rumbled in the distance. Thunder was a rare occurrence in Ireland, and an eerie feeling settled over Brianna as the hairs on the back of her neck perked up. She tilted her face to the sky and supposed she had a little time still before she needed to head back. The platter was nearly clean and seemed almost ready to reveal its secrets. She continued polishing and could see the etching a bit more clearly. She brought it closer to her face to inspect it when a loud crack jolted her and before she could look up, something slammed her to the ground as the world went black.

Brianna awoke to cold water splashing on her face. She reached up to clear it from her eyes and tried to roll onto her back, but pain shot up her leg. Groaning, she blinked and tried to focus. The world around her was dark, and heavy rain continued to pelt her as someone pinned her legs down.

"Let me go!"

When no answer came, she tried to kick them away, only to be rewarded with more shooting pain. She groped through the rain and mud until her hands found what held her fast. A massive tree limb had fallen over her legs. "*Dia cuidiú liom!*" She pushed against it with all her might, but it wouldn't budge. Her right leg throbbed incessantly, and pain radiated up to her hip with each heartbeat.

After struggling to free herself for several minutes, exhaustion overtook her. She collapsed back into the mud and crossed her arms over her face as the storm grew even more intense. She was too tired to cry and forced herself not to think about the possibility of another branch careening down onto her head.

"Help! Help me, please!" she screamed. But the gales ripped her voice and tossed it away like dandelion fluff. After a few more attempts to call for help, she resigned herself to the fact that no one would come for her. Her fate was solely in God's hands now.

Maureen paced in the kitchen, seething. That girl had gone rogue one too many times. She'd missed both the midday meal and dinner. She wasn't in her room and hadn't been seen since breakfast.

To make matters worse, Adeline had had a run-in with

one of the other girls and Mister Wray had kept her with him in his cottage all day, with mention of keeping the girl out of the house a night or two. So Mary, once again, had to step in and help Cook prepare both of the big meals. If Maureen didn't know any better, she'd swear Brianna was doing this on purpose.

Suddenly the outside door to the kitchen burst open. Mister Wray came in, sluicing water from his slicker sleeves and shaking his hat. "Good evening, Mistress Magee. Would it be possible to get some more tea for my cottage?"

Maureen glared at him. "Help yourself. I trust you know where it's kept?"

He nodded, a quizzical look on his face.

A pounding on the door through which he'd just entered drew both their attention. Maureen groaned and stormed over to open it. Her jaw dropped at the sight of the hunched old woman. "You. What are you doing here?"

"May I come in?" Water dripped from the woman's hood and she trembled.

Maureen sighed and stepped aside. The visitor entered and removed her hooded cape, shaking it before hanging it on the coatrack.

"Finnuala?" Mister Wray asked.

Maureen looked back and forth between the two. "You—you know Finnuala?"

"We've met," he said, crossing the room and handing the old woman a towel. "Are ya alright?"

"A bit o' rain never hurt me," she said, patting her face and hair. "Please tell me Brianna made it back here?"

Maureen scoffed. "Funny you should ask. No, she did not."

"What?" Mister Wray and Finnuala asked in unison.

"She's been gone since breakfast." Maureen crossed her arms. "She's shirked her duties one too many times."

Mister Wray stepped closer to her. "Why didn't ya say something when she missed lunch?"

"Well, Mister Wray"—she balled her fists on her hips, annoyance churning within—"had you kept your cousin under control, you'd have been in here and found out yourself. Don't make that ragamuffin's insubordination my fault."

"Ya can't be serious!" he shouted.

"Have ya not seen the weather?" Finnuala added.

Before Maureen could reply, Mister Wray snatched his slicker from the rack and stormed outside, slamming the door in his wake.

After a quick stop at the stables for a lantern, Michael leapt on his steed bareback and raced into the woods. Holding the lantern aloft, he barreled into the gale, heading to where instinct told him Brianna might be. Grateful for all the afternoons he'd spent in the woods with Cara, and that he could trust she knew the paths better than he did, he flew on.

As he rode, he called out for Brianna, but his voice was swallowed by the torrential rain and gusting winds. Suddenly, Cara stopped short, sending Michael flying to the ground. Miraculously, neither the lantern nor his bones had broken in the fall. Returning to Cara, he found her forelegs bogged down in the mud. After digging them free, he sent her back to the stables, choosing to continue on foot. He couldn't risk either one of them getting hurt out here.

With the rain stinging his eyes and the mud and muck slowing his steps, he slogged onward toward Brianna's tree. Every few moments he'd call out her name, but to no avail. As he approached the opening of the small glen where her tree stood, he slowed and scanned the area with the dim lantern light. A strange lump on the ground pulled his attention and he rushed to it.

A large branch, at least half the size of Cara, had fallen, and he looked more closely, dismayed to see Brianna in a heap beneath it, her legs trapped. "Brianna!" He rushed to her side and swiped her hair from her face. She moaned but didn't stir.

"Brianna! It's me, Michael. Can you speak?"

"Mi-Michael?" She coughed, shaking her body. "Help."

He tried to lift the branch, but it wouldn't budge. Moving around to the other side, he crouched down in the muck and wedged his shoulder underneath the limb. He heaved and pushed and eventually it gave ever so slightly. He stood again and used all his weight to shake it back and forth. Brianna cried out.

"I'm so sorry. Bear wi' me one more minute." He squatted down once more, and this time the branch lifted enough for him to slide it off her legs. Lightning flashed, revealing a pile of large boulders nearby that created a cave-like opening. He scooped one arm under Brianna's shoulders and the other under her knees. She whimpered again as he picked her up. "Shh," he crooned in her ear. "I know it hurts, but we need to get you to some shelter."

He hurried to the rock outcropping and settled her inside the opening. He started to go back for the lantern, but she grabbed his arm. "I won't leave you." He squeezed her hand.

"I promise. I'm just goin' to fetch the light." She held fast to his sleeve for a moment and then released him.

When he returned, he held the lantern closer to her face. She had a scratch across her forehead, but it appeared to be just on the surface. He scanned the rest of her, relieved to find she looked relatively unharmed. Until he reached her legs. A long, shallow cut ran the length of her left shin—though the damage was minimal. Unfortunately, the same could not be said of her right. From the knee down was severely swollen, and her foot twisted awkwardly to one side. He grimaced in the dark, racking his brain for what to do.

Shifting so he was up against the rock, he studied her face once more. "Are ya alright?"

Her eyes were closed but she nodded. Her hair trailed down her face, clinging to her skin and hanging over her shoulders. Her clothes were soaked through and she shivered violently. He gently pushed the hair from her face, taking care not to disturb the scrape he knew hid underneath.

"You're soaked. We need to get you dry."

"I have to get back—Cook needs help."

"'Tis a bit late for that, I'm afraid," he said, removing his slicker and tugging his jumper over his head. Thankfully it was mostly dry, except for the sleeve ends and neckline. He slid his arm behind her shoulders to lift her up and carefully pulled the sweater over her head.

"No, I couldn't," she said in protest. "You'll get cold."

Michael laughed. "I'll be fine. Here, slide your arms through."

Brianna did as instructed and then tried to push herself up to stand.

"Whoa, there. Ye're not goin' anywhere." He took her hand and tugged gently to keep her in place.

"But I have to get back." She turned to look at him for the first time. Michael tried to ignore the way the lamplight danced in her eyes and her breath warmed his neck as it came in huffs. The cave—if one could actually call it that—was very small, and they had to press together to keep themselves completely under its shelter.

"We will, but not anytime soon." He yanked on the sleeve of his button-down shirt until it ripped free. "If we venture back now, we're likely to get ourselves into worse trouble. We need to stay here until the worst of it passes."

"Ugh." Brianna's head dropped back to rest on the stony makeshift wall behind them.

"I know." He shifted down near her feet. "We need to brace this ankle as best we can." He looked back up at her. "This is probably going to hurt."

She kept her head back and eyes closed, then nodded. Michael lifted her right foot and moved it toward him as gently as he could. Brianna whimpered. When he began wrapping it with the sleeve he'd torn off, she cried out and reached for his hand.

"I'm so sorry." Michael rubbed tender arcs with his thumb for a moment. "I'm almost done. Let's finish this and then ya can rest." Brianna took a deep breath and Michael made quick work of finishing his task, taking care not to jostle her foot too abruptly.

When finished, he sidled back up next to her so that their shoulders were touching, then he draped his slicker over them both.

18

Brianna breathed a sigh of relief at the warmth that enveloped her when Michael laid his slicker over them. Rather than being uneasy at his nearness, she found unspeakable comfort. Between the thick, dry sweater he'd made her put on, and his coat that blocked the rain, she was warmer than she'd been in hours. Despite this, she continued to shiver.

"Ye'll warm up soon," Michael said. "We both need to stay as dry and warm as possible to make it through the night." Then he wrapped his arm around her shoulders and pulled her even closer. It must have been the arm he'd torn the sleeve from because she could feel the heat of his bare skin against her neck, not to mention each muscle flex as he rubbed his hand up and down her arm.

She didn't resist when he gently nudged her head to rest on his shoulder. There, in the crook of his embrace, she drifted off to sleep.

When she awoke, the rain had slowed to a patter and the wind had finally died down. But outside was still pitch-black.

It was most likely still the middle of the night. The lantern was nowhere to be seen, and Michael's soft breathing told her he was dozing.

Her ankle throbbed terribly, but she'd finally stopped shivering. Her back ached and she shifted, careful not to put any pressure on her injured leg.

Michael groaned, shifted his own weight. "Good morning."

Despite the dire circumstances, Brianna chuckled. "Good morning to ye, sir."

She heard his hair rustle against the rock as he turned his head in the blackness. His nose brushed hers. "Oh, excuse me." They shifted apart, which ushered in a rush of frigid air between them. Within seconds, they were both shivering. He reached over and tugged her gently back to his side. Allowing him to wrap his arm around her once more, she laid her head on his chest again.

"How're ya feeling?"

She shrugged. "Better than I was." He chuckled and Brianna felt it rumble in his chest.

"And the leg?"

"It hurts." She felt him nod.

"I'm just glad I found ya." His voice was rough. With fatigue or emotion, Brianna couldn't tell.

"Me too," she said. "How did ya know where I was?"

"I'd spent the day in my cottage with Adeline, who was in fine form. When I ventured to the kitchen to replenish my tea stores, Magee was ragin'." He shifted his slicker and continued. "She acted like ye'd shirked your duties on purpose and therefore hadn't informed anyone you were missing."

Brianna shook her head. "Naturally."

"Then Finnuala showed up. Did ya know she and the head-mistress know each other?"

Brianna's head shot up, wincing as the movement jostled her leg. "Beg pardon?"

"Mm-hmm." Michael nodded. "When Magee opened the door and saw her there, she said, 'You,' as if the woman was her archnemesis."

Brianna's head began to spin, and she returned it to his chest. "Strange. I had no idea they were acquainted." They sat in silence for several minutes, and Brianna listened to Michael's heartbeat. His breaths were coming and going slowly.

"What were ya doing out here, anyway?" he asked at length.

"Oh, you know me." She laughed, but he remained quiet.

"But . . . why did ya not return when the weather turned bad?"

Brianna sighed, then told him of the platter she'd found, how she was so close to having it all cleaned up and was about to leave when the branch had fallen on her. "It must've knocked me unconscious, because next thing I knew, I woke up and it was storming. And then you found me." She inclined her head to look up at him. She could just make out the outlines of his features in the darkness. "I'm glad ya did."

He ran his fingertips tenderly along her hairline and tucked a strand of hair behind her ear. He then stroked the backs of his fingers down her cheek. "I'm glad I found ya too." Both their breathing stilled, and all Brianna could hear was the pounding of her own heart in her ears.

He leaned forward and slowly brushed his lips against her forehead. Brianna's eyes fluttered closed. He kissed it two more times and then shifted away. "Sorry," he whispered.

"I'm not," she replied, surprised at her own boldness, yet wasn't sure she'd said it audibly or not. Letting her head settle into the crook of his embrace, she slid her arm around the front of his waist. When he didn't protest, she squeezed in tighter. "It's cold."

"Mmm." He wrapped both arms around her now, and the pair dozed once again.

When they awoke, it was still dark, but rather than the inky blackness of midnight, it was the silvery darkness of predawn. They shifted and stretched, and Brianna noticed how the aches encompassed her whole body now, instead of just her foot.

Michael yawned. "So, tell me more about these treasures."

Brianna had told him some of her secrets the first day they'd met in the woods, but now, before she could stop it, she found the rest of her life story tumbling out. She recounted how the headmistress's cruelty had only grown over the years and worsened the older Brianna got. She talked about her first jobs at the house—collecting eggs when she was just four years of age and sweeping the hearths at five.

Michael's jaw clenched and he shook his head. "I remember ya saying how she'd let ye wander the woods alone at that young age. But working at four?"

"Mm-hmm." Brianna nodded. "It's not terribly uncommon for the poorer families of Ireland."

"It shouldn't be that way."

She shrugged. "No, it shouldn't. But lots of things in this world aren't the way they should be."

"True." He shifted to face her more fully. "And you've no idea about your parents—who they are or what happened to them?"

"*Níl aon rud.*" She shook her head. "And I lost the only physical thing that connected me to them. So I truly have nothing." She fought against the tears choking her voice.

He searched her face for a long moment. "So much pain," he said. Brianna wasn't sure if he was saying it to her or himself.

When a tear escaped and slid silently down Brianna's cheek, Michael reached up, rested his hand softly on her cheek, and wiped it away with his thumb. He held her gaze before it dipped to her mouth and back up. He then brushed his thumb over her lips. Brianna's breath hitched, and she lifted her hand and placed it over his. Their eyes spoke volumes to each other in the silent morning.

Slowly, Michael lowered his head. Just before his lips touched hers, he straightened. "I'm sorry," he said again.

"Don't be." Once again, her boldness surprised her. The only thing that surprised her more was the strength of her desire for him to kiss her.

He met her gaze once more, and when he spoke, his voice was low, measured. "Don't mistake it—I want this. More than ya could know."

A shaky smile tipped Brianna's lips. "But?"

"But I don't want to give anyone any reason to question you or yer virtue." He took her hands in his. "I want everything I report when we return to be aboveboard. And when I do kiss ya, I want it to be right."

Brianna blinked long and steadied herself with a breath. She'd never dreamed she'd ever fall in love—if that's what this was—let alone be in such a position with a man the caliber of Michael Wray. She appreciated his thoughtfulness more than she could express, but it only served to deepen her desire to have him near. How were they to continue on as though nothing had happened—or almost happened?

His chest rose and fell in a jagged breath. "So," he continued, "tell me about this platter ya found."

As she told him about what she'd discovered once she cleaned up the tray, she wondered if he was trying as hard not to look at her lips as she was his. When she mentioned the etching she'd seen on the platter, his interest piqued.

"I wonder if it was stolen from one of Donegal's ascendency families?"

Brianna looked toward the area she'd left her things. "I'd had a similar thought."

Outside their cave, dawn was breaking. The storm had passed, though the sky was still overcast. Fog hovered just above the forest floor, and the whole scene seemed plucked right out of a fairy tale. Michael craned his neck for a better view of the sky.

"Time to go home." He crawled into the open and stood. In the morning light, Brianna got her first true look at how disheveled they both were—well, assuming she looked worse than he did. Michael's hair was mussed, and his trousers were caked with mud. His button-down shirt was untucked, and his bare arm must have been freezing. Brianna could only imagine how she must appear after lying on the forest floor for who knows how long in the downpour.

Michael reached down to help her up, and she gritted her teeth as she pulled herself to stand, taking care not to put any weight on her right foot.

"Where did ya last see your belongings?" he asked as he set her hands on the large boulder that had acted as their roof.

She pointed in the general direction she'd last seen them.

After several minutes of searching, Michael returned with the tray. "I couldn't find anything else," he said, examining it closely as he returned.

"This etching"—he tapped it—"I've seen the crest before, I believe."

"Oh?" She shifted her weight to her left foot, craning to get a better look at the image. Michael stepped over and steadied her with an arm around the back of her waist.

He nodded. "Mmm. It seems familiar, but I can't place it for sure."

"Shame," Brianna said, studying the tray before turning her attention back to Michael.

"My family is friendly with most of the other ascendancy families, so I could have seen that design any number of places. Whether it was one of them to whom this once belonged, I'm not sure." He handed the platter to her.

"That's why I love these treasures so much. Each one has a story, a history. And even if I don't know it, I feel connected to the past through them somehow." She regarded him once more. "Is that odd?"

He cocked his head. "Not at all. I'm the same way when it comes to history, particularly the rugged and colorful history of this amazing country."

She nodded but winced as the pain in her foot had returned with a vengeance.

"Ye've lost the color in your face. Let's get ya home." He made sure she had a good hold of the tray, scooped her up, and gave her an apologetic look. "I'm afraid Cara ran back home in the storm. So you'll have to settle for me."

She smiled. "I do believe there are worse ways to travel."

19

"Oh, *buíochas le Dia!*" Finnuala came running into the courtyard as soon as she saw Michael.

Resisting the urge to press a kiss to Brianna's forehead, which grew increasingly warm, he hurried to meet the woman. "Where's her room?"

Finnuala pointed upward. "All the way on the top floor in the gable."

Michael followed her gesture and shook his head. "It's bound to be drafty up there. And she shouldn't be so isolated."

When Magee appeared in the kitchen doorway, Michael called to her, "I'm takin' her to the cottage. Fetch the doctor." He made sure his voice left no room for argument.

When he carried Brianna over the threshold, Adeline shot to her feet. "What— what's going on?"

"She's hurt," he said, brushing past his cousin. "And sick." He entered his room and carefully lowered Brianna onto his bed. He pressed the back of his hand to her forehead. Roasting.

"*Tsk. Créatúr.*" Finnuala rubbed the skirts of Brianna's dress between her fingers and palm. "She needs dry clothes." Michael nodded and scratched at his beard. "Use whatever ya need from the press there for now. We can have someone fetch some of her own things later." He scooped up the clothes he'd draped over the chair yesterday so he could get himself into dry togs and left Finnuala to help Brianna change.

Back in the sitting room, he dropped his clothes in the corner and crossed the room to warm himself by the fire. Adeline's characteristic smugness was painted on her face like cheap rouge. She opened her mouth to speak—some snide comment, he presumed—but with one look at Michael's face, she clamped it shut. When she finally spoke, her voice was quiet, though not soft. "What happened?"

"Tree limb," he said, clearing the lump from his throat. "Had fallen and trapped her."

Adeline shook her head as the kettle began to whistle. Michael removed it from the heat and poured it into the teapot.

"I can't imagine what it must've been like for you out there." She watched him from her spot near the fireplace. "It was hellacious here. There's all sorts of damage. Thought the roof would be blown off this place, but it wasn't, thank God."

"I'm glad you're safe," he replied absently, the tea in his hand already all but forgotten.

The door to his room scraped open and Finnuala came out. "She's dry and already asleep."

Michael nodded and turned back to the flames.

"You should change," Finnuala said.

"I'm fine." His response came out all but a growl.

171

A weathered hand took his and pressed the steaming cup up toward his mouth. "I canna care for both o' ye if ya catch a dose too. We'll step outside. You change into yer dry togs." She squeezed his hand and waited until he looked at her. When he met her gaze, she nodded so slightly he could've missed it if he wasn't looking right at her. She gently nudged the cup again and he took a sip. The warmth radiated all the way down to his stomach.

"Thanks," he whispered and offered her a smile.

"Come, lass," Finnuala said to Adeline. She flicked the curtains of the two small windows closed and led the girl outside.

Michael took another bracing sip of hot tea and then made quick work of changing his clothes. When he opened the door to invite Finnuala and Adeline back inside, Magee and the doctor were walking up the path. Adeline had disappeared to who knows where, and Michael didn't have the energy to try to figure it out.

"In here," Michael called to the doctor.

When they entered, Magee introduced Doctor O'Donnell and insisted on the pleasantries of offering the man a cup of tea. Michael, instead, explained the manner in which he'd found Brianna and what he'd done to try to stabilize the ankle and keep her warm and dry.

"Ye're a good man yerself," the doctor said. "I'll go take a look."

Michael showed O'Donnell to his room, and then forced himself to return to the fireplace. As much as he wanted to hear what the doctor had to say, he had no place being in the room while the man examined her.

After draining his cup, Michael checked his pocket watch.

Only a few minutes had passed, but it felt like hours. The hushed voices of Finnuala and the doctor filtered under the door but remained unintelligible.

"Inexcusable."

Michael jumped at Magee's voice. He'd forgotten she was there. He pivoted on his heel. "Beg pardon?"

She flapped her hand through the air. "This whole mess is utterly inexcusable. Her irresponsibility nearly cost her her own life, as well as yours."

Michael narrowed his gaze and his jaw ached from clenching it so tight. "Where do you get the nerve?" His voice was low, almost a growl.

"Me?" Magee blanched and fluttered her hand to her chest. "You should ask that of Brianna. The nerve of her being out in weather like that. Disgraceful."

"You—" Michael pinched his lips together and ran his fingers through his hair. Swallowing hard, he paced the room, efforting to measure his words so he didn't say something he couldn't take back. "What have you against that girl, huh?"

The headmistress plastered a look of innocence on her face. "I don't have anything against her. Except maybe her lack of judgment." She poured herself a cuppa and took a long, lazy sip.

"*Seafóid!*" His hand slammed against the mantelpiece, punctuating his outburst. "That's nonsense and you know it. Don't think it isn't obvious that it pains ya to even give Brianna a day off, let alone the idea that she might find any sort of enjoyment out of it."

Magee scoffed. "I would nev—"

"Save it," Michael interrupted. "Ya know full well the weather was fine when she left on her outing. 'Twas your nonchalance about her absence that caused her to be stuck out there in the elements so long. Make no mistake—one of these days, you'll get your comeuppance for the way ye've treated her all these years."

Magee closed the distance between them until they were almost toe to toe. She looked him dead in the eye and held his stare for a long beat. "Do not be fooled by her stories, Mister Wray. I'd expect a man of your class to be a better judge of character."

"Oh, I think that's exactly what you're afraid of, Mistress Magee."

She blinked and broke the gaze. "*Psh.*" She set her cup on the table and stomped to the door. "Have the doctor report to me when he's finished," she said, then slammed the door in her wake.

Michael gritted his teeth and swung his arm as though he was going to swipe Magee's unfinished cup across the room. Instead, he pulled at his hair. How had a woman as bitter and vindictive as Maureen Magee ever come to take over the day-to-day care of a place like Ballymacool? Was there not someone better suited for the job? Someone more . . . maternal and nurturing?

He crossed the room and took out his frustration on the briquettes of turf in the fire grate, poking and prodding at them with great vigor before tossing a couple more on.

"Eh, Mister Wray?" Michael spun at the doctor's voice, nearly dropping the poker. "Would ya join us for a moment, please?"

Michael held his hands up, palms facing the doctor. "Are ya certain 'tis proper?"

Doctor O'Donnell stepped closer, clapped his hand on

Michael's shoulder, and chuckled. "It's not often ya find a man of your standing hesitant to visit the woman in his own bed."

Heat crept up Michael's neck and warmed the skin under his beard. He knew he carried himself differently from other upper crust men when it came to matters of women, but he'd seen the example his father set. And he'd seen the consequences his schoolmates faced from the more popular approach.

"I appreciate that about ye, sir," the doctor continued. "With both myself and Finnuala present, it's quite appropriate, I assure you." He led Michael into the dimly lit room.

Michael's breath caught in his chest. Brianna was awake now, and though exhaustion clouded her eyes, the pinkness in her cheeks—and the sight of her in his bed, wearing his clothes—was most becoming.

"I'm so terribly sorry for invading your private quarters, Mich—Mister Wray," she said, her voice raspy.

He waited until her gaze locked with his. "Don't give it another thought. What's important is that you're alright."

She dipped her head. "I am. Thank you. I'll be out of your way in no time."

Doctor O'Donnell cleared his throat. "Now, Mister Wray, I wanted to show ya how I'd like for her care to proceed over the next week or so until I return." He showed Michael how he'd wrapped Brianna's foot and ankle. "Soak the wrap in a warm tea of sphagnum moss, comfrey root, and marshmallow leaves. That will need to be changed ev'ry three hours. Miraculously, I don't believe the bone to be broken. But I won't know for certain 'til the swelling goes down quite a bit." He then explained about the tincture of dandelion leaves, feverfew, meadowsweet, and willow bark Brianna needed to drink three times a day. "To fight the fever she's developed and help with the pain and swelling in her leg," he added. "She's not to be moved other than at the utmost of necessity until after I return in a week."

"We'll see to it she's well taken care of," Finnuala said, taking Brianna's hand.

Michael nodded. "Absolutely."

The doctor moved to the door and motioned for Finnuala and Michael to join him.

"Just rest, Brianna," Michael said as he turned to join the others. She smiled at him and laid her head back.

O'Donnell pulled Finnuala and Michael close and spoke in hushed tones. "She needs rest. Even if her leg is just badly sprained, it's goin' to take a long time for it and the cuts on her other leg to heal properly."

They all nodded.

"I have a feeling that Mistress Magee might disagree wi' my course of action. I wanted to take Brianna in to Letter-kenny to be more fully examined, but the headmistress made it abundantly clear that I was not to remove the girl from the grounds here at Ballymacool. And as she is Brianna's guardian, I must abide by her wishes."

Michael tossed his hand up and let it fall against his leg. "You're telling me, even if Brianna *needed* to be treated at a hospital, Magee wouldn't allow it?"

The doctor removed his glasses and polished them with the hem of his tie and returned them to the bridge of his nose. "I willna speak to speculation. But I *will* say that Brianna needs an advocate here. Someone who knows her and the lifestyle of Ballymacool House." He fixed his eyes on

Michael. "Someone strong enough to stand up to the head-mistress when need be."

Michael nodded slowly. "Understood." He almost hoped for the chance, and prayed if—nae, when—the time came, he could do so in a way that honored the good Lord.

20

Brianna watched as the doctor huddled with Michael and Finnuala, and she strained to catch any words their hushed voices uttered. But to no avail. In her heart, curiosity warred with the jolting fear that something was far more wrong with her health than any of them had let on. Perhaps the tree had done more damage than she realized and they were hiding it from her. Maybe she'd caught her death of cold or pneumonia after being in the elements so long. Her skin prickled with sweat and her heart raced. Who knows how long she was pinned under that limb? Maybe she was in such a state of shock she didn't realize that vital organs had been damaged or some crucially important vessel had been severed. The idea slammed onto the floor of her soul like an anchor. After all, what purpose would it serve to tell her if her life was in mortal danger? If nothing could be done, what point would there be in letting her know? Surely they figured such news would only serve to send her into a state of panic. But didn't they know that's exactly what they were causing with their whispers?

She squeezed her eyes shut and forced herself to take slow, deep breaths. She drew in for a count of three and back out. After repeating that process two more times, the pounding in her chest eventually calmed, and the trembling in her limbs began to subside.

The doctor quit the room, and Michael followed after him. Finnuala, however, moved to her side. "Are ya alright, peata?" Her old friend pressed her fingers against Brianna's forehead and cheeks. "Are ya in a lot of pain?"

Sighing, Brianna took her hand and tugged until she sat next to her on the bed. "What aren't you telling me?"

Finnuala fussed with the blankets, tugging them up and tucking them around Brianna's waist. "What do ya mean?"

"I'm going to die, aren't I?" The strength of her own voice caught her off guard.

Finnuala's mouth flapped open. "Och! Where'd ye get a morbid thought like that?"

"Be honest with me, Finnuala. What did the doctor say?"

"Ya heard the same thing I did, dearie. It'll take time, but ye'll be right as rain in a few weeks." She smiled and kindness lit her eyes, softening the severe signs of her age and rugged life.

The corner of Brianna's mouth lifted in a shaky half smile. "Truly?"

Confusion and questioning clouded Finnuala's face.

Brianna's hands flopped on her lap in frustration. "I saw him talking to ya both out there, and all three of ya were whispering. I just got worried that . . . that I didn't know the whole truth."

"Aw, sweet girl"—she patted Brianna's hand—"'tis only One who knows the whole truth, and it's not our job to take that mantle upon ourselves. We'd crumble under the weight of it. But in this matter of your health and recovery, ya know the whole of it."

Tears stung Brianna's eyes once more and she blinked them back. "Thank you."

Finnuala raised up and brushed a motherly kiss to Brianna's forehead. "*Tsk.* Time for your tincture."

As her friend shuffled across the room, Brianna became keenly aware of the fatigue settling over her. Her head spun as though she'd just spent an afternoon swaying in the treetops of the woods, and her ankle pounded like the drums in the military parades she'd overheard Master McDaid speak about once. She allowed her eyes to drift closed while Finnuala prepared the warm, earthy drink.

A vision of Michael's face materialized a scant breath away. Like it had been in the cave. She could almost feel his arms around her, his skin on hers as his fingers skated across her lips. "Don't leave me," she whispered.

"I'm not goin' anywhere," Finnuala's voice answered.

Brianna flinched and her eyes flew open to find the woman at her side, holding a steaming cup of medicinal tincture.

"I'm stayin' right here fer as long as ya need me. I sleep in ma chair more often than not these days, anyway," Finnuala said, "so I'll set up camp in that fancy one out by the fire. Now drink up." She lifted the cup to Brianna's lips.

"Where"—she coughed at the pungent aroma—"where will Michael stay? I've displaced the poor man after he's already been displaced from his home." She took a swig of the medicine and grimaced at its bitterness.

"Batty's gonna get him set up in one of the other cottages, I believe."

Sleep was already weighing her lids as Brianna finished the liquid. "That's good," she managed to say before fully succumbing to the sweet slumber that beckoned her.

In all his time at Ballymacool, Michael had never seen Batty so flustered. He dithered around the bunkhouse off the back of the stable like Michael's mother always did before guests arrived for a dinner or cocktail party. Somehow the sight of rugged and capable Batty fussing over homey details was a mite more amusing than that of his mother in a similar state. Still, a pang of regret chimed in his gut. Though grateful for his station and all it had afforded him and allowed him to do in the community, he hated how it often made others feel like they had to be a certain way. Or that their daily circumstances were somehow less than what Michael deserved. When in truth, Michael was in awe of Batty's immediate hospitality and how he offered it without thought to his own comfort.

"I'm sure 'tis a far cry from what ye're used to, but ye're welcome to it as long as ya need." He gestured to the private room. The rest of the bunkhouse was open, with several beds, a small stove area, and a rustic grouping of chairs near a fireplace, but this corner had clearly been set apart long before Michael ever arrived. It was unclear if the private room usually served as Batty's residence, and Michael knew he'd never get the man to admit if it was, for it was now Michael's quarters for the foreseeable future.

"'Tis a shame the other cottages were damaged in the gale," Batty said. "But a miracle that the one you occupy was spared."

"I can't thank ya enough, Batty," Michael said. "Truly."

Batty nodded and shuffled to the stove to retrieve the kettle. He held it aloft in silent question. Michael denied with thanks and settled in a chair near the fire. The pair sat and enjoyed the calm for a long while.

"The thatcher should be comin' by in the next few days," Batty said, breaking the silence. "So, with any luck, ya won't be stuck in this ole place for too long." Batty nursed his own cuppa.

"I can think of far worse places to rest one's head. I'm deeply grateful for your hospitality."

Batty snorted as if to say, *I doubt that*, but he didn't argue. Finally, he said, "We're all sure glad ye're here. We've not seen this much drama at Ballymacool since the Brits took over."

Michael scowled. "Took over? As in, after the Uprising and all that?"

"Well, sorta." Batty shifted in his seat. "After the Uprising, things were crazy all over. Ye were just a wee lad, aye?"

Michael's eyes rolled upward, calculating. "I was five at the Uprising."

"Just a wee *babaí*." Batty chuckled. "Ya likely won't remember how the whole country went mad, then. Folk were either answerin' the call to fight, scared to death the world was endin', or raring to defend the cause of king and country."

"Even up here, this far away from the fighting?"

"Oh, boyo, the history books focus on that Easter Sunday at the post office—and right they should—but folk have no idea the ripples that started, which turned into tidal waves in every corner of Ireland." He shook his head and blew out a breath. "The Brits felt they'd better get ahold o' things outside of Dublin and went on a rebel witch hunt, which led them directly to Ballymacool."

Michael leaned forward and rested his forearms on his knees. "Here? Why?"

The corners of Batty's lips tugged downward, making him look like a large-mouth bass. "No one knows, really. All I know is the Boyds were here at that time. Ballymacool was their private home." He snapped his fingers, an idea dawning on his face. "Did yer family know them?"

Michael's head bobbed. "Aye, they did. In fact, now that you mention them, I do have vague memories of coming here for some sort of picnic or some such event as a child."

"Ah." Batty thrust an index finger upward. "That'd be the Boyds' big Easter shindig."

Michael shrugged. "Could be."

"Anyhow, one day the Brits showed up an' kicked out the Boyds, claimin' they were traitors to the Crown and a disgrace to their ascendancy class standing." He shrugged. "To this day, no one knows what exactly the Boyds had done or how the Brits figured out whatever it was. But after that, the Brits shacked up in the house for a while, then it was handed over to Magee to become the boarding school." Batty lumbered to the basin and set his cup in it.

Michael's head spun. How could he have forgotten all that had happened? Ballymacool was practically in his own back garden. Guilt settled on his shoulders like the stocks of old. He'd forgotten because it had meant nothing to him at the time. He was only a small child when it had begun, and as he grew, it did him no good to remember or learn more. He'd settled for what little he'd been taught from his formal schooling and left it at that.

"Now, if ye'll excuse me, Mister Wray, I'm afraid I hafta turn in. The day starts a mite early for me 'round here."

Michael stood. "Of course. On one condition."

Batty shifted his weight and gave Michael a questioning look.

"Call me Michael. If we're to be housemates, I think we've moved beyond the necessity for such formality."

Batty cackled. "Fair enough, Mist—er—Michael. Fair enough. *Ouiche mhaith.*"

"Ouiche mhaith."

21

rianna awoke with a start, grateful to see daylight seeping through the crack of the curtains. While the tincture she'd had to drink morning, noon, and night for the past several days helped with the pain in her leg, her fever was now gone and she was quite ready to be done with the liquid medicine. It trapped her in a deep sleep, and she was unable to wake herself to escape the hazy, all-too-realistic dreams that accompanied each dose. An endless loop of reliving the hours trapped under the tree limb or once again being back in the cave with Michael, only without his warmth or the ability to speak, or some other ailment the visions created.

She scanned the room. Finnuala was nowhere to be found. If she wasn't awake, it mustn't be very late—though with daylight peeking through the window, it couldn't be too terribly early. Longing for a glimpse of the outside world, Brianna eyed the curtains. It seemed utterly ridiculous to have to wake an old woman from her sleep just to slide open a couple pieces of fabric. It had been several days. Surely

Brianna could manage to get to the window and back. Her body aching from hours stuck in this bed, she relished the idea of standing, even if just for a moment. She pushed herself up to sit with tiny movements. At length, she pulled back the covers and got her first real look at her leg. She'd avoided looking too closely at it when Finnuala had changed the wrapping. Because it had been so painful, she had usually squeezed her eyes shut and tried to just hold on until she was finished. But now, without the intrusive gaze of others, she took her time to finally examine the damage that had been done.

She ran her hand down her leg, starting at the knee. It was still incredibly swollen, but she could tell from the tightness of her skin that it had already gone down significantly. What she wasn't prepared for was the bruising. Purple and green splotches covered her shin and calf. Three of her toes that peeked out of the end of the bandage were almost black. She attempted to wiggle them, but it sent pain shooting up the side of her ankle. Flopping back to rest on her elbows, Brianna let her head fall backward. Her eyes drifted closed. If it was still so painful after several days, how long would it take to heal enough for her to get back to her normal life? She couldn't live in Michael's cottage forever.

A realization suddenly dawned on her. This wasn't Michael's cottage. He was still a guest here, and he had his own life to get back to. He couldn't live here with Adeline forever. Brianna allowed her thoughts to drift back to what her so-called normal life was like. A lonesome existence of servitude, wrought with constant uncertainty as to how she would be treated at any given moment. She sighed. Perhaps her current situation wasn't so bad, after all.

Determined to see the sunshine, she carefully swung her legs over the side of the bed and let them dangle until the stars stopped twinkling in her eyes. After a long moment, she slowly slid until her feet touched the ground and flinched at the frigid wood. Then, taking care to keep all the weight on her left foot, she pushed herself up to stand. Faint drumbeats returned in her toes and marched up to her ankle, then her calf. She estimated the window to be about three feet away. But there was nothing to hold on to between here and there, and she certainly wasn't going to be able to walk. She'd thought it would work to quickly press just her toes down and hobble forward, but it was clear that was not going to do. Perhaps she could just reach over without having to take any steps.

Bending at the waist, she stretched her left arm out as far as it could go. Wiggling her fingertips, she tried to reach the edge of the curtain fabric, but it was too far away. When she straightened, the floor tilted and the ceiling swirled downward. Before she knew it, Brianna was in a heap on the ground. Her stomach roiled and the room continued to spin around her. She squeezed her eyes closed and laid her cheek against the floor, grateful now for the bracing cold of it.

"Brianna?" Finnuala's groggy voice called.

She tried to respond but could manage only a trembling groan.

Footsteps rushed to the doorway, followed by a gasp. "Brianna!" In a flash, Finnuala was at her side. "What're ya like?"

Brianna opened her mouth to answer but was afraid last night's dinner would be the only thing to come out, so she closed it again.

"Never mind. Let's get ya back in bed." Knobby fingers

wrapped around Brianna's forearms at the elbows. After lots of tugging and slipping and changing of grips, Finnuala managed to get Brianna to a seated position, but by then, both women were panting, and sweat trickled down Brianna's neck.

"Let . . . let me just sit here for a spell," Brianna said.

Finnuala rested on her knees and nodded, breathless. "Wha'—did ya fall out of the bed?"

Brianna shook her head. Her breaths were coming easier now, but still in puffs. "I wanted to open the curtains." She offered a sheepish look to her friend.

"Och, child! Why did ya not call fer me?"

Brianna shrugged. "I didn't want to disturb ya." She rested her head against the side of the bed. "And I thought it would be a simple enough task."

Finnuala *tsked* and sighed. "I can imagine this is difficult for ya. I know ye're used to being the one to do things fer everyone else, but Doctor O'Donnell was verra clear that ya aren't to move from this bed fer at least a week." She looked at Brianna from head to toe and then began to chuckle. "And this is why."

Brianna couldn't help but return the laughter. She must look so ridiculous sitting on the floor in her bedclothes. But Finnuala was right. While Brianna didn't necessarily miss her daily tasks, she missed being able to do them. She'd never had anyone wait on her before, and every time someone had to help her do some mundane little thing, she felt more guilty than the time before. Surely they all had much more important things to be doing, rather than answering her every beck and call. But it was also becoming more and more clear to her that she truly had no choice in the matter.

If she wasn't able to accomplish opening the curtains, there was no way she would be able to dress, prepare food, or bathe without assistance.

"Now"—Finnuala slapped her knees—"let's see if we can't get ya back in this bed."

Finnuala reached a shaky hand out to her. While probably the heartiest person Brianna had ever known, Finnuala's own physical strength was clearly waning. Brianna couldn't live with herself if the woman caused herself injury trying to help her. She was trying to think of who Finnuala could summon to come help when a knock sounded at the door. Brianna's heart quickened and she smoothed her hands over her hair, tucking a few unruly strands behind her ears. She hoped both that it was Michael and that it wasn't. While she couldn't deny her desire to see him again, the thought of him discovering her in such a state sent pangs of dread with every heartbeat.

"Wait here," Finnuala said. "Although, ye've nowhere else to go, have ye?" She cackled at her joke as she shuffled to the front room.

Brianna heard the door open and strained to hear Finnuala's interaction with whoever it was. "Good mornin', Miss FitzGerald. Ye can put that right over here."

Brianna stifled a groan. Adeline was the last person she needed.

"Cook said I should bring this to you." Dishes rattled and Brianna could just envision the girl trying to carry a tray full of dishes and food.

"That's verra kind of ya. Thank you."

"I'll be back later to fetch the dirty dishes when you are done." Adeline's voice was flat. Resigned.

"Actually, could ye do one more thing?"

No, no, no, no. Please, Finnuala, not her.

"We've had a wee mishap, and I could use a pair of young hands to help me."

"Eh, alright." The hesitation in Adeline's voice was palpable. But Brianna appreciated that the girl had not submitted Finnuala to her typical caustic attitudes.

Footsteps drew near. "Just in here."

"What do you nee—" When Adeline rounded the foot of the bed and saw Brianna on the floor, a look of shock sprang to her face, then melted into an expression of confusion and disgust.

"I canna get her back in bed on me own, and she lacks the strength still to do so without aid. Will ya help me get her up?" Finnuala was already on the other side of Brianna, reaching down to grab her arm.

"Oh, okay." With a grimace as though she was about to shovel dung, Adeline scooted closer.

"Right," Finnuala said. "Hook one arm under hers like this"—she slid her right arm under Brianna's until her elbow hooked into the armpit—"then cup her elbow with the other hand."

Adeline sucked in a deep breath. Her cheeks puffed out as she held it, then followed Finnuala's example.

"On three," Finnuala instructed. "*A haon, a dó, a trí.*"

Brianna clamped her eyes shut and pushed against the floor with her left foot as the two women hoisted her up. Stumbling, they finally managed to rest Brianna's backside against the edge of the bed. Once it seemed Brianna was secure, Adeline hastily released her grip and backed away, wiping her hands on her apron as though they were filthy.

"Thank you," Brianna said as Finnuala helped her sit up against the headboard before the room could resume its twirling.

Adeline crossed to the washbasin and scrubbed her hands and arms up to the elbows, then started to reach for the towel but stopped short, staring at it. Forgoing the rough cloth, she wiped her hands dry on her apron and hurried to the bedroom door. "As I said, I'll come back later to collect the empty dishes." She paused. "Though it will likely not be until after lunch." She pinned Brianna with a glare. "Everything is taking much longer now."

Brianna's chin sank down to her chest. "I know. I am sorry. Please send my apologies to Cook—and Mary as well."

"*Wheesht.*" Finnuala pulled the blankets up to Brianna's waist. "They know ya didna choose this course for yerself. I'm sure they're all just happy ye're going to be okay." Finnuala gave Adeline a look full of motherly reprimand.

She blinked hard but said nothing for a moment, then, "I'll see if Mary or someone can bring over some hot water and bathing soap."

While she was certain Adeline meant it as a barb, Brianna couldn't deny that a bath—even of the sponge variety—sounded wonderful. And if Adeline's reactions were any indication, Brianna needed it much more than she realized and was even more grateful that Michael wasn't the one to have to help her up. "Thank you," she said at length.

Adeline nodded slightly and lingered for a second before turning and hustling outside.

Being clean felt even better than she'd imagined. The warm water was like a hug from an old friend as it splashed over her head and down her arms. Brianna closed her eyes while Finnuala combed her still-damp hair. When Brianna had reminded the woman that her arms still functioned and she was perfectly capable of brushing her own hair, the woman practically scolded her. Deep down, Brianna assumed Finnuala—who had no children—needed to nurture someone just as much as Brianna needed nurturing. So, she'd not fought her on it. And now, sitting in bed in a fresh nightgown, with Finnuala humming a soft tune and braiding her hair, Brianna wondered if this was what it was like to have a mother. If this was how the nights in her childhood might have gone had her parents never left her on Magee's doorstep. Instead, she'd spent her nights curled up alone, pretending the threadbare blanket Magee afforded her was a mother's embrace. She swallowed against the lump in her throat.

"Thank you, Finnuala," Brianna managed to say. "Thank you for taking care of me."

Finnuala leaned over and kissed the top of Brianna's head and mumbled something she couldn't quite make out.

The front door creaked open as someone rapped on it. "Knock, knock."

Brianna smiled and breathed a sigh of relief that Michael had chosen to call now that she was refreshed. She tugged at the sleeves of her borrowed gown. Mary had brought it along with the hot water and said Brianna could use it as long as she needed.

"How's the patient faring today?" Michael scooted around the door, balancing a tray of tea and sandwiches on the palm of one hand and gripping a vase of fresh wildflowers in the other.

"I'm doing just fine, thank you," she said.

Finnuala tied the end of Brianna's braided hair and set the comb on the bedside table. "I just remembered, I've some wash on the line. I'll just go collect it."

Brianna's brows drew together. "Finnuala, ya didn't do any—" But she was out the door before Brianna could finish.

"I come bearing gifts." Michael set the tray on the table without spilling so much as a drop of tea. Much unlike Adeline's tray, which had so much tea sloshed from the pot that the plates were swimming in it. "That's from Cook," he said.

"Thank you," she said. "And thanks to Cook."

"And these," he said as he set the vase down next to the comb, "are from me." He smiled and sat in the chair next to the bed.

Brianna studied the flowers, which Michael had obviously picked from various places on the house grounds. "They're lovely, thank you."

"So, how are ya doing, really?" He studied her face, intensity Brianna couldn't place flaming behind his eyes. "I feel like I haven't seen ya in ages."

Brianna's cheeks warmed. "'Tis only been a few days." And yet, she knew exactly what he meant. Those few days had felt like an eternity. "I'm alright, though healing is coming more slowly than I'd like. However, I feel much improved today."

"Glad to hear it." He reached over, squeezed her hand, and let it go.

"*Haigh?* Hello?" Batty's voice carried from the front doorway. Finnuala must have left it wide open. Batty's slight frame filled the bedroom doorway. "Oh, hello, Michael. Eh, Brianna, do you think ya might be up to some visitors? There are a coupla people here who've asked to see ya."

"Me?" Brianna's mind spun. Just about everyone she knew was on the grounds of Ballymacool House. "Um . . . aye, I suppose so."

Batty grinned. "*Iontach!*" He called over his shoulder and two more silhouettes filled the frame. "G'on in, Sean."

"Sean!" Brianna gasped as her old friend walked through the door, a warm smile spread across his lips. "Michael, this is Sean McFadden, a local thatcher. He keeps all our thatch in tip-top shape."

Michael stood and shook the man's hand. "Michael Wray," he said.

"*Deas bualadh leat,*" Sean said, then turned his attention back to Brianna. "Movin' up in yer social circles, eh?" They shared a good-natured laugh.

"It's a long story," Brianna and Michael said in unison.

"I was called out to fix some of the roofs on the property after the storm last week and just wanted to stop in and say hi." A boy came around and stood next to Sean.

Brianna's eyes widened. "This can't be young Colm?"

"Aye, 'tis, indeed. Can ya believe he's nearly eleven?"

"Eleven? My goodness!"

"Colm, say hello to Brianna and Mister Wray."

"Hiya," Colm said, tipping his flatcap.

"Moira sends her love. She wanted to come, but the wee one'll be here in a few weeks, and the journey over Errigal Pass is just too much."

"A new babaí? Congratulations!"

Sean beamed. "Thanks. We're absolutely chuffed." Colm

held up a basket to his father. "Oh! I almost fergot. Along with her love, my better half sent over a few other bits and bobs. Some of her freshly made brown bread, a crock of stew, and some herbs for poultices." He gestured to Colm, who sheepishly brought the basket to Brianna.

"How did ya all know I was . . . what happened?" she asked, taking the basket from Colm.

"This is Donegal, Brianna. Very few secrets go unknown." He laughed. Then a voice called him from outside. Sean answered it, then turned back to Brianna. "I'd best get back to it. My apprentice has some questions for me."

Through the window, Brianna saw a lanky young man with red hair who looked to be in his early twenties. He waved and she waved back.

"'Twas lovely to see ye, Sean, Colm. Please send my deepest gratitude to Moira for the thoughtful gifts."

"*Go cinnte*," Sean said as he crossed the room and placed a kiss on Brianna's cheek. "Ya get better soon, now."

"Thanks, I will," she said.

Sean and Colm each shook Michael's hand and left. As they rounded the corner, Finnuala came back in, her arms conspicuously empty of any laundry.

"Alright now," she said. "That's enough excitement fer the moment. Brianna needs her rest."

Brianna's heart sank. Michael had only just arrived, and they'd not even had a chance to talk. While it was wonderful to see Sean and she was so grateful for the care basket—even now her stomach growled at the enticing aroma wafting up from it—she'd truly wanted nothing more than to talk with Michael. She looked up and met his gaze.

"Alright," he said on a sigh. "I'll be 'round later to look in on ya."

"Yes, yes, verra good." Finnuala was shooing him to the door as she spoke. "Word came from the doctor while I was out. He'll be here this afternoon to check on Brianna. 'Twould be good if ye were here fer that."

Michael cast a glance back over his shoulder at Brianna, nodded, and left.

22

"*An mhaith, ar fad.*" Doctor O'Donnell finished rewrapping Brianna's ankle. "Very good, indeed. It's comin' along quite nicely."

Michael watched his every move, brow furrowed. "And you're certain it isn't broken?"

The doctor sniffed and shrugged one shoulder. "Well, yes, as certain as I can be. Miraculously, it appears to be just a severe sprain an' bruising." He looked at Brianna. "The good Laird was watchin' out for ye, that's for sure."

Brianna smiled and squirmed under the direct attention of so many people.

"I could be surer if we had access to an X-ray machine, but, alas, she'd have to make the trip to Dublin for that, and I'm afraid she's just not up for that journey." Doctor O'Donnell stepped around Michael to the head of the bed and took Brianna's wrist in his hand. He stared at his watch, lips counting silently. He patted her hand and smiled, the kindness in his eyes warming her. "Nor do I think you warrant it. Yer fever's gone, the swelling is down greatly since I last looked in on you, and while it will be a few weeks yet before you're ready to return to all yer duties, I have no doubt ya will make a full recovery."

In the corner, Magee cleared her throat. "Good," she muttered. "Very good," she repeated more strongly.

Doctor O'Donnell turned and eyed the headmistress. "That is, provided she's allowed the proper rest and recovery time." He kept his gaze pinned on her overlong before he shot a look to Michael and Finnuala in turn.

"She will," Michael said, and then turned his attention to Mistress Magee as well. "You have our word." Michael slipped his hand behind him and gave Brianna's fingers a squeeze. Her skin came to life at his touch, and heat flashed up her neck. Everyone else in the room seemed oblivious to Michael's small, silent act of rebellion. Even after all that had transpired between them during the storm, and the days since, Brianna couldn't help but wonder if he'd truly meant what he'd said that night in the woods. And yet here he stood, holding her hand in front of what might as well have been the whole world. She squeezed in return and his thumb arced circles over her fingers.

The doctor faced Brianna again and Michael deftly slid his hand away. Brianna bit her lip to keep the grin from belying their connection. Doctor O'Donnell began packing up his bag. "Rest for a few more days, then you can start making short trips."

"Short?" Finnuala asked.

"To the sitting room or over to the press to get clean clothes," he said. "Ye'll know what's too much. And as your strength returns, ya can venture farther. But no stairs, and no lifting or carrying anything for at least a fortnight. I'll check back in, in a week."

The doctor shook Michael's and Magee's hands and tipped his hat to Finnuala, who was on the opposite side of the bed from them all. He patted Brianna's arm and headed for the door. Finnuala, Michael, and the headmistress followed him.

Michael closed the door behind the doctor and Finnuala headed for the kitchen.

Magee huffed and crossed her arms. "So, she gets to continue to get room and board for free while the rest of us break our backs doing her share of the work in addition to our own." She shook her head. "Typical."

Michael cupped his hand over his chin, rubbing at his beard. Had this woman no heart at all? Why did she hold such vehement animosity toward Brianna? "Is that truly what you think is happening here?"

Finnuala stacked some sandwiches on a plate, took them into the bedroom, and shut the door.

Magee chortled. "You have no idea. That girl has been taking advantage of my hospitality her whole life. And now she sits in here like a queen, being served hand and foot around the clock. Meanwhile, the rest of my staff has to pick up her slack."

Michael stepped to the door and reached for the handle. "Well, if she's truly as poor of a worker as you've said, then it shouldn't add too much to their plates, now, should it? I'd think it a relief to have her out of your hair for a bit."

She scowled but said nothing. An emotion flashed in her

eyes that he couldn't place. Anger? Perhaps. Sadness? No. Fear? Yes, it was a livid fear that clouded her vision, and Michael wondered all the more what had transpired to place it there.

"Now," he said, "I believe ya have a school to run." He opened the front door and waited for her to exit.

The pair regarded each other in strained silence for a long moment before Magee sniffed, tipped her chin upward, and said, "Indeed."

Michael closed the door after her and raked his fingers through his hair. He'd been here mere weeks and had already tired of Magee and her haughty ways. How had Brianna and the rest of the staff put up with her for so long? Then it dawned on him—they had no choice. Brianna in particular was stuck in this special sort of trap, with no foreseeable way out. He paced a few lengths of the room before stopping at the fireplace. He rested his palms on the mantel and released a long, slow breath.

Then he slid one of the books from its place and headed back to Brianna's room. He knocked and was invited inside. Brianna was adjusting her position in the bed, and Finnuala was collecting dishes from around the room.

"I'll put these in the basin to soak. Then I'm gonna help myself to a cuppa and a wee rest by the fire."

"Goodness knows ya deserve it," Brianna said. "Thank you, Finnuala."

She flapped a dismissive hand and carried her load out of the room. Michael dragged a chair from the corner over to the bedside. As he sat down, he waggled the thin copy of *The Collected Poems of W. B. Yeats* in his fingers. "Shall I read to ya for a spell?"

Brianna smiled. "That would be lovely, thanks." She settled against the pillows Finnuala had tucked behind her.

Michael thumbed through the book, searching for just the right line of verse to read. He opened his mouth to begin and paused. He stared at the page. The words on it might as well have been in Greek. He couldn't focus for the questions clanging in his mind. He shut the book and dropped it to his lap. "Remind me again, how long have ya been at Ballymacool?"

Brianna blinked, clearly taken aback at his abrupt question. "Well, I've been in my current position for ten years, but I've been working here in some capacity since I was a young girl."

"Aye, that I remember." Michael shifted in his seat. "But, were ya born here?"

"No. Well, I was born in the area, but I don't know exactly where. I was a small infant when Magee found me on her doorstep. She took me in and raised me. I was just a toddler when she took over Ballymacool and opened the boarding school."

"But . . ." Michael absently opened the book cover and let it fall closed over and over. "Why does she treat ya like a maid rather than her adopted daughter?"

Brianna's head lowered and she picked at a thread on the duvet.

"I'm sorry, I don't want to hurt ya. I shouldn't pry." He chided himself.

"No, it's fine." Her voice was barely above a whisper. "I've wondered that myself many times." She shrugged, and when her gaze met his, her eyes were rimmed red and swam with unshed tears.

Michael's heart lurched and he instinctively reached for her hand, letting the book clatter to the floor. "Brianna," he said, his own voice thick with emotion.

"She's said several times before"—her voice cracked and she cleared her throat—"she's said things about how I deserve this or that, but I've never understood what she means. I've only ever done what she's asked."

Michael nodded. "She's made similar comments to me, and at times alluded to your history." He scooted to the edge of his chair and placed his other hand over hers. "Ya know nothing of your parents?"

She shifted slightly and moved as though she was going to reach with her free hand, then stopped. Michael dropped his gaze to his lap and waited, giving her time to collect her thoughts.

"All I know is what she's told me," Brianna said at length. "That before Ballymacool was a boardinghouse, she was the teacher at the local primary school. She found me on her doorstep in a basket with a note asking her to take care of me." She paused again, her chin quivering. A single tear slid down her cheek. "Besides the note and the blanket I was wrapped in, they'd left one other thing with me, but it's been lost."

Michael reached up and wiped the tear from her cheek, just as he'd done in the cave. "You'd said something like that the night of the storm. I'm so sorry it's lost. Would ya like to tell me about it?"

Her right hand slid from his, and her delicate fingers traced along the bottom of her neck. "'Twas a necklace," she whispered. She turned her head toward the window and seemed a long way off for a moment. Then she looked back at Michael and the sorrow that filled her eyes broke his heart. When she spoke again, her voice had found more strength. "A pendant. Actually, just part of one."

As she described the shard, its design, and how long it had been gone, Michael's pulse quickened. Equal parts hope and ire rose in his chest. "Did it have part of a word engraved on the back?" he asked, working to keep his voice calm.

Her gaze shot up to meet his, and her mouth fell open. "Yes! How did ya know that?"

"And ya say that it's still missing? Ya haven't found it or gotten it back yet?" When she shook her head, confusion etched on her face, he clenched his teeth. His mind swirled with all he wanted to say to that despicable Magee the next time he saw her. He would tell her—

"Michael?"

Brianna's voice jolted him from his spiraling, angry thoughts. "Brianna, I—I found your necklace."

She sat up straight. "What? Ya did?" A wide grin split her face before it faltered. "Why didn't you tell me?"

Michael shook his head. "I found it weeks ago but didn't know who it belonged it. It was wedged under the door of the cottage." He jammed his thumb in the direction of the front room. "I figured it must belong to someone at Ballymacool, but since I was so new here, I had no guess as to who. So I gave it to Magee, and she assured me she would find its owner."

Brianna fell back against the pillows. "Ya gave it to Magee?" Pain laced her voice. "And she . . . she kept it."

Michael took her hand once more. "I don't know what she's done with it. She had to have known it was yours. If ya had it with you when she found you . . ."

"She knew." Brianna swallowed hard.

Michael stood and took a step toward the door. "I'll have a word with her. I'll make sure ya get back what's rightfully yours."

Brianna held her hand up, palm out. "Wait."

He stopped and looked back at her.

"Don't say anything to her."

"What? Ye're joking, right?" He stuffed his hands in his pockets. All he wanted to do was throttle that hateful woman for what she'd done to Brianna. Now, he had a chance to make things right, or at least a tiny bit better, and she wanted him to wait?

"Sit down, Michael," she said, gesturing to the chair. "Please?" Her eyes searched his, and urgency yet calmness shone in them. He did as she bade.

She chewed her lip and shifted in the bed, wincing as she adjusted the position of her leg. "I've no idea why she would keep such a thing from me. But I can't help but feel it best not to confront her about it. Not yet, at least."

Michael took a deep breath and released it slowly. The head-mistress did have a shadiness to her, he couldn't deny. And Brianna was a grown woman, capable of making her own decisions. Much as he wanted to protect her, he had to trust that if she didn't want to pursue it with Magee just yet, she had good reason for it. Even if she couldn't quite articulate that reason.

"I'd just like to wait a bit longer. Please."

Michael nodded. "Very well." He tugged the sleeves of his jumper up to his elbows. "But when ye're ready, I'm here for whatever you need."

She smiled and reached for his hand. "Go raibh maith agat."

23

Maureen watched over the dining room, annoyance churning in her gut. The girls had continued the methods Mister Wray had shown them when he first began to meddle in her affairs. And now with Brianna out of the picture for who knows how long, they had expanded their participation in the serving and cleaning up from meals. Recently, rather than a quiet, dignified meal full of decorum and silence, Maureen was forced to endure the clanks and clangs of inexperienced hands stacking dishes and flatware. How long had it taken Brianna to learn not to do such things? Too long. And just when she'd gotten it to Maureen's liking, it was starting all over again. A few of the girls even deigned to sing—some godforsaken sea shanty, at first. But Maureen had put a stop to that nonsense. A few of the girls had pleaded with her to allow it, and she had acquiesced. But, she'd said, if they insisted on singing, it must be something that provided some sort of edification. So they'd resorted to a few old hymns.

"Now, isn't this nice?" Mister Wray's voice broke into Maureen's thoughts.

She glanced at him from the corner of her eye. He was wiping crumbs from his beard with his serviette. She grimaced. "Not exactly how I'd describe it."

He tossed his napkin onto his plate. "Oh? How would you describe it then?"

"Tiresome, Mister Wray. Most tiresome." She turned to face him. "And that's quite the same way I'm beginning to feel about your presence here. You were summoned to aid us with Adeline and her . . . issues. For that, I am grateful. She is much improved. But I did not invite you here to meddle in our affairs and disrupt nearly twenty years of tradition we've put into place here."

He leaned back in his chair, folded his arms, and stretched out his long legs, crossing them at the ankles. "Happy to help, Mistress Magee. Though I fear my work here is far from done. In fact, Adeline's requested that I stay for the duration of the semester."

Maureen blanched. He wouldn't.

"And as for yer traditions . . . ya know, some might say that traditions were made to be broken." The smirk that tipped his mouth was like a red-hot poker, stoking the flames of her irritation.

"Spoken like an adolescent spoiled brat." Her heart lurched at her boldness. Could she afford to insult the Wray family in such a way? Likely not, but she didn't truly care. She'd been manipulated and pushed around for far too long by people of their ilk. It was clear she was going to have to make her own way in this world if those currently in it were going to resist what she was trying to accomplish.

The room fell quiet, and Maureen realized she'd shouted her last statement rather than uttered it through clenched teeth as was her intention. She swallowed hard. Mister Wray simply raised his brows and deepened his smirk.

The astonished girls took turns gaping at them. Mister Wray stood, straightened his jumper, and sauntered from the room. Once he had gone, she stood. "Carry on, girls. We've a schedule to keep."

Michael slowed his pace as he walked the path back to the bunkhouse after helping Cook clear up the evening meal. The night air was cold and the sky clear. While he'd managed to keep his cool in the dining hall, the truth was, it took every ounce of his strength not to tear into Magee and put her in her place right there in front of everyone. The scene replayed in his mind, and his jaw clenched. He didn't even care that she'd insulted him. The last thing he wanted was to be accepted by the likes of Maureen Magee. No, what grated him so deeply was her belief that she was in the right. In how she ran Ballymacool, in her view of the way society should be, and in the way she treated Brianna.

Michael's steps stilled and he tipped his head back. The wind was unseasonably calm, just barely tickling the tops of the trees. Their whispered laughter the only sound to be heard. The ebony sky stretched overhead like bejeweled velvet. He breathed in deep, letting the frigid air fill his lungs, resisting the reflex to cough it out. It made him feel alive and hushed his angry thoughts so they stretched like cold honey rather than rushing and crashing over his mind like Astelleen Burn Falls.

Finally releasing the breath, he continued on to the bunk-house. Its windows glowed amber, and conversation spilled out through the open door. Michael entered to find Batty, Sean, and Sean's apprentice gathered around the fireplace like old friends, comfortable in each other's company. Sean was commenting on the state of affairs with Italy and Mussolini, and the lot of them shook their heads.

"Evenin', gents."

"Ah, Michael, welcome in." Batty stood and fetched another cup from the shelf. "Will ya have yer evenin' cuppa wit' us?"

"Cinnte." Michael shook Sean's hand and settled in one of the empty seats near the fire. "Will ya stay long?" he asked.

Sean took a swig from his cup and shook his head. "Níl. Colm and I'll leave tomorrow." He looked to one of the bunks where Colm was already asleep. "We were able to finish up the repairs today, but by then it was already dark. Batty offered for us to stay rather than chancing Errigal Pass in the dark."

"Smart." Michael took the steaming cup from Batty, who sat down.

"Have ya met my apprentice, Áedach?"

The red-haired young man shook Michael's hand. "Nice ta meet ya."

Michael returned the greeting.

Sean went on to explain to Batty all the repairs that had been done, and what Batty would need to watch for in the coming days. He then offered to return if need be. "But dependin' on what happens with Moira and the babaí, I may send Áedach in my stead."

"Go maith," Batty replied. "And how was yer evenin', Michael?"

Michael was midsip and just widened his eyes, drawing a spate of laughter from the lads.

"That sounds about right," Batty replied. Sean nodded heartily. "I don't suppose auld Magee's too happy wit' Brianna bein' laid up as she is?"

"Not at all." Michael watched the fire crackling in the grate. He was curious how much Batty had seen—though he presumed it was more than was apparent. He wanted to spill his thoughts so they could be filtered through the lens of someone familiar with Ballymacool, yet not fully part of his current predicament, but he couldn't bring himself to do it.

Batty looked to Sean and gave him a condensed version of the situation so far—about Adeline and why Michael was there, and what had happened with Brianna. "An' the headmistress is none too happy aboot any o' it. I think she hoped bringin' Michael here would calm t'ings back down. But they only seem ta have gotten more stirred up, though not truly through any fault o' his own."

Michael shrugged and swallowed another mouthful of tea. "'Tis true. I've managed to get myself right in the middle of a sticky thicket, and I don't foresee the headmistress and I seeing eye to eye over any of it."

Sean's head bobbed. "That's a tough one, so it is."

"And how're ya feelin' about it all, Michael?" Batty asked.

Michael leaned forward and rested his elbows on his knees and sighed. "I find that to be a complicated answer."

The other men chuckled.

"But I will say that I do not appreciate the lack of compassion, or justice, I see being shown to Brianna by Magee."

"How so?" Sean asked. The question didn't hold any challenge to it, just a curiosity to know more.

Michael turned to Sean, weighing his response. "Ye've done the thatch work for Ballymacool for a while?"

"Aye," Sean said. "It was one of my first accounts when my apprenticeship ended nearly fifteen years ago."

Michael nodded. "And ya seem to be quite well acquainted with Brianna."

"'Tis true. Folk in service are often well-known to one another. She sees to it that I always have what I need when working at Ballymacool, and that I am well fed, that sort of t'ing."

"The more I learn about Brianna, about her upbringing"— he paused—"the more . . . questions I have."

Sean drew a deep inhale through his nose. "Brianna's story is a tragic one. But one not uncommon to this area—nor to the whole of Ireland." Batty murmured his agreement. "Surely ye're not unfamiliar with the plight of the impoverished?"

Michael shook his head. "Not at all. And my family does all we can to help, but my issue at Ballymacool isn't one of money. It's that Brianna's treated as less than. She's constantly the target of Mistress Magee's anger. I've not seen the sort of vitriol she spews toward Brianna directed at any o' the other staff. Magee is strict and firm with them, but not cruel. She's cruel to Brianna. It's not fair, and I mean to see justice is done."

Sean blew a low whistle.

"Ye know a thing or two about justice, doncha, Sean?" Batty rose and patted Sean on the shoulder before collecting the men's cups and taking them to the basin.

"Tá, I do." Sean's glance flitted to Áedach and back to Michael. He seemed deep in thought for a moment and reached up to rub the back of his neck. "I don't know all the details of what ye or Brianna are facin', but I do know this—when it comes to seekin' justice for a perceived wrong, a man can easily become blinded by his own definition of the word."

Michael sat back in his chair. "I see."

Sean must have read the confusion on Michael's face because he continued. "See to it that ye're seekin' His justice"—he pointed a finger upward—"and not yer own version of it. Ya can never go wrong if ye're seekin' Him first."

Michael worked his jaw and nodded.

Sean stood and stretched. "A wise man once told me, 'The Lord said to pray for our enemies. But he didn't say 'twould be easy.'" He nodded to Áedach and Batty, then Michael. "It's gettin' late, lads. Ouiche mhaith."

Michael bid them his good nights as well and made his way to his little room. As he readied himself for bed, Sean's words echoed in his mind. He wasn't entirely sure that his quest was misguided, or that his motives were selfish. He rolled his eyes at himself. Well, they weren't entirely selfish. And while the immediate solution wasn't clear, a few things were becoming increasingly so. Maureen Magee held something against Brianna Kelly. Brianna was not perfect, but she did not deserve the treatment she'd been receiving most of her life. And Michael was fairly certain he was beginning to fall in love with her.

24

"Are ya ready, peata?" Finnuala stood by the bed, hands held out like a mother encouraging her baby to take her first steps.

After nearly two weeks in bed, Brianna was more than ready for a change of scenery. But after what happened the last time she attempted to stand up, apprehension now chained her to her spot. She glanced at her leg. No doubt it was healing. The swelling had gone down even more, and the bruising had changed colors yet again.

"C'mon. Ye'll be grand."

Brianna floated a look to her friend.

Finnuala's expression changed, and the look in her eyes grew more serious. "Ya won't know how it's doin' unless ya give it a go. Here, take my arm." She held her elbow aloft and motioned for Adeline—who stood on the other side of Brianna—to do the same.

"I thought I was only supposed to be helping with kitchen things," Adeline said, eyeing Brianna warily.

Finnuala rolled her eyes. "If ya don't sow in the spring, ya won't have anything to harvest come autumn."

Adeline snorted and looked at Finnuala like she was a madwoman. "What on earth are you on about?"

Finnuala kept her eyes fixed on Adeline's. "What ya do in life when ye're young sets the foundation the rest of yer life will stand on. If ya don't sow the seeds of kindness, compassion, and friendship now, they won't be there for you to benefit from later on." The two stared at one another for a long minute. Adeline opened her mouth as if to speak but closed it again.

Slowly, Adeline lifted her elbow out for Brianna.

"Anois," Finnuala said.

Brianna eyed them for a moment then slipped her hands into the crooks of their arms and slid forward until her toes brushed the ground.

"Just take her slow and steady like," Finnuala said, widening her stance so she was better anchored to support Brianna's weight.

Taking a deep breath, Brianna stood. Her muscles already protesting, she steadied her balance so the bulk of her weight was on her left foot.

"Let's try a step," Finnuala said.

Putting as little weight as possible on her right foot, Brianna hobbled forward. All three women breathed a sigh of relief, and Brianna was grateful that Finnuala had had the presence of mind to start on the side of the bed closest to the door. The trio managed a few more shaky steps, and then Brianna stumbled. Adeline quickly changed her grip on Brianna's arm so that she could wrap her other arm around Brianna's waist. Brianna's gaze shot to Adeline's. "Thank you."

Adeline kept her eyes trained on the floor ahead of them and simply nodded. At last, they made it to the chair near the fireplace. Brianna collapsed into it and all three huffed and puffed as they recovered from the arduous journey.

"Now"—Finnuala said between breaths—"that . . . wasn't . . . so . . . bad . . . now . . . was it?" Brianna, Finnuala, and Adeline burst into laughter. Anyone passing by would think they'd gone mad.

When the hilarity had faded, and the three were wiping their eyes and shaking their heads, Brianna was finally able to appreciate her new location. As Finnuala went around and opened the curtains of all the windows, Brianna gazed out onto the courtyard and drank in the new surroundings. The emerald lawn stretched out and sparkled in the midautumn sunshine. The gorse bushes in the distance swayed in the breeze, and stretches of clouds skated across the azure sky. Of course, the scene wasn't really new, but after a fortnight of staring at the press in Michael's room or the limited view from the bedroom window, it all felt quite fresh and exciting.

"Now, can I get ya an'thing?" Finnuala mopped her brow with her handkerchief.

Brianna shook her head. "You've done plenty. Go rest awhile."

"Bah." Finnuala flapped her hand. "I don't need ta rest." She looked down at her apron. "But I could stand to fetch a few things from my own cottage. 'Tis early enough in the day that I can get there and back."

Brianna nodded. "Alright. Be careful."

Adeline stood and started to follow Finnuala out the door but Finnuala turned and pointed to the chair opposite Brianna. "I need ya to stay here. Brianna shouldn't be alone, in case a need arises. She canna get anywhere on her own."

Adeline folded her arms and huffed. "I wanted to go back to the main house. There's nothing to do here."

"There's plenty ta do if ya look for it." Then she lowered her voice. "And sometimes the most useful things we can do, don't look useful at all." She winked and slid the door closed behind her.

Adeline stood awkwardly in the entryway for a moment before slumping over and sitting in the chair across from Brianna.

"Thanks for staying with me," Brianna said.

Adeline just rolled her eyes and shrugged.

Brianna watched her for a long moment. Despite her best efforts to appear mature, Brianna could see just how young the girl was now that they sat so close. She couldn't be more than thirteen or so.

"How old are you, Adeline?"

She slumped back in the chair, folded her arms again, and stared into the fire. "Fourteen," she said with the attitude of a four-year-old.

Brianna nodded. "How long have you been at Ballyma-cool?"

Adeline was quiet so long Brianna wasn't sure she would answer. Just when Brianna was about to reach for one of the books above her on the mantel, Adeline said, "Almost a year."

"Do ya like it here?"

"What do you think?" she snapped.

Brianna just smiled. "I know the feeling."

Adeline looked at her for the first time this whole encoun-ter. "Isn't this, like, your home?"

Brianna shrugged. "It's where I live."

"What about your family? Why aren't they helping you right now?"

"I'm an orphan."

"Oh." Adeline's gaze dropped to her feet. After a pregnant pause, she added, "Sometimes I feel like an orphan."

Brianna's brows arched up, then lowered back down. "I'm sorry to hear that. Ya don't hear from your parents much?"

Adeline's eyes took on a sheen as she stared a million miles away. She shook her head.

"I'm sorry," Brianna said softly.

Shrugging, Adeline straightened in her seat. "Never mind. It's fine. I don't need them anyway."

"What about your cousin? It was nice of him to come and assist ya."

"He's only here because they forced him to be. He didn't want to come." She glared at Brianna. "And he's only still here because of you."

Unsure what else to say, Brianna let Adeline's comment hang in the air. Surely that wasn't true. Michael wouldn't stay at a place like this just for her, would he? Clearly Adeline still needed him. Brianna wanted to ask more, but before she could, the cottage door burst open and Mistress Magee, breathless, carried in a basket of potatoes.

She lumbered over and dropped it at Brianna's feet. "Cook needs these peeled." She tossed a peeler on top of the spuds.

"The doctor said I'm not to do any work," Brianna said, annoyed by the catch in her throat.

"Well, it's your foot that's damaged. Your hands still work, don't they?"

Brianna looked to Adeline, who had suddenly become quite engrossed with a thread on her sleeve. "I—"

"Don't tell me it will harm your leg for you to peel a few potatoes? You still have a job to do here, lass, and if you're not going to do it, perhaps you don't need a roof over your head anymore either." Magee's bootheels clacked against the wood floor as she made her way back to the door. "It's up to you."

Brianna flinched as the door slammed. She stared at the basket of potatoes, at a loss for what to do. She supposed Magee had a point. She was capable of doing something simple, like peeling spuds. Slowly reaching for the peeler, she asked, "Would ya hand me that bucket, please?"

Adeline set the waste bucket next to the basket and Brianna started in, letting the peels drop into it. When she was about halfway finished, Michael came in looking for Adeline.

"Ah, here you are. Cook sent for ya." He smiled at his cousin, then stopped short, his eyes fixed on Brianna. "What— What are ya doing?"

"Magee wanted her to peel spuds," Adeline answered nonchalantly.

Michael spun to face Adeline again. "And you let her?"

"Oy!" Adeline shot to her feet. "Don't yell at me, it was her choice to agree to it."

Raking his fingers through his hair, Michael said, "No, it wasn't. Don't you get it?"

Adeline fell into her customary pouting stance, and Michael shook his head. He stepped closer to Adeline, and when he spoke again, his voice was calmer. "Brianna has fewer choices in matters than you might expect."

Adeline just looked at him, then at Brianna.

Taking a deep breath, Michael reached down and took the peeler from Brianna. "You don't have to do this." His voice was calm, but fire blazed behind his eyes.

"I . . . well," Brianna whispered, feeling like a foolish child. Her head dipped forward. "It's just peeling potatoes. I figured it would be fine. Though I am tired." Not so long ago, she could've peeled those spuds in record time and not even broken a sweat. But her injury and illness had taken a toll on her stamina, it would seem.

Michael crouched down in front of her and took both her hands in his. "Brianna, you are one of the strongest people I've ever known. You've overcome so much, and you've done it all by yourself." He hooked a finger under her chin and lifted it up so she met his gaze. "I've no doubt you're capable of making your own way, but you shouldn't have to. And you will never have to face it alone again if you don't want to." He raised her hand to his lips and pressed a slow, tender kiss to it.

Brianna's eyes fluttered closed. Her head spun at his touch and when she opened her eyes, he leaned in closer and whispered, "I'd be honored if you'd allow me to stand in this gap for you."

Realizing he was speaking about much more than just potatoes, Brianna's breath caught in her chest. Not trusting herself to speak, she simply nodded. "Thank you," she managed at length.

Michael rose and grabbed the bucket, set it on top of the basket of peeled potatoes, and hoisted both up. "Let's go, Adeline. Cook's waiting."

Michael burst into Magee's office and dropped the basket of potatoes on her desk.

"You forgot something in the cottage." He brushed his hands together a few times and slid them into his pockets.

The headmistress slowly rose, mouth agape, and stared at the basket as if it were a pile of dung. "Mister Wray! Have you lost your mind?"

Michael pushed his bottom lip up and shook his head. "On the contrary. I'm seeing more clearly by the moment."

"Take these down to the kitchen this instant." She planted both fists on her hips.

"You managed to get them all the way over to the cottage. You should have no problem getting them down to the kitchen."

Magee peered into the basket. "I see she couldn't even finish the job. *Tsk.*"

"I told her not to finish."

"How dare you? You had no right."

"Doctor O'Donnell specifically said she is not to resume her duties."

The edge of her mouth slid up in a smirk. "He said full duties, by my recollection. There's nothing wrong with her arms."

Heat flashed up Michael's face. "Ya truly are a piece of work, Mistress Magee."

She simply stared at him and cocked a brow.

"Oh." He snapped his fingers. "I've been meaning to ask ya. Did you ever find out who that pendant belonged to?"

Magee's eyes widened for a split second before her stoic countenance returned. "No. The owner never came forward."

"Hmm. Shame, that."

"Indeed." She swallowed hard.

"Well, it's getting closer to dinnertime. Ye'd best get those down to the kitchen." Michael opened the door, then turned back. "Brianna is not to do so much as wash a dish or boil a pot until O'Donnell clears her. I'd advise you not to test me on this." He closed the door after him, with Magee still standing behind her desk, mouth bobbing like a fish.

25

Brianna closed her eyes as the cool breeze kissed her face. Even on this autumn afternoon, the sun shone, warming her skin and setting the grass gleaming like an emerald in a crown. Michael had helped her out to the lawn of the courtyard so she could sit and enjoy the fresh air.

"I've missed this," she said, eyes still closed, face turned upward.

Michael chuckled. "I thought you might."

In the distance, the church bells tolled and next to her, Michael stirred. She glanced over as he checked his pocket watch. "Do you need to go?"

"Not yet," he said, staring toward the main house, squinting against the bright afternoon light. "I've another hour or so before I need to check on Adeline. She's been doing much better with Cook, so I've been slowly keeping more and more distance to see how she fares."

"Tell me about her." Brianna shifted her body to face Michael.

He looked at Brianna. "What do you want to know?"

"Where exactly is her family?"

"My uncle Thomas runs an estate in County Dublin."

"Dublin?" She blew out a breath. "That's a long way off. Why did they send her here and not somewhere closer to home?"

Michael sighed. "With all the civil unrest down there, they felt it would be safer for her here." He looked back toward the kitchen, as if he could see through the walls to Adeline. "At least, that's what they say."

Brianna nodded. "Ya think it's something else?"

Shrugging, he said, "I think it's a combination of things, really. Namely that she's burned all their bridges around them."

Brianna's jaw fell slack. "She burned them?"

"Metaphorically speaking." He grinned and his beard dimpled.

"Oh, right. Of course." Brianna's cheeks warmed and she laughed. "Why—" She paused to choose her words carefully. "Why is she so angry all the time?"

Michael released a long sigh as the breeze picked up and stirred the ends of his hair. Brianna resisted the urge to reach over and brush them away from his face. "I don't really know, to be honest," he said in answer to her question. "But I think she misses her sister, Ciara."

"Oh." Brianna shifted in her seat. "Can she maybe come for a visit?"

Michael shook his head. "She died at six months old. Typhoid. Adeline was three or so."

Brianna clutched her chest. "Oh, how awful. I'm so sorry."

Michael swallowed hard. "'Twas a terrible time. My uncle's always been a hard man, and Ciara's death hardened him further. He and *m'aintín* Kathryn sort of . . . withdrew. And wee Adeline was left to her own devices a lot."

"That's— That's horrible." Her gaze drifted to the grass.

"She had her nanny, but it wasn't the same. In truth, I think every time her parents looked at Adeline, they saw Ciara. And it was too much." He scratched his beard and sighed. "I think Adeline tried to get their attention any way she could."

When Brianna didn't respond, he continued. "Her behavior grew worse the older she got. And the more they pushed her away, the more she rebelled. Eventually, she had ostracized her family from the whole of the community with her destructive choices, and they couldn't handle her anymore."

"She mentioned the other day that she often feels like an orphan. Now I see why." She wagged her head. "It's so sad. But surely they still love her?"

"Oh, aye, I'm sure they do. But they don't know any other way."

"Poor Adeline. No wonder."

Michael was quiet for a moment, then said, "Y'know, I never really put it all together until now. She has always just been my annoyin' little cousin, but it makes perfect sense. Maybe I've been goin' about it all wrong with her." He sat back in his chair.

"I think ye've done a great job with her. As ya said, she's gotten much better." She placed her elbow on the back of her chair and rested her head on her hand. "I've even seen an improvement in the way she treats me."

His eyes widened. "Have you? Good, very good."

She laughed. "But then, 'twas back to normal."

He echoed her laughter. "Ah, families. Doncha love 'em?"

Brianna blanched and sank back in her chair. When she didn't answer, Michael reached over and placed a hand on her arm. "Aw, geez, I'm sorry."

"It's fine." She offered him a shaky smile and covered his hand with hers.

"It's not fine. I should've been more thoughtful."

"Michael." She waited until he looked at her. "Truly, it's fine. Yes, it's painful not to have my parents or the hope of any siblings, cousins, and the like. But I've made my peace with it. I know you didna mean anything by it."

They were quiet for a long time, but Brianna wanted to know more about him. She wanted to know everything. "So," she said, "tell me about your family. Do you get along with your parents?"

For the rest of the hour, Michael shared stories about his childhood. About how his parents were firm, but fair, and while he felt his mother was a bit too preoccupied with appearances, she had a good heart.

He confided in her that he often struggled with his family's position. He wanted to be more accessible within the community, to be treated like a normal bloke rather than handled with kid gloves. And he shared his concerns with the changing society and how his family would fare with it all.

They laughed together as he described the time he tried to run away to join the pirates he just knew were waiting for him around the bend in the River Swilly, and tears stung Brianna's eyes when he shared about the time his first beloved horse passed away.

All too soon, the bells tolled, and Michael had to head back to the kitchen. He stood and tugged his tweed waistcoat back into place. Brianna reached up and took his hand and he stilled. "Thank you for sharing your family wi' me."

He held her gaze for a long moment and then nodded. "Anytime." He took his chair inside, then returned. He reached down and scooped her up with one arm under her shoulders and the other cradled under her knees. He carried her inside and carefully set her in the wingback chair by the fireplace.

When she was settled, he knelt down and took her hand. He kissed the back of it and then turned it over. He traced the lines on her palm with his finger. "I wish I didn't have to go."

Brianna could barely hear him for the sound of her own heartbeat pounding in her ears. Every nerve in her body stood at attention. Her mouth suddenly dry, she licked her lips and whispered, "Me too."

He lowered his head and tenderly eased his lips onto her palm then brushed them against her wrist. Her fingertips. Finally, he rose and looked down at her. "Tea later?" His voice was thick with emotion. Or was it longing?

Brianna could only nod and follow him with her gaze as he walked to the door. When he left, she finally released the breath she'd been holding for fear of breaking whatever spell they'd been under. She stared at her palm and brushed her fingers over the places he'd kissed. She rested her head back and let herself drift off to sleep, hoping to relive the moment in a dream.

The embers glowed orange in the fireplace grate, but the rest of the kitchen was dark and quiet. Cold. Maureen stood in the blackness, listening to everything and nothing, willing her pulse to slow. It had been happening more frequently of late—the racing heart, the impending sense of dread. The feeling that everything she'd worked so hard to build was on the verge of crumbling around her.

She jumped at the knock that sounded at the back door. Even though she was alone in the room, she looked around as if someone else would admit they were expecting a visitor. Of course, no such admission came, and she was forced to answer the door herself. Her face crumpled at the sight of the old woman.

"What do you want?" Maureen hissed.

Finnuala seemed unfazed. "Just a moment of yer time."

Maureen stared at her. What on earth could this woman want with her? When she didn't respond, Finnuala asked, "May I come in?"

Sighing, Maureen stepped aside and Finnuala shuffled past her. The only place to sit were a couple of stools at the counter, and they each settled awkwardly on one.

"Do ya remember me?" Finnuala asked.

Maureen scoffed. "I'm half your age, *a mhantach*. I have no trouble remembering what I did yesterday or even a fortnight ago. I know you were there the night Brianna went missing."

Finnuala kept a steady gaze on Maureen, and it unsettled her. "Before that," she said. "Lang before."

In a flash, Maureen was back to that night. That awful night when the soldiers rumbled past her door on the road to Ballymacool. She could still hear the screams when she let her mind get quiet enough. She could hear a plaintive voice crooning the lingering lullaby that haunted Maureen's dreams. "Before?" she repeated.

Finnuala smiled and leaned in closer. "Y'know, the seekin' fer one thing will find another."

"Och. Don't speak to me in proverbs, old woman. Speak plainly." Maureen stood and crossed to the fireplace. She grabbed a poker and stabbed at the embers. With each jab, they glowed brighter before dimming once more.

"Did ya know that Brianna lost her pendant?"

Maureen stilled.

"Weeks ago. Did she tell ya?"

Clearing her throat, she efforted to keep her voice light. "No, no she didn't. What a shame."

Suddenly Finnuala was next to Maureen in the dim, and she flinched when the old woman spoke again. "Ye have no idea the treasure ya have in that lass, do ya?"

Treasure, *right*. That girl had cost Maureen everything. "A lazy, half-hearted worker, that's what."

"*Tsk, tsk, tsk.* Ye've had twenty years with one of the most wonderful human beings the good Laird ever created, and ye've missed it. Ye've missed it all." Finnuala shuffled to the door. Maureen watched over her shoulder as the woman crossed the threshold. Just before Finnuala closed the door, she murmured, "Just remember, 'tis no secret that's known to three."

26

When Finnuala left, the door closed with a thud, echoing like a gavel and sending Maureen fleeing to the solitude and sanctuary of her private chamber.

Once there, she lit the lantern and hurriedly dug through her vanity drawer. Both the pendant and photo were still safe. What else could Finnuala have been referring to? She was the second person in the last couple of days to bring up Brianna's necklace. And then there was the veiled threat the old woman had uttered as she left. *"'Tis no secret that's known to three."* The woman had always spoken in proverbs, and clearly time and old age had done nothing to change that. But to which secret was she referring?

It had to be the pendant. There's no way she could have known anything else. Surely she knew nothing of Richard or it would have come to light long ago. And no one knew of everything else. Maureen had made certain of that. Besides, all those involved were long gone. There was no other logical explanation.

Unwrapping the broken necklace, Maureen let her thoughts tumble over her possible courses of action. She could, as she'd planned, keep it hidden and continue to play ignorant. Then again, Mister Wray knew it was last in her possession—he'd been the one to give it to her. Were he to confront her about it, and it came to light that it was Brianna's, she'd have no reason to deny knowing to whom it belonged. No explanation as to why she'd delayed returning it to her. And Maureen suspected Wray already knew whose it was or he would not have inquired about it after spending so much time with that wretched girl.

Another option was to return it and claim she'd simply forgotten, lost track of it in all the hullaballoo of late. But the thought of having to appear apologetic to Brianna churned Maureen's stomach. If anything, it was the girl who should be apologizing to Maureen for destroying everything she'd ever loved or truly cared about.

Eyeing the piece in her hand, the temptation to destroy it swelled within her. Throw it in the fire or smash it beyond recognition. But logic punched those reactions down again. Wray. He knew she had it. She crossed the room and stared out onto the darkened front lawn. Cold radiated from the windowpanes, sending chills down Maureen's back. An idea dawned. A way for her not to have to approach the girl with humility, but rather appear thoughtful about it. A way that allowed Maureen to keep it hidden until absolutely necessary that gave her a reasonable explanation for doing so. Yes, this would work. It had to.

Rewrapping the shards, she placed them back in their hiding place, ignoring the call of Richard's photograph. She didn't want to remember him. Not tonight. In truth, she wanted to be free of him and his haunting memory and betrayal. Yet she couldn't bring herself to fully let go so she slammed the drawer shut, hoping to trap him—and her thoughts of him—away for at least another night.

Another week had passed and Brianna and Finnuala once again sat at the kitchen table, discussing what they might want to eat for lunch when a commotion outside caught their attention.

"But, Mrs. Wray—" Batty's voice mixed with the scuffling of feet.

Brianna opened the door to find Michael's mother standing next to a very flustered Batty. Her face swung from shock to suspicion as she eyed Brianna.

"Have I interrupted your cleaning?" She stepped inside and began removing her gloves as her eyes scanned the room.

"Oh, no, I . . ."

Batty pushed past Brianna and gently tapped Mrs. Wray's arm. "As I was tryin' to say to ya, your son's had to change his lodgings."

Ignoring his touch, the woman turned a slow circle, still inspecting her surroundings. "Why? What's hap—" Her words cut off abruptly as her gaze fell onto the rusted platter on the counter. It had been there since the day after the storm. Brianna had gotten so used to seeing it there, she'd almost forgotten about it.

Mrs. Wray set her gloves down and picked up the tray, turning it over in her hands. She grew still at first, then lifted it closer to her face and studied it for a long, quiet moment.

Then she traced a trembling finger over the engraving. "Boyd," she whispered.

"Pardon?" Brianna stepped closer. "Do ya recognize the design?"

Mrs. Wray was silent for so long, Brianna thought she'd forgotten the question—or perhaps was ignoring it completely. But then she turned and looked at Brianna with glassy eyes. "It's the Boyd family crest."

Brianna blinked. "Boyd? As in the Boyds of Ballymacool?"

Nodding, Mrs. Wray murmured, "Mm-hmm." She was silent for another moment and then asked, "So, where's Michael? And why has he had to adjust his lodging arrangements?"

Batty scurried to the door. "I'll just go find him, marm." With a tip of his hat, he was gone, and Brianna couldn't help the smile that curled her lips. She'd never seen a man look so uncomfortable.

"Would you like some tea, Mrs. Wray?" Brianna asked.

"No, thank you." She clasped her hands in front of her waist. "Don't let me keep you from your work. Carry on."

Heat radiated up Brianna's cheeks, and her gaze dropped to the floor. Trying to think of a concise way to explain why she had taken up residence in her son's cottage, she limped to the chair across from Finnuala and sat down. "I'm actually not working at the moment." She pointed to her ankle. "I was injured, and the doctor forbade me from climbing stairs."

Footfalls hurried up the path. "Mother?" Michael burst into the open doorway. He hugged her hastily. "What are ya doing here? Is everything alright?"

She patted his cheek. "Everything's fine, worrywart. Sometimes a mother just needs to see her son."

Michael wrapped his arm around his mother's shoulder and pulled her in for a proper hug. "'Tis good to see you."

She smiled and then said, "You too, dear." Gesturing to Brianna, she added, "This one was just explaining why she's in your cottage."

"Brianna," he said. "Her name's Brianna. Ya met her last time you were here."

Mrs. Wray nodded absently. "Oh right, of course." Then she turned and whispered rather loudly from the corner of her mouth, "She hasn't gotten you into some sort of trouble, has she?"

In the corner, Finnuala snickered. Brianna's mouth fell open, and her hand flew to her chest.

Michael stepped back. "Mother! Of course not."

"Alright, alright." Mrs. Wray waved her hands in front of her. "It's a mother's job to ask questions."

Michael gave his mother a reproving look and then sat her down and explained about the storm, Brianna's injury, and her recovery.

"What a harrowing experience," she said when he was finished. She laid her hand on Michael's shoulder. "I'm so glad you're okay."

"I'm quite fine, Mother. 'Tis Brianna who needed our worry." He looked to her, and she warmed under his gaze. Then, becoming keenly aware of how closely Mrs. Wray was watching her, she shifted her attention to the fire and busied herself stoking it.

"I believe I'll have that cup of tea now, Brianna."

She blinked. "Yes, of course." She stood and started to limp to the kitchen when Michael held his hand up.

"I've got it. You rest." He sent his mother a pointed look. "Join me, won't ya?"

Brianna watched Michael pull the kettle from the burner and arrange the teapot and cups. Mrs. Wray returned her attention to the platter. She ran her hand over the engraving again. "Such a shame."

"Pardon?" Michael asked.

"The Boyds," his mother replied, brushing the rust from her fingers. "Do you remember them?"

Michael shrugged. "Not much. I have a vague memory of an Easter picnic, but that's it."

"That's all you remember?" His mother laughed. "I can't believe you don't remember every detail of our visits out here."

Michael poured the tea. "Why's that?"

"Well, your father and I weren't the closest of friends with Richard and Margaret, but we ran in the same social circles, of course." She lowered herself into one of the chairs at the table. "We used to come to their annual Easter picnics. Oh, how your father loathed them." She laughed again, shaking her head.

Michael joined her at the table, and Brianna leaned forward, eager to learn anything she could about Michael, as well as the treasure she'd found in the woods. Across from her, Finnuala remained quiet but stirred in her chair, fidgeting with her fingernails.

"And they weren't your favorite," Mrs. Wray continued, "but you always had fun. Anyway, all that changed once they had that baby."

"Baby?" he asked.

Mrs. Wray nodded. "Oh, yes. We came to visit after she was first born and then again for the picnic a few months later. You were so enamored with that wee child. You wouldn't leave her alone!" More laughter.

"Really? I have no memory of that 'tall." He looked to Brianna, his brows tipped up, light dancing mischievously in his eyes. His glance flitted to his mother and back and he shook his head. Brianna chuckled. "Are ya telling me stories?" he added.

"No, no, I'm not. In fact, I think we have a photograph somewhere back at Castle Wray. I'll show you next time you're home." She sipped her tea and seemed lost in memory.

"What do you think it was that drew me to a baby of all things?"

His mother shrugged. "I'm really not sure. She was the first baby you'd seen, and you were awestruck at how tiny she was. When you held her at the picnic, you noticed she had a small heart-shaped birthmark on her neck." She smiled at him. "You were convinced the heart was put there for you and refused to let anyone hold her the rest of our visit."

Michael scoffed. "Be serious. Why would I think that?"

She laughed heartily. "Why does a five-year-old boy think or do anything he does?"

"What did I do the next time we saw her?"

Mrs. Wray's laughter faded, and her gaze dropped to her hands. "You didn't see her again. The whole family was killed when the British soldiers raided Ballymacool." She wagged her head slowly. "Such a shame. They were a lovely family."

"The soldiers killed the whole family?" Brianna asked in dismay.

Mrs. Wray flinched as though she'd forgotten Brianna was there. "'Twas a dark time in Ireland, full of horrors and heartbreak."

Silence stretched long in the room, the weight of memory hanging heavy in the air. In the distance, the church bells tolled, and Mrs. Wray stood from the table.

"I'd like to eat with Adeline before I return home." She tugged her gloves back on her hands. "I suppose I had more reason than just you to come, dear." She kissed Michael's cheek and scrunched her nose at his beard.

"I'll walk you over for lunch," Michael said, pressing his hand to the small of his mother's back. When she was in front of him, he turned and smiled at Brianna.

A knock at the door was quickly followed by its opening. "Oh, hello, Mary," Michael said, gently pulling his mother aside to let the housemaid in before they exited.

"Goodness, but ye're a popular lass today," Finnuala said with a chuckle.

Brianna shook her head. "Am not. Mrs. Wray didn't come to visit me, if you recall," she said with a smile. "Welcome, Mary! 'Tis lovely to see you."

Mary had been coming and having lunch with her and Finnuala the past several days, and it had been utterly delightful. She'd shared about her life before coming to work at Ballymacool and confided that she had a crush on the stable lad, Pádhraig, when she first arrived. They'd giggled together and even shared a few of their personal fears. It had been the balm to her soul that Brianna hadn't known she needed.

"Oh, you simply must come," Mary crooned as she placed the freshly washed linens in the press. "We have the best *craic* at our weekly get-togethers!"

"Are you sure you want me there?" Brianna asked.

"Absolutely," Mary said. "We've all always thought ya were lovely to be around. It's just . . ." Mary flashed a glance in the direction of the main house, and Brianna understood immediately. These last three weeks since the storm had been more eye-opening than Brianna could have ever imagined. And more bittersweet. She'd gotten to know Mary, Batty, and the others better and had been with Finnuala and Michael almost constantly. She'd never spent so much time around friends—she'd never actually had friends, really. The bitterness came from the realization that she could have had more of that throughout her life. Instead, she had been locked away in solitude and servitude—intentionally isolated from the life-giving connections she was now forging. Reality was beginning to set in. When it came to Maureen Magee and Ballymacool, Mary, Batty, and Cook were staff. Brianna was a servant.

These last few weeks had opened her eyes to see that the one person who was supposed to care for her the most was the one holding her back. While anger churned down in her heart, it was tempered by a deep, abiding sadness. A newly resurrected grief at all she'd truly lost. It was more than her parents, more than the loneliness. It was losing the last score's worth of possibilities. Swallowing against the lump in her throat, she closed her eyes and pulled in a slow, deep breath.

She didn't want to ignore the pain and pretend it didn't exist. But she refused to let it keep her locked away any longer. She'd tasted the fresh air of freedom and never wanted to go back. There had to be a way to acknowledge the grief without letting it bury her. And the first step was to accept Mary's invitation.

"I'd love to come, thank you." She smiled and finished the last bite of her sandwich.

"Grand, so!" Mary collected the empty plate from Brianna's lunch. "We gather outside the bunkhouse after the students have finished their dinner. I'd best be off. *Go dtí sin.*"

Finnuala shuffled over and settled in the seat Mary had just vacated. "That should be a lovely time."

"Yes, I think it will be." Brianna imagined the staff gathered around a fire at dusk as music lilted around them. She pictured Mary and Pádhraig dancing a reel and Batty playing the concertina. Then her heart sank. She'd never participated in such a thing. She didn't even know how to dance—another hidden blessing of her injury. And she had only one dress now that the one she'd been wearing in the storm had been damaged beyond repair. "Do . . . do you think what I'm wearing will be alright?"

Finnuala chuckled and reached over and patted her hand. "Ye're not goin' to a royal ball, peata. 'Tis a *grúpa* service staff havin' a bit o' craic on a Saturday evenin'."

Brianna laughed. "I guess you have a point."

Finnuala tipped her head from side to side. "Still, maybe let's bathe ye and plait yer hair real nice." She winked. "Just in case."

The afternoon had stretched on like the taffy she'd once seen a student eat. Endlessly. Brianna had been unable to nap with all the thoughts and images that swirled through her mind every time she closed her eyes. She tried to read but found her mind constantly wandering back to tonight.

At last, Finnuala had awoken from her rest and helped Brianna get ready. It was lovely to wear something other than a nightdress or the robe she'd borrowed from Mary. With her hair freshly washed and braided, Brianna felt like a new woman. The bells finally tolled eight, and Brianna could picture exactly what was happening inside the main house. The girls would be marching to their rooms to prepare for vespers, Cook and Adeline would be cleaning up, and Mary and the rest of the staff would be making their way to the bunkhouse for their weekly informal *céilí*.

"Shall we?" Even Finnuala had cleaned up nicely and looked more put together than Brianna had ever seen her. She held out her elbow and Brianna pushed herself up to stand and hooked her arm around Finnuala's. The doctor had been right—once Brianna started moving around, it came more easily each time. And while she was still far from back to normal, she was able to cross the room on her own and didn't need nearly as much assistance to make it to the sitting area. But the bunkhouse was a whole other beast. Down the long stone path and around the bend, it was by far the farthest Brianna would have ventured since the accident. She worried that just the journey there would wear her out, but she was not going to miss this for the world.

As the pair stepped outside, Michael rounded the corner. Brianna sucked in a breath at the sight of him and willed her pulse to steady. He carried a lantern, which glowed against his skin. His thick hair was neatly combed back and settled in waves behind his ears, curling up at the nape of his neck.

He wore his oat-colored wool jumper and dark trousers, the combination of which set his hazel eyes gleaming.

He tipped his imaginary hat to Finnuala and Brianna in turn. "I heard ya were coming tonight and thought you ladies might like an escort."

"Much obliged, sir." Finnuala dipped a curtsy and chuckled. Then she held her hand up to the side of her mouth and said, "In truth, I wasna sure how I was goin' to get her there m'self." If she'd meant to whisper the statement, she'd failed and all three laughed, though Brianna's cheeks burned in embarrassment.

"Allow me." Michael handed the lantern to Finnuala and stepped to the other side of Brianna. He slid his left arm around her waist and gripped her right hand in his. He inclined his head until she looked at him. His eyes seemed to ask if the positioning was okay, and Brianna nodded, hoping he couldn't feel her heart pounding as he held her. "Just lean into me an' we'll take it nice and slow."

The first few feet weren't too bad, but then Brianna started to tire. Her left leg burned from holding the bulk of her weight. "Can we stop for a moment? I just need to catch my breath." They'd made it to the end of the path where it forked off into the woods and veered left, toward the barn and bunkhouse.

"Of course," Michael said. "Take all the time ya need."

The trio stood still, and Brianna rested in the grip of her friends. The night breeze blew gently, cooling Brianna's face. On it floated the lilting notes of a lively jig. If this were a weekly occurrence, how had she never heard the music before? Then she remembered that her Saturday nights were typically spent doing a deep clean of the kitchen and dining room.

"I'll tell them ye're on the way," Finnuala said. Brianna turned to tell her she didn't need to, that they'd be there soon enough, but Finnuala had already released her hold on Brianna. "They'll be wonderin' what's keepin' ye." She winked at Brianna and scurried as quickly as her old legs could carry her up the path, the lantern bobbing in her hand as she went.

Moonlight bathed them in a soft, silvery glow. "'Tis a lovely evening," Brianna said, watching after Finnuala.

"Mmm," Michael replied, and she could feel him bob his head. Brianna tried to adjust her weight on her left foot but stumbled as she hopped. "Here, rest against me." He tugged her closer so her whole side pressed up against his. Brianna closed her eyes and laid her head against his shoulder in relief.

"Better?" he asked.

She tried to say yes, but her voice wouldn't come. She nodded. In the distance, the jig ended, and a slow waltz began. Instinctively, they began to sway gently to the tune. Their movement was barely noticeable at first, and it seemed neither of them realized they were doing it. Brianna's eyes remained closed. She let the fresh breeze, the feel of Michael's embrace, his heady, musky scent, and the melodic notes wash over her.

Michael shifted so they faced each other. He stepped back half a pace and asked, "May I have this dance?"

When Brianna smiled, he gently pulled her closer again and tightened his arm around her waist. They continued to sway, and she wrapped her arms around his shoulders and laid her head on his chest. The sounds of his breathing, the beating of his heart, and the music floating in the air around them entranced her. "I've never danced a waltz before."

He eased a soft kiss to the top of her head. "To be fair, ya still haven't. We're just swaying."

Brianna looked up into his face, and they both laughed. "Fair enough," she said.

Their laughter died down and he held her gaze. Then, letting go of her hand, he brushed a strand of hair from her forehead. "Whatever this is, I don't want it to end."

She searched his eyes and found nothing but sincerity. "Me neither."

He settled a kiss to her forehead and held it long. When he looked in her eyes again, their swaying stilled. Brianna reached up and brushed her hand to his cheek. His beard was soft under her fingertips and she tenderly ran them down the strong line of his jaw, not breaking their gaze.

Michael hooked his finger under her chin and tugged her even closer. He lightly brushed his lips to hers and lingered, his mouth barely hovering over hers. He grazed them again, even softer. At last, he tightened his hold and melted into a deep, tender, unhurried kiss. Brianna relaxed into his embrace, sliding her arms around his neck and letting herself get lost in the moment.

When it ended, Brianna looked at him again, breathless. "I should've waltzed a long time ago." They chuckled together once more, and he enveloped her in a warm hug.

"Oy!" Finnuala's voice called in the distance, breaking the spell of the moment. "Are ye gonna join the party or stand in the dark all night?"

Brianna and Michael looked at each other, and he bobbled his head as though weighing the options. "I suppose we'd better join them," he said.

"Aye, I s'pose we should."

In a flash, Michael scooped her up and Brianna screeched. Cradling her like he did when he carried her out of the woods after the storm, he brought her to the bunkhouse lawn.

"There ya are," Mary said, jogging over to greet them. "I thought maybe ye'd gotten lost."

Brianna looked up at Michael as he set her down carefully. "Not quite."

Batty was sitting on a tree stump with a concertina in his lap. He waved her over. "We've saved ye a seat, Brianna. Over here." He gestured to a chair that must have been brought out from the bunkhouse. Finnuala and Michael helped her over to it.

"*Tá fáilte romhat, a Bhrianna!*" Batty then let out a long, swooping whoop and kicked off into a jaunty reel. Pádhraig sat in a chair next to him playing the *bodhrán*, and one of the other housemaids was on the tin whistle. Everyone else clapped along to the beat. The jovial tune was punctuated by a whoop or a holler here and there, and not a single face was without a wide grin.

When they launched into a slower-tempoed hornpipe song, Mary performed a traditional céilí dance, tapping away at the ground with her hard-soled shoes. Brianna marveled at the talent of her newfound friend and let her spirit be buoyed by the lively atmosphere. Next was another jig. Pádhraig thrust the bodhrán at Michael. At first he protested, but then Pádhraig whispered something in his ear and he acquiesced. Taking a deep breath, Michael's head bobbed along to the beat, and he silently mouthed as he counted along. Finally, he took the tipper in his right hand as though he was holding a pencil and started flicking his wrist. He settled in and his eyes drifted closed. Nothing about him moved except his knee bouncing in time with the lively tune, and his hand as it battered out a driving beat. Brianna's jaw dropped. Was there no end to this man's surprises? He opened his eyes and caught her staring at him. He winked and then turned his attention to the center of the circle.

Pádhraig had gone over and caught Mary before she could sit and was now twirling her around the makeshift dance floor. Brianna laughed and clapped, but her gaze kept drifting toward Michael. He was tapping away on the drum, a huge smile on his face, dimples in full force. Brianna couldn't remember a time when she'd been happier. The song ended in a flourish, and Mary and Pádhraig collapsed in their seats, breathless. The musicians shook their hands from the cramps that no doubt plagued them after such a demanding set, and laughter filled the air.

"Michael Wray," Finnuala said. "Where did ya learn to play the bodhrán like that?"

Michael was already handing the drum back to Pádhraig. He shrugged as he went and sat next to Brianna. "My mother was insistent that I be well-rounded in my education. Though when she demanded I learn an instrument, I think she had something more like the guitar or fiddle in mind, not a drum. I always seem to be doin' the opposite of what she has in mind fer me." He scratched his beard, and the group laughed. Then he reached over and took Brianna's hand.

"An' thank God fer that," Finnuala said, keeping her eyes trained on Brianna.

Throughout the rest of the evening, Brianna and Michael stole little glances here and there, and they even shared another dance. Only this time, she remained seated while Michael danced around her seat like a leprechaun, much to the delight of everyone there. But for Brianna, doubt began to set in. The private moment they'd shared had been wonderful— she could still taste his kiss and feel his embrace when she closed her eyes. But what did it mean for her, truly?

She could never belong in his world, and he couldn't stay at Ballymacool forever. She would be foolish to think anything of substance could ever come about between them. Her thoughts were interrupted by Michael's hand on her arm.

"What's the matter? Are ya in pain?" He glanced down at her ankle then back to her face.

Brianna shook her head, dropping her own gaze to her lap.

"Are ya tired, then?"

"No. Well, yes, but that's not it. I'm fine." Brianna rested her head against the back of her seat and closed her eyes.

Next to her, Michael stirred, and the case to his pocket watch clicked shut. "We'd probably better get ya back home. It's late and has been a long day for ya."

Brianna nodded and stood. He reached over as though he was going to pick her up, but she held her hand up in protest. "I can walk. Finnuala, are ya ready?"

Finnuala hobbled over. "Aye, lass. M' auld bones canna take much more dancin'." She took Brianna's arm, and the pair barely made it a few steps before Brianna needed to stop.

"Ladies, please let me help." Michael rounded Brianna's other side, and they managed to limp back to the cottage.

At last, in front of the door, Finnuala excused herself inside. To see to the fire and kettle, she'd said, but in the darkness, Brianna thought she'd seen the woman wink again.

She clasped her hands behind her back. "Thanks for a lovely evening. And for seeing us home."

He stepped closer. "I wouldn't have it any other way." He

looked around before lowering his voice and adding, "I'll never think of the waltz the same way again."

Heat crept up Brianna's neck and spread across her cheeks. She wouldn't either. But she couldn't afford to let herself get hurt. Not like this. She dropped her chin and whispered, "Good night."

"Brianna?" All hint of levity was gone from his voice, and the intensity she heard in it beckoned her to meet his gaze. "I don't know what the future holds for me, but I know I want you in it."

Her heart clenched. Oh, how she wanted that too. But how would it work? There was no way. "Michael."

"Do ya not want that as well?" Doubt clouded his words— or was that disappointment? He ran a tender hand down her shoulder and arm, setting goose bumps with his touch.

How could she express everything she was feeling? Did he truly not see the obstacles between them? She studied the outline of their feet in the darkness.

"Will ya not look at me?"

She turned her head, taking her gaze to the courtyard. "I just—"

"Brianna." Oh, how she loved the sound of her name on his lips. She'd never felt so seen, and like she belonged, as she did when she was with him.

She finally met his eyes with hers. She could feel his breath on her skin. She laid her hand on his chest, his heart racing like the bodhrán beneath her touch.

"Do ya not want—" He closed his eyes and cleared his throat, then met her gaze once more. "What do ya want?"

Brianna clenched his sweater in her fist. "I . . ." Dare she admit to herself, to him, what her heart truly longed for? She searched his eyes, which shone with glassy, unshed tears. "I want . . . you."

He released a puffed breath, and his lips tipped up in a smile. She tugged his sweater, pulling him closer until their lips met once again, the sensation even sweeter than before.

But logic flashed in her mind, and she pushed back. "I'm sorry. We . . . can't."

Before she could get lost in him again, she turned, hopped into the cottage, and closed the door behind her.

27

Michael stared at the closed door, confusion swirling in his mind. As if on cue, clouds slid in and hid the stars, blanketing the earth in the same dim uncertainty Michael himself felt buried under. Had he misinterpreted things? Had he forced his advances on her and missed cues that she didn't welcome them?

He raked his fingers through his hair and then cupped his hand over his mouth. His fingers drifted until he touched his lips and he remembered her words.

"*I want you*," she'd said. And she'd initiated that kiss just mere moments ago. She felt the same way—a way in which he'd never felt for anyone else. Many a pretty lass had caught his eye over the years, but none had captivated him like Brianna. He wasn't going to let her just slip away.

He knocked on the door and poked his head inside. "Brianna?" The interior was dark save for the soft orange glow of the burning turf in the hearth. Finnuala was already snoring softly in the chair next to it.

Outside, the clouds slithered along and broke apart,

allowing a gray light to spill in onto the floor of the cottage. The door to the bedroom was open, and no light shone within. He scanned to the kitchen area, freezing when his eyes fell on her, sitting at the table. A steaming teapot was in front of her, and she sat in a pool of silvery light, tears staining her cheeks. "Oh, *mo chroí.*"

He hurried forward and knelt down by her side. Taking his handkerchief, he wiped her tears. "What is it?" He kept his voice low so as not to wake Finnuala.

Brianna shook her head, but when Michael placed his hand over hers, she gripped it and held tight, as though it were a lifeline on a stormy sea.

Finally, she looked at him. "What are we doing, Michael?" she whispered. "This is *craiceáilte.*"

He smiled. "I'm okay with crazy."

She sighed. "I'm serious."

"I've never been more serious about anything." He traced circles on her hand with his thumb.

"You know who I am, right?" Her gaze drifted to the fireplace. "I'm nobody."

Michael's heart ached. She had no idea. "Nobody" was the furthest thing from what she was. Who she was. Over the last several weeks, he'd grown to see how much he needed her, how much the world needed her.

"Don't misunderstand," she continued, keeping her face turned away. "It's been amazing. Tonight was . . . breathtaking. Our whole time together. But it could never work. We're from two different worlds."

"I think it's you who misunderstands," he whispered, his voice hoarse with emotion. "Brianna, I love you."

She spun to face him. "I beg yer pardon?"

He raised up on his knees and cupped her cheeks in his hands. "I love ya, Brianna."

"But . . ." She blinked hard and puffed out a disbelieving breath. "How?"

He laughed and she shushed him, wincing and flinging a glance toward Finnuala who still snored in the corner. "'Tis easy," he said.

"But how would it work? I can't— I can't leave. Can I?" She laid her hands over his. "I have nothing to offer ya."

"Ya have everything. You *are* everything."

Brianna dropped her hands and her gaze to her lap. "I can't let ya. Magee will never allow me to go. And you . . . it'd cost ya too much. I can't. I don't have anything."

"It's easy to halve the potato when there is love."

Both Michael and Brianna shot their attention to Finnuala, who was eyeing them from the corner. Then they looked back at each other, shock and amusement on their faces.

"You are worth whatever it might cost me." Michael stroked Brianna's hair then rubbed the backs of his fingers down her cheek. Fighting against the stinging in his eyes and the lump in his throat, he added, "It would cost me far too much to be without you."

"Michael." Her tears had returned, but so had the light in her eyes. She laid her hand on his cheek, and for just a second, his eyes drifted closed at her touch. He turned and pressed a kiss to her palm.

"We'll figure it out together?" he asked.

She nodded. "Will ya tell me again?"

"*Tá mé i ngrá leat.*"

Her mouth widened in a grin, and she scooted to the edge of her seat. She swept her hand down his cheek, then brushed his lips with her fingertips. "I'm in love with ya too." As Michael pulled her into an embrace, she met his lips with her kiss and his head spun with elation.

"Alright, alright. That's enough o' that outta ye two." Finnuala groaned as she unwedged herself from the chair. "Now that ye both have figured out what the rest of us already knew, can we all get some sleep?"

"Aye," Michael and Brianna answered in unison.

He leaned in close and let his lips skim her ear. "Sweet dreams, my love."

She giggled and turned her head away and Michael's breath caught. Could it be? The darkness plays many tricks on a man's eyes. After the events of the day, it must be fatigue fooling his senses.

"They'll be very sweet, I'm sure," she said, interrupting his thoughts. Then she tugged him forward and kissed him quickly once more.

The next morning Brianna and Finnuala were sitting out in the courtyard. The grass was still damp from the rain that had moved in overnight, and the sky hung heavy and slate overhead, but in Brianna's heart, spring was in full bloom.

"'Tis about time, ya know?" Finnuala said after a while.

"For?" Brianna replied, unable to keep the smile from her face. Her cheeks ached. She'd never smiled so much in all her days.

"*Wheesht.* Ye know verra well what." Finnuala wiped her nose with a hankie. "What will ya do now?"

Brianna shook her head as her shoulder rose and fell. "Ya heard as much as I did. I guess we'll figure it out together."

Just then, Master McDaid stepped out into the courtyard. Dark circles hung beneath his eyes and his shoulders hunched slightly. He looked dead, nae, asleep on his feet. As he held the door open, a line of girls filed out and marched down the stone path toward the recreation field. He started to go back inside and stopped short when his eyes fell on Brianna and Finnuala. He huffed as his lips sank into a thin line, then he stomped toward them.

Brianna looked to Finnuala, who had the same questions in her eyes that Brianna was asking herself. "Morning, Master McDaid," she said.

He harrumphed, removed his spectacles, and polished them with the end of his tie before perching them back on his nose. "Ya look just fine to me," he barked.

"Beg pardon?"

"Well, ye're just sitting out here like the queen of England surveying her subjects while the rest of us slave away inside. You know, while Mary has to cover for your laziness, I'm left having to escort the students from place to place." He shook his head. "Disgraceful."

Finnuala shifted in her seat. "If ya have issue wit' it, ye can take it up with Doctor O'Donnell."

He started to retort, then stopped abruptly and turned his attention back to Brianna. "You do realize you're spending time with a madwoman, don't you?"

Brianna pursed her lips, trying to make sense of anything the man had said since he'd come over. "I'm sure you're a busy man, Master McDaid. Ya must have places to be," she replied, at a loss for anything else to say.

He narrowed his eyes. "I'm trying to do you a favor, miss. If you want anyone to ever take you seriously, you should think carefully about the company you keep. Did you ever stop to think that there's a reason she lives out in the middle of nowhere, hiding away from the world?"

Brianna looked back and forth between Finnuala and Master McDaid. "You know each other?" Brianna asked Finnuala.

He scoffed, a look of sheer disgust on his face. "We do not. I simply know *of* her." He sniffed. "There's a difference."

"Easy there, Johnny, don't hurt yerself." Finnuala cackled and turned to Brianna. "John-boy and I were acquaintances in our younger days. But I wouldn't say we ran in the same circles."

"You can say that again," he said. "You be careful, Brianna. And perhaps a little bit wiser with the friends you choose to keep." He cocked one brow at them, then sauntered back inside the main house.

Brianna turned and looked at Finnuala, who simply shrugged. "They say it helps to be a teacher if ye're half-cracked yerself." She started cackling at her own joke, and Brianna couldn't help but join in.

"I'm going to go inside." Brianna poked her thumb toward the cottage, then stood and waited for her balance to steady.

Finnuala started to get up, but Brianna waved her off. "Will I not help ya?"

"I'm okay," she said. "You just enjoy the weather."

"Ah, yes, and what a fine Oi-rish day 'tis, says I." She comedically thickened her accent and shaded her eyes from the absent sun. Brianna chuckled again.

Once inside, she collapsed in a chair at the table and tried to collect her thoughts. The past twenty-four hours had been an emotional whirlwind, and she was still trying to make sense of it all. The platter, still on the table from Mrs. Wray's visit the day before, caught her eye. She lifted it closer to the light. How could she have forgotten about it already? The memory of Michael's kiss floated across her mind, and she let it linger for a moment. Oh, that's how. Smiling to herself, she limped to the window and studied the tray. She tilted it in her hands, each shift shedding clarifying light on a different section of the etching.

Finnuala came in a few minutes later, wiping her forehead. "Startin' to rain. 'Sides, I'm ready for a cuppa." She looked at Brianna and her eyes widened.

"Can you believe what Mrs. Wray said?" Brianna asked, shaking her head. "That poor family."

Finnuala nodded absently and shuffled to the stove.

Maureen was climbing the stairs to her private chamber when an eerie feeling washed over her, raising goose bumps on her skin and prickling the back of her neck. Never one for superstitions or ghost stories, she marked it up to a draft and continued on. Muted gray light poured in from the window at the end of the corridor as she walked to her room. A low moaning sound halted her steps. She strained to listen against her quickening breath. Nothing. She continued on, and just as she got to her door, it came again. A low, mournful sound that gave way to a haunting melody. Her eyes widened in dread as she recognized the lullaby she'd heard outside her door the night Brianna had been left on her doorstep.

Though she'd not lived on Ballymacool grounds at the time, the screams had still carried through the night air, painting unwanted pictures in Maureen's mind of what kind of horrors were taking place there. She squeezed her eyes shut against the memories and clamped her hands over her ears, refusing to listen, refusing to remember. She hurried into her room, slammed the door, and fell against it. What was happening?

Why were those events, long gone and buried, coming back to haunt her now? She'd made her peace with what had to be done. Hadn't she? Richard's face flashed in her mind, quickening her pulse and sending her gut seething. Perhaps not.

She studied herself in the looking glass, hating the eyes that stared back at her. The severe lines of her face, the dull black of her hair. Ripping the pins from the bun, she tore at the strands until they came free. Then, clawing at her dress, she yanked and tugged until she stood before the mirror in just her shift. Her hair was wild, and so much more than her skin laid bare in her reflection. The woman she truly was shone back at her in the dim glass. A mere shell of who she'd been. A woman whose heart had been made alive, then used, and finally discarded. Everything she was meant to be died when she left the arms of Richard Boyd, and nothing would ever be right again.

She slid the drawer open and slowly pulled out his photo and hugged it to her chest. Then, tilting it back, she looked into his eyes and let the memory of her love for him take over. A mournful, empty howl swelled up from somewhere deep within. It ballooned in her chest until she feared she'd burst. The moan exploded from her lips like a siren. Her limbs trembled with a wildness she'd hidden and stuffed down for twenty years. She gripped the edges of the framed photograph until it dug into her skin, then she pulled her arm back and threw it across the room, shattering the glass on the ground. She swiped the books and brushes from her vanity, sending them careening to the floor. Yanking the drawer from its place, she tossed it aside, scattering its contents across the rug. All the heartache and humiliation from Richard's rejection poured out through her tears and her cries.

"Mistress Magee? Mistress, are ya alright?"

Maureen spun to face the door. "Don't come in." Her throat stung, and her voice held a painful rasp.

"Are ya okay?" Mary asked again through the closed door.

"I-I'm fine." She put on the calmest voice of decorum she could muster. "I tripped."

"Do you need help?"

"Good night, Mary!"

Maureen huffed and waited until Mary's footsteps faded down the corridor. She heaved shaky breaths and surveyed the damage to her room. Bending down, she picked up her brush, only to drop it again. She'd take care of it in the morning. Pulling back the blanket on her bed, she started to get in, but stopped. Padding across the room, stepping around the debris of her tirade, she picked up Richard's photograph. Shaking it free from the splinters of the broken frame, she then clutched it over her heart and collapsed into bed and a dreamless sleep.

28

Brianna sat on a stool in the kitchen. While she hadn't missed her grueling schedule, she had missed her conversations with Cook and the predictability of the routine. As though summoned by thoughts of her, Cook turned and smiled.

"Sure is nice to have ye back, Brianna. 'Tis a lovely way to kick off a Monday marnin'." She turned back to the pot she was stirring. "And it'll be even nicer when I don't have ta be here so bleedin' early in the mornin'." Her robust cackle filled the kitchen.

"I can't say I've missed that part too much," Brianna admitted.

Cook sighed. "Ye've been livin' a life o' luxury, lass. Now 'tis time to get back to the real world."

Brianna's gaze drifted to the back door. She wasn't ready to return to this life. She'd tasted freedom and it had been satisfyingly sweet. To give that up for good was already proving to be more difficult than she anticipated.

"Just an hour or so a day," Doctor O'Donnell had said

yesterday morning when he checked in on her. "I don't want ya jumping back to everything right away and hurtin' yerself again."

Brianna whispered a prayer of thanks for his instructions. At least she had a little bit more time to pretend her life was normal.

"Have ya seen Mistress Magee?" Mary's head popped around the door to the hallway.

"Níl," Cook said, then muttered something else under her breath. Brianna couldn't make it out for sure, but it sounded something like, "I try to avoid that."

"I've not seen her," Brianna answered.

Mary huffed and checked the time. "She's late for breakfast, she's not in her office, and I've an appointment in town to collect the linens she sent in for repair. Can ya look for her?" she asked Cook.

"Don' look at me. I've got m' hands full down here." Cook stirred her pot with more vigor than Brianna assumed necessary.

Brianna slid off the stool. "I can."

"No, no. Ya need to stay off that leg."

"Actually, Doctor O'Donnell said I need to start using it more. Working up to being on my feet all day and all that."

Mary again checked the watch pinned to the bodice of her dress. "If ye're certain. 'Twould be a massive help. I'm already late as it is."

Brianna waved her off. "Don't give it another thought. I'll find her."

"Thanks." Mary sighed. "I owe ya one."

Brianna started to protest, remembering all Mary had done for her, but she'd already disappeared around the corner.

Brianna made her way to the courtyard, relieved with how much easier her steps were coming lately. She still limped, but the pain was mostly gone now, and her stamina had grown greatly as well. Scanning the grounds, she noted that Mistress Magee was nowhere in sight. Pádhraig bounded around the corner on his way to collect more turf for the bunkhouse. Brianna asked him if he'd seen Mistress Magee.

"Sorry, Brianna, haven't seen her."

If Pádhraig hadn't seen her, then she wasn't anywhere at the rear of the property. So, she must be in the house. Brianna checked the dining room, just to be sure the headmistress hadn't shown up already, only to find a mass of hungry girls waiting for their breakfast.

When she arrived at the staircase leading to the class-rooms, she stood there for a long moment, staring up. Had they always been so tall? Yesterday Doctor O'Donnell hadn't said that she should start taking stairs . . . but he hadn't said she shouldn't either. She gripped both the handrails and picked up her right foot when Master McDaid appeared at the top of the stairs. He seemed quite flustered and in a great hurry.

Brianna asked him if he'd seen Mistress Magee.

"Do I look like my master's keeper, eh?" He grunted, a scowl like he'd just eaten a lemon creasing his face. He shook his head, *tsked*, and brushed past her.

Sighing, Brianna leaned up against the wall. She'd done more unassisted walking in the last ten minutes than she'd done in almost a month, and her ankle was beginning to ache. While she rested, she racked her brain, trying to think of where the headmistress could be. If she wasn't at the back of the property and she wasn't in the classrooms, the only places left were the front of the property and the residence floor. A quick glance from the front door revealed that Magee was clearly not there. All the girls were already in the dining room, which meant the headmistress likely wouldn't be in any of the students' rooms. That left her private chamber.

After another brief rest, Brianna pushed off the wall and slowly made her way to the stairs leading to Magee's room. Hesitating at the bottom once more, she worked up the courage to begin her ascent. The first step sent a sharp pain shooting up the side of her ankle and leg. So she turned and stepped sideways, placing both feet on a stair before attempting another one. At last, she made it to the top and crept down the corridor.

Faint memories swirled around Brianna—her as a wee girl, playing with blocks on the runner. Running down the hall with a ribbon in her hand, watching it trail behind her. She stopped and looked behind her, as if she was reliving someone else's daydreams. Passing the doors of the empty rooms leading to her guardian's chamber, more memories flooded her mind. Brianna had actually stayed in Magee's room with her when she was very young. At three or four, Magee moved her to the room next to hers. The older Brianna got, the farther away Magee had put her until, finally, she had banished her to the makeshift attic room in the top of the gable.

Brianna wrapped her arms around her waist as the memories continued to bury her. She scanned them as they whirled by, hoping to find some clue as to when or why she'd lost Magee's favor. But nothing. She gave up trying to understand what it would take to earn approval from the cold, callous woman long ago. And she thought it best not to pick up the baton of that race again. Taking a deep breath and straightening her shoulders, Brianna continued until she came to Magee's door.

Once there, Brianna pressed her ear to the wood and listened. Silence. She knocked softly. No answer. She knocked again, a little stronger. "Mistress Magee?" Still nothing. "Mistress Magee? It's Brianna. Are ya there?" All was so quiet, it sent shrill ringing through Brianna's ears. Where on earth could she be? It was so terribly out of character for the headmistress to be late for anything. The woman thrived on routine and prided herself on the efficiency with which she ran her school. For Magee to be this late, she'd have to be—

Icy chills clawed up her spine, raising bumps on her skin. With equal portions urgency and dread, Brianna placed her trembling hand on the doorknob. "Mistress Magee, I'm coming in," she barely eked out the words.

She turned the knob and cracked the door. "Marm?" As the door opened, so did Brianna's mouth. The room was a disaster. The bed was in disarray, drawers strewn about, and Magee's personal effects lay scattered all over the floor. Brianna stepped inside and looked behind the door, as though she expected the headmistress to be hiding there.

"*Cad a tharla?*" she whispered to the room.

She was about to go find help when something glinted in the light. She stepped near the window and stooped down. A dingy white handkerchief was crumpled on the floor with a piece of chain sticking out, reflecting the light pooling in from the window. Brianna scowled and cocked her head. Ever so slowly, she reached out and peeled back the corner of the fabric. Brianna sank to the floor. There, in the wad of material, were three broken sections of chain—and Brianna's pendant.

Brianna felt like she'd been socked in the stomach. Magee had had it all this time? She looked to the door and back to the pendant. Disbelief dizzied her while relief struggled to surface. But the cool, refreshing waves of relief sizzled out under the flames of anger that burned in her chest hotter than any fire in any grate.

Snatching her necklace from the floor, she wrapped it back up and shoved it in her apron pocket. She clambered to her feet and, ignoring the searing pain in her ankle, she bounded down the stairs and out into the courtyard.

Raising her arms, she clasped her hands on top of her head and forced her breathing to slow while trying to rein in her thoughts. But they refused to settle. Her mind spun with unanswered questions and accusations that had been lurking in the shadows of her mind for too long.

"Shouldn't you be in the kitchen?"

Brianna froze, her skin crawling at the voice. Slowly, she turned to face Magee. Her hair, though pulled back, was a mess, and dark shadows circled her eyes. Her skin had lost its color, and her eyes held a wildness Brianna had not seen before.

"I'm told Doctor O'Donnell cleared you to get back to work yesterday morning. Did he not?" she asked.

Brianna's jaw ached as she struggled to keep her voice calm. "He did. Some."

Magee's brows rose and she turned her palms up to the sky. "Then what are you doing out here?"

Brianna studied her for a long moment, weighing her response. Now that rational thought was beginning to return, she remembered Michael telling her he'd given the necklace to Magee. But something in her had shifted when she saw it in Magee's room. Whatever shred of loyalty she'd held for the headmistress had dissolved, and she no longer desired to comply just to keep the peace. "I was trying to decide what to do with this." Brianna held out her hand, letting the handkerchief fall away to reveal the pendant.

Magee blanched and fell back a step. She held her index finger up in front of her, shaking it, when suddenly her gaze darkened. Her brow furrowed and she raised to her full height. "Thief!" she shrieked. "How dare you enter my private chambers!"

"I'm the thief?" Brianna's eyes burned from opening so wide. "You're jokin'!"

Michael came jogging up the path. "I heard shouting. Is everything alright?" He stopped near Brianna, hands on hips, breath puffing. He looked between the two women.

Brianna kept her stare fixed on Magee but pivoted her arm to show Michael what she'd found.

"Ya got it back!" he said, a smile lighting his face.

"Where was it?" Michael asked, his gaze pinned on Magee.

"Yes," the headmistress squawked, "tell him where you found it." She folded her arms as a pious smirk darkened her face.

Michael pursed his lips and sighed. Then he looked to Brianna.

She tossed her free hand out and let it fall against her leg. "She had it. In her room."

"So you admit it! You went into my room without my permission." She jabbed a finger at Brianna. "Thief! I want the *gardaí*."

Hot coals burned in Michael's chest, but he willed himself to remain calm, if for nothing else than Brianna's sake. He held his hand up. "There's no need for that, mistress. Let's just take a moment."

Brianna slipped the pendant into her apron pocket while Magee looked on with a glare.

"Now, Mistress Magee," Michael said, his eyes on the woman, "I recall turning this necklace over to you over a month ago. Why have you not returned it to Brianna before now?"

Magee's face paled and her eyes darted all around. "I was holding on to it . . . for safekeeping." Seeming to have found her footing, she continued, "Clearly it was not in a state to be worn, and I didn't want her to lose it." She hoisted her chin and pinned Brianna with a stare, equal parts disdain and pride in her expression.

Michael fought the urge to roll his eyes at the absurdity that Magee would think such a load of malarky was believable. Instead, he said, "Well, since ya were concerned that it would be in a safe place, surely ye're happy that it's back with its rightful owner."

Magee's eyes clouded as she narrowed them. Then, she stepped forward. "I still would like to know what you were doing in my private chambers. You'll be lucky if I don't call the police anyway."

Brianna straightened her posture, and Michael smiled when she did not back down from Magee like he'd seen her do in all the other encounters he'd witnessed. "I was looking for ya. Mary asked me to find ya since ya were late and she had an appointment in Letterkenny. When I'd looked everywhere else, I went to your room and knocked. There was no answer and no other explanation for your whereabouts. I began to worry that you had fallen ill." She swallowed. "So I opened the door to ensure ya were alright. When the room was empty, I was going to leave, but my necklace caught my eye."

"*Humph*. Likely story."

Michael shrugged. "Seems likely to me."

"I will say," Brianna continued, "when I first looked inside, I was quite alarmed. I thought the place had been burgled and ransacked."

Magee clapped her hand over her mouth and spun around to look up toward the window of her room.

"What happened in there?" Brianna asked.

"Nothing!" Magee snapped. She cleared her throat and tugged at the bodice of her dress. When she spoke again, her voice was calm but tight. "Nothing of your concern."

Brianna looked to Michael, her eyes questioning. He shook his head, to communicate what they were both thinking. *I have no idea.*

"Well," he said, "clearly, Brianna entered your room only to check on your well-being. And she didn't steal anything since the necklace belongs to her and was given to you for the sole purpose of finding the owner. I see no need to call the gardaí. Do you, headmistress?"

Magee glared at Brianna again, then batted her hand as though swatting a pest. She released a sort of hissing grunt as she turned and stomped away.

29

ichael walked Brianna back to the cottage. Her leg throbbed and she needed to sit down after all the extra activity of the morning. A good half a foot taller than hers, Michael's sturdy frame filled her peripheral vision, radiating a silent strength that bolstered Brianna's own. His eyes, squinted against the morning light, seemed set ablaze in a caramel glow. As they approached the door, his hand bumped against hers and she grasped it. The touch of his skin, warm and roughened from his increased physical labors of late, soothed her weary heart.

He stopped and looked at her, his eyes searching her face. "Thank you," she said.

His nose crinkled and he cocked his head. "For what?"

"For helping me." She dropped her gaze to their hands and shifted so their fingers intertwined. "With Magee just now, but more than that. For all of it."

His mouth tilted up in a lopsided smile. "The pleasure was all mine, Brianna Kelly." He brought her hand to his lips.

After a tender kiss to it, he winked and pushed the cottage door open.

Brianna limped inside and sank into one of the chairs at the table.

"Would you not be more comfortable over by the fire?"

Yes, she probably would be. Truth was, she couldn't stand to be on her feet one second longer. "I'm fine here." She smiled at him and watched as he knelt down, added another brick of turf, and stirred the embers.

Finnuala emerged from the bedroom and greeted them both. "Ah, ye're a good man yerself, *a Mhicheál.*" She shuffled over and settled near the fire, a look of complete and utter contentment on her face.

Brianna enjoyed the idyllic scene unfolding before her while she pulled the handkerchief from her apron pocket and set it on the table in front of her. Carefully unwrapping it, she took the pendant in her hand. She let her eyes drink in every familiar stroke, then ran her finger along the sides, tracing the jagged edges that she could've drawn in her sleep. Her throat tightened and her vision blurred. She blinked hard, not wanting to conceal her most treasured—her only— heirloom after being so long without it. Especially after having resigned herself to the fact that it was gone forever.

Michael scooted a chair over and sat next to Brianna. "I'm so glad ye've got it back."

Brianna nodded and could feel him studying her.

After a long moment, he held his hand out, palm up. "May I?"

She set the pendant in his hand and watched as he turned it over and over, finally squinting at the back side. He pointed to the *c-o-n* engraved there. "I wonder what it says?"

"I've spent untold hours thinking about that very thing."

He turned to her. "Any guesses?" Outside the cottage, clouds slid in from the west, diffusing the sunlight filtering in through the window.

Brianna shrugged. "I've had thousands of guesses over the years but finally decided it was no use because I'd never know if any of them were right."

Michael flipped it over to look at the front, tilting his head one way, then another, then back again. He hunched his back until his nose almost brushed the design, then sat up straight and extended his arm out in front of him. He stilled. "Wait a min—" He tilted his head toward his left shoulder, then reached beyond the pendant to the platter. He slid the tray over and set the pendant on it, next to the engraved design.

"What?" Brianna asked. "What is it?" She leaned into his shoulder, trying to get the view from his perspective.

Michael lifted the necklace close to his face once more, then set it down and studied the tray more closely. "Look," he said. He traced the double-walled outline on the pendant, then did the same on the lower left quadrant of the platter's design.

"Let—let me see." Brianna's voice quivered. She studied the two etchings and looked up at Michael. "They're the same."

A funny little grin played on his lips. "And look here." He pointed below the engraving on the platter. "It looks like letters too."

Brianna stood and bent low over the tray, but the shadows were too dark. She picked it up and shifted it so the light could hit the design. Sure enough, a clear *d* and *o* were engraved there. They looked to be the last two letters of the word. The rest were rusted away or too damaged to decipher. She took the pendant and turned it over. "*C-o-n* . . . *d-o.* What could it be?" She repeated the letters to herself over and over but couldn't figure it out for the life of her.

Michael appeared to be doing the same thing. He ventured a few guesses, but none of them made sense. Then, from the corner, Finnuala uttered a word in a low, solemn voice, "*Confido.*"

Michael's and Brianna's heads shot up to look at the woman. "It says *confido*," she said, repeating the Latin word. A few raindrops splattered on the windowpanes.

Finnuala stood and slowly crossed to the table. Her eyes held a sadness Brianna had never seen before, and her countenance was fallen. "I need to tell ye two a story," she said.

Brianna shifted in her seat and flung a glance in Michael's direction. He did the same.

"Alright," Michael replied.

"'Twon't be easy. For any of us." Finnuala's gaze remained fixed on the floor, and she fidgeted with the hem of her apron.

"It's alright, Finnuala. Sit down an' tell us." Brianna patted the seat to her left. But Finnuala stayed where she was, and her lips rolled in and out, as if trying to form the words. Michael took Brianna's hand, and they waited for her to begin. Outside, the pitter-pattering of raindrops crescendoed into a roaring downpour.

Sinking into one of the chairs at the table, Finnuala cupped a hand over her mouth and squeezed her eyes shut, sending tears streaming silently down her face.

"Finnuala?" Brianna reached over and took hold of the woman's other hand, just as she'd done so many times for her.

"*Cheap mé—*" Her voice broke and she shook her head. Then she tugged a hankie from her sleeve and patted her cheeks dry and blew her nose. "I thought it was gone. Forever." She sucked in a breath as though she had more to say, but remained quiet.

"Shall I give you a minute?" Brianna asked.

Finnuala nodded.

"Táe?"

Finnuala blew out a sigh of relief and bobbed her head again.

By the time the water had boiled and the tea steeped, Finnuala had managed to compose herself. Brianna poured her a cup and added the milk. Before the two liquids could fully combine, Finnuala lifted it to her mouth with shaky hands and drew a long sip, her eyes closed.

After setting her cup down, she rested her hand on the rusted platter and repeated her words, "I thought it was gone forever."

Confusion knit Brianna's brow. "Ye've seen it before?"

"'Twas awful."

Brianna shook her head. "I don't understand. What was awful?"

Finnuala slowly raised her gaze to meet Brianna's. Her eyes held a wildness and fear that unnerved Brianna. "The night the Brits came to Ballymacool."

Brianna locked eyes with Michael, the confusion on his face matched that swirling in her own heart.

"In 1916, after the Uprising," Finnuala said, her voice barely above a whisper, "the British gov'rment got scared."

"And rightly so," Michael added.

She ignored his comment. "They were afraid of losin' their

grasp on this country an' wanted ta keep the chaos from spreadin'. I think they thought if they could send a message in the places awee from Dublin, it would deter any further rebellion."

Brianna and Michael nodded. "Batty said the same thing," Michael told them.

Finnuala only bobbed her head then crossed over to the window, lost in the memory of whatever had happened. "They went on the hunt fer rebel sympathizers. Not just the folk who'd be apt to fight but anyone who mightn't be fully on the Brit's side, or who might stand against 'em in any way."

Brianna listened on in horror as Finnuala described all the ways British forces had invaded towns and homes.

The old woman turned back to them. "Then one night they came ta Ballymacool." Tears filled her eyes once more and her chin trembled. Brianna feared Finnuala might not be able to continue, but she took a shaky breath and carried on. "The soldiers ransacked the house, destroyin' priceless heirlooms that didna interest them and lootin' the ones what did. Mrs. Wray was right when she said that *pláta*"—she pointed to it—"belonged to the Boyds. Had been in their family fer generations. Since Mary Queen of Scots's weddin', if legend's ta be believed."

Michael's and Brianna's eyes widened. "Really?" he asked.

Finnuala nodded. "I've lost track of all they took. They stayed in the house fer a few weeks, an' then suddenly they were gone an' Magee was startin' up the boarding school." She shrugged. "I t'ink everyone figured it was all lost or sold or hidden in some soldier's trunk."

"Incredible," Michael said, and Brianna bobbed her head.

Finnuala rolled her lips together and blew out a long breath from her nose. "But they did far more than steal valuables. They were tryin' ta send a message that the same fate would befall anyone who appeared ta be a threat to the Crown. Richard an' Margaret Boyd were badly beaten."

"Oh, how awful." Brianna slid her arm through Michael's and tugged him closer.

"My mother said they'd been killed?" he asked.

Finnuala looked away. "I can still hear the screams." She left the window and reclaimed her chair. "Eventually, the Boyds were brought into the courtyard an' the abuse continued. Each squad took their turns beatin', tauntin'. All I could do was hide an' watch helplessly, hopin' they didn't find us."

"Us?" Michael's voice was tender as he asked the same question plaguing Brianna's thoughts.

"The Boyds had a wee daughter. She was just a few months old. When the raid began, Margaret had thrust her at me and begged me ta take her away ta hide. She gave me a name an' address. Said when it was all over, if an'thing had happened to 'em, that person would take care of the baby." Finnuala's voice cracked and she blew her nose. "I had no choice. I took the baby an' tried to run. But the soldiers were everywhere. So I hid in the bushes an' I watched 'em—Richard and Margaret—die, right there on the lawn." She pointed out the window, her eyes reflecting fresh pain. "While I cradled their wee babaí in m' arms."

Brianna rounded the table and wrapped her arm around Finnuala's shoulders. She could think of no words that could possibly comfort her. All the while, a sinking feeling grew in the pit of her stomach.

Michael looked between them, his forehead creased. "I thought— Mother said the baby had died as well."

Finnuala shook her head and her face crumpled. "Oh, I wanted so badly ta take care o' that sweet babaí. But I couldna."

"Why not?" Brianna's voice was barely a whisper.

"Because I was the nanny. I was the first person they'd look fer her wit'." She buried her face in her hands. "I had no idea what the soldiers would do if they found her, so I waited 'til it all died down an' took her to the address Margaret had given me. Richard had tried to protest when she gave me the name, but Margaret wouldna have it.

"'There's no time!' she'd hissed at him in the melee. So, wantin' ta keep her safe, I took her where Margaret had instructed. I sang her the same lullaby I'd sang to her every night of her life as I laid her basket on the doorstep, even though m' heart was breakin'. I just prayed she'd know how loved she was. I wrapped her up tight, kissed her wee face, an' slipped away."

Brianna sank to her knees. "Finnuala, whose doorstep did you put that baby on?"

Finnuala swallowed hard. She met Brianna's gaze and whispered, "Maureen Magee."

Brianna gasped as though a knife had pierced her back. She pushed herself to stand, ignoring the jabbing pain in her ankle, and backed away.

"Brianna," Finnuala said, her hand extended.

Brianna shook her head, her vision blurring. Then she turned and limped outside as fast as she could. Rain pelted her face, mixing with her tears. She started to run toward the woods, but her ankle gave way and she fell onto the muddy path.

"Brianna!" Michael called into the downpour. He rushed to her and knelt down at her side.

"How could she?" Brianna cried, slapping the side of her fist onto the ground, sending mud splattering across her face.

He gently took hold of her arm. "Let's get back inside."

"No!" She pushed him away. "Don't you see? She knew! All these years she knew where I came from and said nothing. Did . . . nothing!" Sobs shook her body, and she collapsed into the muck. All this time she'd thought Finnuala was her friend. Brianna had come to think of her as a mother figure when in truth it was Finnuala who had condemned Brianna to her fate of a lonely, rootless life of solitude and slavery.

Next to her, Michael settled down to sit. Warmth enveloped her as he leaned over and wrapped his arms around her. He didn't say anything, but rather held her as she cried. They were soaked to the bone, and when all her tears were spent, Brianna feared she might wither away completely from the pain of her heart crumbling inside her. With just a word from Finnuala, she could have been spared nearly twenty years of heartache and despair. But instead, for whatever reason, Finnuala had chosen to remain silent, driving home for Brianna the fear that all the trusted people in her life had only ever been lying to her.

Suddenly Michael's embrace felt less like a comforting safety net and more like a prison. Her own mother had failed to keep her safe. Her supposed one true friend had sentenced her to a lifetime of misery. What was to stop Michael from doing the same? For all she knew, he had known who she was all along. No. She refused to let it happen again. If the last month had taught her anything, it was that she was far stronger than she ever realized. And if the whole of her life had taught her one thing, it was that she didn't need anyone. She'd been doing it all alone until now, and she could—she would—continue it alone.

Rolling onto her knees, she tried to push herself up to stand. Michael gripped her arm, but she shook him off.

"Brianna, please—"

"Leave me be!" She ambled to her feet and limped back to the cottage. She threw the door open and approached the table, not caring about the mud that dripped all over the floor. Finnuala still sat at there, her eyes puffy and red. They held the exhaustion of one finally having unloaded a heavy burden.

"You should go," Brianna said, refusing to meet the woman's gaze.

"Peata, let me explain." Finnuala stood and approached her, but Brianna backed away, shaking her head.

"Ye've explained enough. I don't want to hear any more." She folded her arms across her chest and turned her back to the old woman. When Finnuala didn't move, Brianna spun, grabbed the platter from the table, and threw it across the room. "Go! *Amach!*" She turned away once more, pressing her hands onto the edge of the basin, and let her head hang.

At the sound of Finnuala's feet shuffling to the door, Brianna released a breath. When she was certain the woman had gone, she turned to close the door. Michael was standing there. "You should go too," she said quietly.

"Bri—"

"Just. Go." She slid the door closed and tried not to let the pain in his eyes reach her heart.

Michael jogged after Finnuala and called for her, but she just flapped her hand and kept going. "Finnuala, wait." He caught up to her and circled around to block her path.

"Don't go," he said. "Not yet."

Finnuala shook her head. "'Tis no use. She hates me."

"She doesn't hate you." He gripped the woman's shoulders. "She's just hurt."

"I need ta go home." Finnuala sidestepped him, but he stopped her again. He looked around, searching for a way to get her to stay.

"At least stay until the weather clears. Come to the bunkhouse. You can dry off an' have a cuppa." He bent at the waist until he met her eyes. "Eh? C'mon."

Finnuala allowed him to lead her to the bunkhouse. He got her a towel and led her to a seat near the fire. When the tea was ready, he brought her a steaming cup and pulled up a chair so their knees were almost touching.

"I've ruined it," she whispered, wagging her head. "I've ruined ever'thing."

"No," he crooned, but he wasn't sure he even believed himself.

"Aye, I have. All I wanted ta do was keep her safe."

Michael studied her for a moment. "I know."

"But I couldna. That's why I left her." She crumpled into a fresh spate of tears and Michael waited for them to pass.

"I believe you," he said at length, then repeated himself. "I believe you."

She finally met his gaze. "Ya do?"

He nodded.

"All I've ever wanted was ta keep that girl safe." She let her attention drift to the fire. "But I ended up breakin' her heart."

They sat in silence for a long time, listening as the rain died down. When Finnuala had finished her tea, she said she wanted to go for a walk to clear her head.

Michael nodded. "Do ya mind if I ask you a few questions before you go?"

30

Brianna squinted at the light coming in from the bedroom window and rolled to her side, pulling the duvet over her head. A dull pounding had taken up residence behind her temples and her face ached from her night of tears. Slowly, she peeked her head out and her eyes fell on the muddy clothes heaped on the floor. She groaned. It would take ages to get those clean. She laid in the morning light, listening to the deafening silence. Without Finnuala's constant humming, or her clattering around in the kitchen making tea and porridge, the cottage felt deathly quiet. Brianna chided herself for her weakness. Wasn't this how she'd woken up every day of her life? Alone in the silence, most often in the dark as she rose before anyone else to slink down to the kitchen to start the fire and get breakfast going. Why should it be so different now?

The images of Mary's, Batty's, and Finnuala's faces filled her mind, then came Michael's. His hazel eyes twinkling, his bearded dimples punctuating his perfect smile. Throwing back the covers, Brianna pushed herself out of the bed, trying to shake the images free, but they wouldn't budge. Michael's voice echoed in her mind, "Brianna, I love you. We'll figure it out together."

"There's nothing to figure out," she spoke to the empty room. This life held nothing for her but betrayal and loneliness. She hobbled to the kitchen and sliced bread for toast and put on the kettle. While she waited, she quickly dressed—refusing to think of Mary's continued generosity—and ran a comb through her hair, choosing to leave it down. No reason to plait it if she wasn't going anywhere.

Then someone knocked on the door. Brianna briefly considered ignoring it, but she couldn't bring herself to. Answering it revealed Michael and Finnuala on the doorstep. *Should've ignored it.* She started to close the door, but Michael's hand held it open.

"Brianna," he said, his voice filled with sadness. "I know you're upset, but I think ya should hear what Finnuala has to say."

She scoffed. "What else can she say? That she's really my mother but didn't want me? That I started the Uprising?" She shook her head. "No, thank you. I think I've heard enough."

"Please," Finnuala said, her eyes pleading. "*Le do thoil,*" she repeated.

Brianna sighed and limped back to the table. Michael led Finnuala in and helped her settle there as well. He started like he was going to come sit next to Brianna, but then leaned against the counter instead.

"Finnuala," Michael said, "ya said last night that Richard protested when Margaret gave you Magee's name as the person to give Brianna to?"

Finnuala nodded and fidgeted with her fingers.

"Why do ya think that was?"

"I canna say," she answered. "I assumed he thought they would make it out alright an' didn't want Brianna given to someone else."

"I see," he said and scratched his beard. "And ya said ya couldn't keep Brianna yourself because it was well-known that you were her nanny?"

"Aye." She kept her gaze on a spot on the table.

"When you were her nanny, did ya live in the same cottage ya do now?"

Finnuala's head shot up, eyes wide. "No, no. I lived in Ballymacool House, in a small room next to the nursery."

Brianna fought the urge to roll her eyes. None of this changed the fact that Finnuala had lied to her for twenty years.

"When did ya start living in your cottage?"

"Oh"—Finnuala's eyes rolled to the ceiling as she tried to recall—"not long after the boarding school opened. Y'see, when this all happened, Maureen was the teacher at the primary school. But then, when the soldiers left Ballymacool, it became the boarding school an' she took over not long after."

"Where were ya all that time in between?" Michael asked.

She shrugged. "I was hidin'. To this day, no one knows what caused the Brits to raid Ballymacool. And if the Boyds had been secretly supporting the rebellion, who knows wha' they connected the rest of us to. After I saw what they did to poor Richard and Margaret . . ."

Michael nodded and waited a moment for her to collect herself.

Meanwhile, Brianna grew impatient. "This is all the same as what you said last night. If there's something new, then let me hear it. If not, I'd appreciate being allowed to go about my day." She crossed her arms and sat back in her seat.

"I know this is difficult," Michael said to Brianna, "but I really think ya need to hear it. It's your story too." He looked at her until she met his gaze. When she looked at him, he lifted his brows, imploring her to listen. The compassion she saw in his eyes nearly undid her. She bit her cheek to bolster her resolve and nodded.

"So," Michael said, turning back to Finnuala, "ya told me that you'd been hiding in the woods, sometimes finding abandoned old houses to stay in until ya thought someone might discover you, and ya went somewhere else. Is that right?"

She nodded. "Aye. I never wanted ta get too far from ya." She looked at Brianna. "An' when Maureen opened Ballymacool, I built m' cottage where I could keep a safe distance but still keep an eye on ye."

Brianna sighed and tossed her hands in the air. "That's very kind, but why not say something? Why not go to the gardaí or tell someone else who I was and what had happened?" She stood and limped to the basin, but that was too close to Michael so she hobbled over to the doorway to the bedroom and leaned against the frame, arms crossed. "You let me go my whole life believing I was alone—that I was . . . was nothing! And ya could've changed all that with a word!"

Finnuala was quiet for an aggravatingly long time. When she spoke, her voice was low, laced with pain. "Do ye remember what McDaid said to ya about me?"

Brianna scowled. What did Master McDaid have to do with any of this? "Aye. He called you a madwoman."

"By the time it was safe enough to come forward, I was

already seen as the crazy auld woman in the woods. I'd been livin' in my cottage for a while and had become somewhat of a recluse. Then, when I saw how Maureen was treatin' ye, I wanted to do something. But if I were to bring it to light then, no one woulda believed me."

"And ya didn't even want to try?" Brianna inwardly scolded herself for the crack in her voice.

"Oh, peata, I did. Desperately, I did. But Maureen didna even know I was the nanny, and there was no way to prove ya were who I would say ye were." She stood and crossed to Brianna. Taking her hands in her own, she added, "It would've been my word against hers, and I was afraid she'd send you awee somewhere I'd never be able ta find ya."

Brianna blinked and looked away.

"So I hid and waited for you ta find me. I'll never ferget that day ya came bobbin' through the woods an' we found each other." She flapped her hands, her voice thickening once again. "Oh, I should've told ye a long time ago, but it felt cruel when ya had no way to change your situation—and I had no way to help ye. Ya had no family to speak for ye, except fer a crazy auld woman. So I prayed for God to bring about yer rescue."

Brianna wanted to protest, but something Finnuala had said struck her. "So, ya don't think Magee knows who I am?"

Finnuala drew her lips into a thin line and wagged her head. "I don' think so. The note askin' her to care fer ye had no signature." She gripped Brianna's hands again. "Y'see? I was afraid that if I spoke up, it would serve only to make things even worse fer ye. And I couldn't do that."

Brianna looked to Michael, who inclined his head, eyes questioning. *What are you going to do?*

"I can't tell ya enough how sorry I am. But please know everything I did—or didna do—was for yer best interests. It's messy, and imperfect, and I know I made loads o' mistakes, but it was all done out o' love."

Brianna hobbled to the fireplace and lowered into a chair, resting her forehead in her hands. Finnuala's words didn't change the fact that she'd been lied to for so long. And yet, given how Master McDaid had reacted to Finnuala and all that she'd just shared, Brianna could see how it would've been difficult to know the right thing to do—especially if breaking her silence would endanger their lives. But that threat had been gone for a long time. Had there truly been no way Finnuala could have at least shared the truth with Brianna?

Brianna's back warmed where Michael's hand rested. "Brianna, I know this is a lot. And I know you feel betrayed. But please know that there are people in this world who love you and are willing to fight for you." He stepped back, taking his warmth with him. "I won't press you or force you, but I will do everything in my power to show you that loyalty isn't something that's reserved for everyone else but you."

Michael left her side, and she listened as the sound of his footsteps crossed the room. Brianna assumed he was going to sit with Finnuala, but then he was back next to her. He knelt by her feet and held his hand below her face. Brianna raised her head up from her hands and stared at the pendant resting in his palm.

He placed his other hand on her knee. "You have never been nobody. God spared ya from your parents' fate for a reason. I don't pretend to know why His plan for ya included this road you've been led down, but I do know He doesna waste a single tear."

Brianna shook her head slightly. It was easy for Michael to say such things, what with his fancy life and luxurious amenities. He already held people's respect simply by carrying the name Wray. She doubted he'd known a day of heartache in his whole life, while she'd known little else.

"I fell in love with you, Brianna." He pointed his finger at her. "From the moment I saw you here, I knew there was something special about ya. Something that set you apart. And it wasn't your family or your position—or lack thereof. It was you. Your heart, your fire, your generosity."

Brianna looked away, not wanting him to see the tears pooling in her eyes.

He pressed something into her palm and curled her fingers around it, holding his hand around hers. "But now you've been given this gift. You're a daughter of the Creator of the universe. And now ya know you're also a true daughter of Ballymacool." He leaned in close and whispered, "Ya have a purpose far grander than you could ever imagine."

He stood, then stepped back toward Finnuala. "Thank you. For sharing your story. Brianna's story. I know 'twasn't easy—for either of you. But I'm grateful she's had you to watch over her. I've got to go back to Letterkenny for a coupla days. Will ya continue to watch over her while I'm gone?"

Finnuala looked at Brianna and hesitated, then nodded. Michael smiled and turned his attention on Brianna. "And will ya think about what I've said?"

"I'll try."

He placed a kiss on the top of Finnuala's head, and after one last look at Brianna, he left, leaving her to wage the war in her heart all alone.

Brianna tossed and turned all night. Her thoughts tumbled like a stone over Assancara Waterfall. But one thought stood out among them. *Brianna Boyd* echoed in her mind over and over. What did it mean? She was a Boyd of Ballymacool. Was that enough to free her from her servitude to Mistress Magee? How would she break the news to her? Magee's antagonistic treatment of Brianna made her wonder if perhaps the woman would be relieved. Or would she feel threatened? Or would any of this matter at all, and instead would Brianna simply carry on, business as usual, just with the knowledge of who her parents truly were?

Morning dawned all too soon, and yet the reprieve from her dizzying reverie was welcomed. Brianna shuffled to the kitchen and stopped short when she saw Finnuala at the table. While her arguments had been logical, Brianna still wasn't sure she was ready to face the woman, let alone forgive her. How does one forgive a twenty-year-old web of lies? Brianna shook her head. These questions would be the end of her.

"I've made ya some tea and toast. It's still fresh." Finnuala looked up at Brianna through her lashes and drummed her fingers on her teacup.

"Thanks," Brianna said flatly and stared at the breakfast. Finnuala stood. "I'll go."

Brianna winced. How could she force the woman to abandon her tea? "No, sit down." Brianna kept her gaze on her own food and sank into the chair.

Finnuala did the same. They ate in awkward silence and when finished, Brianna cleared the dishes.

Finnuala started to say something but Brianna opened the front door. "I'm going to see if Cook needs anything." She hobbled out the door and closed it before Finnuala could utter another word.

Cook smiled when Brianna entered the kitchen, which might as well have been a bear hug. Breakfast was already finished, and it would be a couple of hours before she started preparations on the midday meal, so Brianna helped her wash a few dishes as they chatted about mundane topics. Brianna enjoyed the conversation, but in the back of her mind, she wondered if Cook was also harboring some massive secret about her past.

31

The following day passed very much the same, with Brianna avoiding Finnuala, finding mundane tasks to do around the grounds, and managing to stay away from Magee. Friday morning, Brianna was sweeping the front steps when Michael arrived in a motorcar with his parents and a lanky gentleman Brianna didn't recognize. Michael's face was the epitome of discomfort as the automobile's wheels slid on the gravel path as they rounded the corner. Brianna bit her lip to keep from laughing.

The Wrays and their guest emerged from the car and brushed their sleeves and slacks and skirts from dust. "Blasted motorcar," Michael muttered, then he turned to Brianna. "Hello, Miss Boyd."

Brianna blinked, the unfamiliar name fitting like a shoe on the wrong foot. "Mister Wray," she said. "Welcome back to Ballymacool."

Mrs. Wray approached and shook Brianna's hand, though her stance still held some apprehension. Nae, suspicion.

Michael reintroduced Brianna to his father, and then he

gestured to the other gentleman. "This is Robert Blackman. He's a barrister in Letterkenny."

Brianna shook his hand. "Brianna Kelly." Michael shot her a look. "Er, Boyd, so it would seem."

"A pleasure." Blackman removed his hat and smoothed his salt-and-pepper hair with his hand. "And I'm here to see about precisely that issue."

Brianna's gut pinched and her cheeks warmed. "I should tell you now, Mister Blackman, I can't pay you."

Blackman set his hat back on his head. "Today is just a consultation, for which there's no fee. Should we find you have a case, then we can discuss payment." Brianna nodded. "Now, is there some place we can talk?"

"I thought the cottage might be best," Michael said. "Is Finnuala still there?"

"She was a little while ago when I left to help around the main house."

Michael sent a puzzled look her way and then nodded once and faced his guests. "This way, please." He led the way to the cottage, and they shuffled chairs around so the group could all sit together. Finnuala was not there, and Brianna wasn't sure where she would be.

Once they were all settled and the routine offerings of tea had gone around—including the two obligatory refusals before accepting on the third—Mister Blackman asked, "So, where would you like to begin?"

Michael looked to Brianna, who felt as wide-eyed as a deer who'd caught wind of a hunter. She had no idea what needed to be discussed in a matter like this, so she shrugged.

"I thought, perhaps, ya might like to see the platter," Michael said.

Blackman was quite eager and seemed almost giddy at the idea of it. Brianna went to her room, got the platter, and handed it to the barrister.

"Muise," he said under his breath when he first laid eyes on it. He turned it over and over in his hands, wonder lighting his eyes. "Would you look at that? It's . . . well, it's extraordinary."

Brianna's forehead creased. "Is it?"

Blackman nodded his head vigorously while sliding on a pair of wire-rimmed spectacles from the inside breast pocket of his suit coat. "Oh, quite." He perched the glasses on the edge of his nose, tipped his head back, and angled his eyes to look through the lenses. The corners of his mouth pulled downward as he studied it. "Ah, yes. You see here"—he hovered his finger over the engraving and traced it—"that's the Boyd family crest."

"You're certain?" Mrs. Wray asked.

"Undoubtedly." He stretched to hand the tray to Michael's father.

Mister Wray took it, studied it, and nodded his head. Then he tilted it toward his wife. "See, there."

"You were the one who recognized it, Mother," Michael said.

"I know," she replied. "I just . . . wanted to be certain. Memories can be such fickle beasts."

"So, it's clearly the Boyd crest on the platter. Now, I'd like you to see something else." Michael leaned over and whispered in Brianna's ear, but with his breath tickling warm on her neck and his lips brushing her skin as he spoke, she found it impossible to focus on what he was saying. When she didn't respond, he cleared his throat. "Brianna?" he asked, his volume a little louder.

"I'm sorry, what?" she said, hoping her cheeks weren't as pink as they felt.

"I asked if you'd get the necklace for Mister Blackman to see."

"Oh, right. Yes, of course." She reached into her apron pocket, pulled out the handkerchief, and handed it to the barrister.

"What's this?" he asked as he unfolded the fabric.

Brianna told him what she knew about it—how she'd been told it was with her when she was left on Magee's doorstep, and how she'd lost it, and about Magee hiding it from her.

When she was finished, Michael practically jumped out of his seat. "See there? That design? 'Tis a perfect match for the bottom left quadrant of the Boyd crest." Now Michael was the giddy one, and Brianna couldn't help the smile that slid onto her face at the sight of him.

Blackman scowled and studied the pendant, looking from it to the platter and back. "It is similar."

"Similar? 'Tis an exact match," Michael said, his voice growing in volume.

"Could be. It's hard to say."

Michael rounded the table, took the pendant out of the barrister's hand, and turned it over. "And how about that? Those letters are the first part of the word *confido*, the Boyd family motto."

"I trust," Blackman said.

"So, you believe me?"

Mister Blackman turned his gaze toward Michael. "*Confido*. It means 'I trust.'"

Michael blinked, clearly taken aback by Blackman's matter-of-fact manner. Brianna, however, was struck by the irony that her family motto was apparently "I trust" when everything and everyone she'd ever trusted had either turned on her or wound up being a falsehood.

"But look here," Michael continued, "on the platter. The *d* and *o*, like the end of *confido*."

Mister Blackman sat back in his chair. "It is quite a co-incidence."

"Coincidence? How can you not say it's conclusive proof of who Brianna is?"

His father huffed. "Oh, for goodness' sake, son, let the man speak."

Michael eyed his father and then turned his attention back to the lawyer. "So, what are ya saying?"

Blackman shrugged slightly. "I'm saying it's possible. But there's nothing here that's absolutely definitive." He turned to Brianna. "Do you remember your parents giving this neck-lace to you?"

She blinked. "I was only a few months old."

"Oh, I see."

"Finnuala!" Michael said, snapping his fingers. "She's the one that told us who Brianna is. She's the one who left her on Magee's doorstep. She'd been the Boyds' nanny."

Blackman's eyes lit up. "Well, I need to speak with her."

Michael asked Brianna if she knew where Finnuala might be.

"I haven't seen her since breakfast."

Michael ran his fingers through his hair then jumped to his feet. "I've an idea. Sit tight for a wee sec." He hurried from the cottage, leaving Brianna with his parents and their lawyer.

"Do you know this Finnuala well?" Mrs. Wray asked her.

Brianna nodded. "Yes, quite well. I've known her since I was a little girl."

"Well, of course, if she was your nanny," Mister Wray said.

"No." Brianna shook her head. "She was my nanny when I was a baby. Then when the house was raided, she escaped with me and left me on Magee's doorstep. I met her in the woods one day when I was three or four."

"Hmm, I see." Blackman rubbed his chin. "Curious."

Mister Wray looked confused. "But, how di—"

The door burst open and a breathless Michael dragged Finnuala inside. "She's here. I found her."

His father stood up and offered his seat to her. "You didn't have to run the poor woman ragged, son."

Michael made the introductions and then said, "Mister Blackman would like to ask you a few questions."

The lawyer asked Finnuala to tell him the story from the very beginning. It was all Brianna could do not to run from the room. How many times would she have to relive this abandonment and betrayal?

When Finnuala was done, Blackman asked, "And you were the Boyds' nanny, you say?"

"Aye."

"Do you have any proof?"

Finnuala blanched. "Proof?"

Blackman leaned forward and placed his forearms on the table. "Yes, any sort of papers that show when you were hired or anything of the like?"

The corners of Finnuala's mouth tugged downward and she shook her head. "Nae, I don't remember signin' anything. Mister Boyd told me I was brought on at the last minute. I guess the lass they had set before me had to refuse the position or somethin'."

"And you've known Brianna for a long time?"

She bobbed her head. "After I left her wi' Magee, we reconnected when Brianna was a wee girl. Maybe three or so?"

Blackman hummed and scratched his head. He thought for a few moments and then shook his head. "I'm sorry, but there's just not enough to say for sure that Brianna Kelly is actually Brianna Boyd. It pains me to say that were we to take this to the high court, they could argue that you and Brianna planned this story. And without proof, we'd have no way to disprove that theory."

Michael banged the side of his fist on the table. "Blast it. Is there nothing else we can do?"

"I'm afraid not." He shook his head. "I'm terribly sorry."

Finnuala sniffled and dabbed at her eyes while Michael paced behind his chair, seething. Brianna sat, staring at the table, numb. She had no real right to be disappointed—she'd never expected to make any sort of claim. And yet she couldn't help but drown in the tide of betrayal she was now sinking under.

Blackman shifted in his seat and looked around, an odd expression on his face. "Eh," he said, "I'm sorry to bother, but might someone show me to the privy?"

Michael sighed and stepped toward the door, but Finnuala held up her hand, staying him. "I'll show 'im. I need a bit o' fresh air, anyway." She and the lawyer left, leaving the group in a heavy silence.

"Oh," Mrs. Wray said. "Michael, I brought those photos you asked for." She reached into her handbag and pulled out three rectangular, black-and-white photographs and handed them to her son.

Michael stepped over and sat in the chair next to Brianna. The first photo was of a large group of people, all dressed in light clothing. The women were in ridiculously large bonnets. His mother reached over the top edge of the photo and pointed. "There's Richard and Margaret. And here's me and your father." Michael laughed and cracked a joke about his father's hairstyle. "See, there's you. And that's the Boyd baby." Her eyes flitted to Brianna and back to the photo.

Brianna leaned in for a closer look. Michael sat on the ground, legs crisscrossed in tweed short-pants. He wore a white vest and a white flatcap. On his lap sat a little baby with a bald head, wearing a white, ruffled dress. Michael slid his hand onto Brianna's shoulder. She took the photo and lifted it closer, studying the baby's face. Was that really her?

"This one is just our family," Mrs. Wray said.

Brianna looked over at the photo of Michael and his parents. On Michael's lap was the same baby. "You refused to put her down," his mother added with a chuckle laced with nostalgia. "You insisted she be in the photo with us."

Michael handed the picture to Brianna, and she studied it as well. Only this time, she let her gaze linger on young Michael. The same intense eyes stared back at her. His hair was lighter and there was no beard, of course. But there was no doubt that was Michael Wray.

"Oh, and look at this one," Mrs. Wray crooned.

An awe-filled laugh escaped Michael's lips. A close-up showed Michael, a delighted grin on his face, peering down at the baby, completely enamored. Where in the first two pictures the baby was sitting on his lap, facing outward, in this one she was cradled in his arms. The profile of her face highlighted her full cheeks and silken head.

Brianna reached for the photo, but Michael pulled it closer to his face. He brought it so close, it almost looked like he was trying to smell the baby's head.

"Michael, whatever are you doing?" his mother asked.

"Shh!" he hissed, continuing to examine the photo. Then he slowly pulled it away and turned to look at Brianna. She met his gaze, his eyes wide, a grin barely tickling the corners of his mouth. He reached up and Brianna thought he was going to stroke her cheek, but instead he took his index finger and ran it behind her ear so lightly it sent chills skittering down her arms. Gently, he turned her head away from him and lifted her hair off of her neck. He gasped.

Michael turned to his parents. "Look." They moved in closer, and he pointed to something on the photograph. A small, heart-shaped mark behind the baby's left ear. He then pointed to Brianna.

Her chills returned and her pulse raced. It couldn't be.

"Well, I'll be," Mister Wray muttered.

Michael's mother gasped and her voice cracked. "Oh, Michael." She laid her hand on Brianna's shoulder. "Brianna."

Michael hooked his finger under Brianna's chin and turned her to face him. "You have the same exact mark."

Brianna's fingers drifted up and rubbed the place where Michael had pointed.

"You didn't know it was there?" he asked, laughing.

She shook her head. "I had no way to. 'Twould be impossible for me to see on myself."

Michael laughed. "I suppose that makes sense." Then he shot to his feet. "Muise! The barrister!"

Mister Wray hurried out to find Mister Blackman. Michael extended his hand to Brianna and pulled her up to stand. He slid his arms around her in an embrace. Part of her wanted to get lost in it forever, but an even bigger part of her couldn't help but hold back. How could she know she could truly trust him? She pulled away and let her gaze fall to the floor.

"Brianna," Mrs. Wray said, stepping between her and Michael. She took hold of her hands. "I'm sorry if I seemed cold before. It's just, well, when you're in a position like ours, there are people who will try to take advantage. And I suppose I've allowed myself to become more guarded than perhaps I'd realized."

A shaky smile lifted Brianna's lips and she nodded slightly. She wasn't sure how to respond to such a confession. Just then, Michael's father returned with Mister Blackman and Finnuala.

"Mister Wray tells me you have some new evidence?"

"We do," Michael said, and proceeded to show him the photographs while his mother explained what they were. Then they asked Brianna to pull her hair aside.

Brianna tried to ignore the awkwardness gnawing at her gut while Mister Blackman examined her mark and the mark in the photograph over and over again. At last he removed his spectacles and said, "I do believe you are the infant in these photographs, Miss Kelly. Or, rather, Miss Boyd."

Finnuala sucked in a breath and cupped her hands over her mouth. Michael gripped Brianna's shoulder, and his parents hugged one another.

"Give me a day or two to research all the particulars for a case like this, find the information on the Ballymacool property, and so forth," Blackman said. "I'll return with the paperwork in hand and a plan for how to proceed in regard to Mistress Magee."

"Thank you, Blackman," Mister Wray said, shaking his hand. The barrister made the rounds of handshakes and thank-yous, and then Michael's father offered to drive the man back to Letterkenny.

"Much obliged." Mister Blackman tugged his hat onto his head and stepped outside. "See you in a few days."

"Coming, Johanna?" Mister Wray beckoned. "Michael?"

"Yes, dear."

"I'll stay," Michael said.

Mrs. Wray gave him a knowing smile. Then she hugged him and Brianna and said goodbye to Finnuala.

"I'm going to walk 'em out," Michael told Brianna.

She nodded and watched him leave, his arm around his mother's waist.

A shaky hand pulled her attention away from Michael's retreating form. "Brianna. Sit with me?" Finnuala asked, fresh tears filling her eyes.

Brianna chewed her lip while a battle raged in her heart. Relief at all that had been discovered with Mister Blackman mixed with the weighty grief at the deception she'd had to endure up to this point. But no matter what the woman had done later, the fact was that Finnuala had risked her life to save Brianna's during the raid. And out of respect for that, Brianna joined her at the table.

"I know ya hate me, and I know what I did doesn't make a lick o' sense to ya, but I had to try one more time."

Brianna groaned. "I don't hate ya. I just . . . I don't know."

Finnuala nodded. "I've loved ya like me own daughter.

Since the first moment I held ya in that old nursery up there, ye had me wrapped around yer little finger." Her chin quivered. "It killed me to leave ya on that doorstep, but I would've rather died a little more inside each day than risk ya being killed." Her voice cracked and her face crumpled.

Brianna looked to the ceiling, willing her own tears not to fall.

After a shaky breath, Finnuala continued. "Once ya returned to Ballymacool, I didna have the resources to bring it all to light. There wasna a Mister Blackwell to vouch fer us or concrete proof to secure the truth. All we had was the word of a wild auld woman in a woodland cottage versus that of a well-known, cultured headmistress at a respected boarding school. I was afraid if I spoke up, I'd lose ya forever. An' now, to think that I may have done that anyway." Sobs shook her shoulders, and she pressed her hankie over her mouth.

"Finnuala," Brianna said, fighting to keep her composure, "all my life, there's been this . . . feeling . . . bubbling in my soul, that I was meant for something more. Something great. But the more time passed, the more that bubbling faded to a trickle. And in recent years, it nearly disappeared altogether."

Brianna dabbed her middle fingers to the corners of her eyes. "I'd come to accept my lot and had learned to be comfortable with the isolation. When I lost my pendant, I felt this desperate sort of panic that the last vestige of connection to my parents had been ripped from me. And then to find out ye'd known all along. I felt . . . betrayed."

Finnuala nodded. "I know, peata, I know."

"I understand why you couldn't confront Magee or tell anyone else. I know they wouldn't have believed ya. But why couldn't ya tell me? Ye've heard me cry so many times over the years, longing for my family, and ya withheld it from me still. Why?"

Finnuala scratched at a spot on the table and drew in a deep breath. When she released it, she looked Brianna in the eye. "Because I didna want to make an impossible situation even worse for ya. How much harder would it have been for ye over the years to know ya were a Boyd of Ballymacool yet powerless to do anything about it?"

Brianna let the question settle for a beat. "I don't know. But I'm also not sure that it was your decision to make."

"Perhaps not. I'm not yer mammy, and I've never pretended to be. Though I've loved ya as if I were. And like any parent, I've made my fair share of mistakes. But not a single one was made fer my own selfish gain. Any mistake I made was in the pursuit of doing what seemed best for ye." She stood and skirted over to Brianna's side of the table to lay a hand on her shoulder. "I admit that I haven't always made the right choice. But now it's yer choice to make on if ye're willin' to forgive an auld woman fer lovin' ya too much or not." She kissed her fingertips and laid them on Brianna's head, then turned and left the cottage.

32

Two days later the Wrays returned with Mister Blackman. Brianna checked that her plait was neatly in place and her dress fresh and wrinkle-free. She'd never given too much thought to her appearance before—it always seemed pointless given the physical nature of her work, never mind the fact that she was invisible to most people as she went about her duties. But today was different. It felt . . . heavy. Nae, momentous. No matter what news Mister Blackman carried with him, one way or another, everything would be different after today. Even if nothing changed about Brianna's day-to-day life, she herself was changed. A sobering reminder of the difference one's true identity makes—and of the importance of finding it in the right places.

Brianna stepped outside to meet the group as they arrived. Michael was coming up the path, and when his eyes fell on her, a wide smile creased his face, setting Brianna's heart galloping. How could she deserve someone who looked at her the way Michael did? Doubt sidled up and gnawed at her. Would it last? Could it?

"Mornin'," he said, pulling her fingers to his lips and brushing them with a light kiss.

Her cheeks warmed at his attention. "Hello."

He stuck his elbow out to her. "Shall we?"

She slid her hand into the crook of his arm, relishing the firm but gentle strength she found there. They entered the main house through the back and made their way to the foyer. Magee was standing in her office doorway, watching with a shadow of suspicion on her face.

Michael and Brianna greeted his parents and the barrister. Brianna noticed Michael sent a questioning look to his mother, who shrugged subtly. If she had any idea of what Mister Blackman had found in his research, she wasn't giving anything away. They'd just have to wait a few more minutes.

Magee stepped into the hallway. "Welcome back, Mister and Mrs. Wray. It's good to see you again." She turned to the barrister and extended her hand. "I'm Maureen Magee, the headmistress of Ballymacool."

Blackman shook her hand and introduced himself. He removed his hat and tucked it under his arm. "Might we have a few moments of your time?"

Magee scanned the group and then nodded curtly. "Right this way." Then she inclined her head to Brianna. "Thank you for seeing them in. You may go about your duties now."

Blackman cleared his throat. "Actually, this concerns her. I'd like Brianna to join us."

Magee blanched, then sniffed. "Very well. As you wish."

Maureen's heart pounded so heavily in her chest, she feared it was audible from across the room. She'd presumed the Wrays had come on some matter involving Adeline—who had calmed greatly of late. But what could they possibly want to discuss involving Brianna? Making every effort to keep her posture tall and her face stoic, she rounded her desk and gestured for the group to sit. There were only two chairs, so Blackman accepted one and asked Brianna to take the other.

"Thank you for your time, Mistress Magee," Blackman began. "I know you're a busy woman, but we've a matter of some import to discuss. You see, we've discovered something that will likely greatly affect the inner workings of Ballymacool."

Maureen resisted the chill that settled over her shoulders and worked to keep her face from registering the anxiousness that wound up her spine. "Alright," she said, "I'm listening."

Blackman opened his mouth to speak and then stopped. "Eh, perhaps you might sit down. I've a number of documents to show you."

Swallowing hard, she lowered herself into the high-backed chair behind her desk.

"Might you start by telling us how Brianna came to be under your care?"

"Oh . . ." She blinked. "Well, it was late at night about twenty years ago. I was living nearer in to Letterkenny at the time. I heard a commotion out the front of my house, then someone knocked on my door. When I answered it, no one was there—except for a basket in which Brianna was lying."

Blackman nodded and scribbled something on his notepad. "Very good. Thank you." He flipped through some papers, shuffling them back and forth. Maureen watched him, craning her neck to see what sort of documents he was studying so intently.

"Is that all?" she asked.

"No, no. Just gaining my bearings." After more shuffling, he finally continued. "What you say lines up with other reports I've heard of the event. Did you have any idea at the time who the infant's parents were or where she came from?"

Cold sweat prickled the back of Maureen's neck and under her arms. "I— I don't recall."

The lawyer was quiet for a beat. "I see." More shuffling. "How did you come to be the headmistress here?"

Where was the man going with all this? Maureen shifted in her seat. She could think of no reason for which the series of events leading to her taking over Ballymacool was of any consequence here. At least, none that they would be privy to. She'd made certain of that. Her heart thudded against her chest, and she hoped the barrister couldn't hear it from where he sat. She searched for a way to change the direction of the conversation. "I'm sorry. I believe you said you were here to tell me something?"

"Yes, yes, you're right." Blackman set the file of papers in front of him on the desk and launched into a long story, babbling about Brianna, her necklace, and that madwoman from the woods. Maureen watched him speaking, but her mind had stopped listening. She had no desire to talk to, or about, Brianna. Or Finnuala. "—one of the Boyds," Blackman was saying.

Maureen startled at the name, sweat beading on her palms. "I'm sorry, what did you say?"

The man stared at her blankly for a brief moment. "Brianna

is not Brianna Kelly. She's Brianna Boyd, daughter of Richard and Margaret Boyd."

Maureen clenched the arms of her chair, her knuckles burning with the intensity of her grip. They knew? "I see," she managed to say, chiding herself for the quaver in her voice.

"I realize this must be a shock to you. It was a shock to all of us—no one more than Brianna herself." He chuckled.

"Are you certain? Have you any proof?"

Blackman's brow furrowed and he tilted his head. "Perhaps I wasn't clear in how I explained it." He slid a photograph of a young boy holding a baby—Brianna. The photo couldn't have been taken too long before she was left on Maureen's porch. Blackman mentioned a platter Brianna had found in the woods bearing the Boyd crest and how it matched Brianna's blasted pendant. "You see this here?" He pointed to the mark by Brianna's ear in the photograph. "Brianna bears the same mark." He nodded at Brianna, who turned to the side and lifted her plait to reveal what Maureen already knew was there.

Maureen's gut churned. "So her last name is different than we thought," she said. "I fail to see how this changes much."

"She's the rightful heir to Ballymacool Estate," the younger Mister Wray said, stepping forward and jabbing his index finger onto the desktop.

No, no, no, no, no. "I'm afraid you're mistaken, Mister Wray, not that it's any of your affair." Maureen stood. "The deed to Ballymacool House and its lands was signed over to me when the plans were made to turn it into a boarding school."

Blackman patted the air in Mister Wray's direction, while

shooting him a stern look. "I apologize for Mister Wray's overzealousness." He flipped open the cover of a file. "Though I'm afraid he is correct."

Maureen stumbled back into her seat, shaking her head. "No, no. That's impossible. Ballymacool is mine!"

Her jaw ached and the scrolled wood on the chair arms dug into her palms as she watched the barrister slide a thick stack of papers from the file. He turned to a page about three-quarters of the way back and rotated it to face Maureen. "I can understand your shock, and I know this might be upsetting—"

"Upsetting? You have no idea who you're dealing with here. I won't let you take my home. My school. I won't!" She didn't care that she was shouting each phrase louder than the last. There was no way she was going to give up Ballymacool without a fight.

"Mistress Magee." The man's voice was sickeningly calm. "If you please, I'd like to show you this."

Maureen closed her eyes and pulled her lips into a thin line. She needed to hear what he had to say, so she knew best how to fight it. She slowly opened her eyes. "Very well. Continue."

His slid his finger down the page as he tried to read the document upside down. "Ah, there it is. You see here? This line: *The deed and property of Ballymacool is henceforth granted to Maureen Magee.*" He skipped a line or two and then continued. "*Should a direct member of the Boyd family be found at any time in the future, Ballymacool House, its grounds, and surrounding lands will be redeemed to that person, revoking Maureen Magee's ownership.*"

All warmth drained from Maureen's face. There had to

be some sort of mistake. "That makes no sense," she said, her hands starting to tremble. She thrust herself out of her seat and paced behind her desk, one palm clasped to her forehead. "No, no, that's not right. They told me it was mine. It makes no sense to make an allowance for the Boyds to regain possession. The whole point was to—" Her gaze shot to the group, who stared at her, eyes wide. She clamped her mouth shut.

"Mistress, I understand this is a shock," Blackman said.

Then the senior Mister Wray stepped forward and placed a hand on the barrister's shoulder. "Begging your pardon, Blackman, but I'd like the headmistress to finish her statement." He narrowed his gaze. "You were saying something about the whole point? The point of what?"

Maureen stood silent.

"If you believe you have a legitimate claim to ownership, please make your case," Blackman said. "If you can't give just cause for your continued possession, I have no choice but to follow what is outlined in this agreement."

Maureen shook her head and looked at Brianna. With the way the afternoon light shadowed her features, Maureen could see Richard, clear as day, in her attributes. Even in his death, he was still finding a way to break her heart. She couldn't let him hold sway over her anymore.

"Because she doesn't deserve it! None of them did! The arrangement was to get rid of them. For good!"

Blackman slowly rose to his feet. "I beg your pardon?"

"Richard Boyd was a dishonest, philandering traitor to the Crown!" She pounded the desk with each word. "I did what I had to in order to rid the county of his adulterous and traitorous ways."

The weight of Magee's admission flung Brianna against the back of her seat. Michael's hand slid onto her shoulder, and she grasped his fingers. Could she be hearing this correctly?

Mister Blackman leaned forward, flattening his palms against Magee's desk. When he spoke, his words were slow and measured. "What exactly did you do, Mistress Magee?"

"What needed to be done!" Her eyes were wild and the cords in her neck strained.

"What did you do?" Michael growled behind Brianna.

A sudden calm settled over Magee, and a chilling satisfaction shone in her eyes. "The ridiculous Uprising had people all over this country cracked. They were losing their minds, the lot of them. So, when the British military asked for people to tell them of anyone sympathetic to the rebellion cause, I went to them."

"You did what?" Mister Wray hissed.

Brianna tightened her grip on Michael's fingers and strained to listen to Magee over the sound of blood rushing in her ears.

"I turned in Richard Boyd and his household for their treasonable activities." She smirked. "And they were so pleased with the information I provided that they agreed to give me ownership of Ballymacool in exchange."

"How could you?" Brianna cupped trembling fingers over her mouth.

Magee leveled a glare at her. "Oh, don't act so surprised. You come from a line of dirty liars. The daughter of an adulterer. You have no business running anything, let alone a school where the moral well-being of young ladies is at stake."

Mister Blackman straightened. "That's the second time you've referred to Richard and adultery."

Magee blinked. "And?"

"Do you have any proof of this? Who did he supposedly have these affairs with?"

The headmistress's demeanor faltered. "It was one affair. And with whom makes no matter."

Blackman flashed a look to the Wrays and Brianna. "Perhaps you're right," he said, urging the group with his expression not to say anything else. "But the fact remains, as it stands right now, Brianna Boyd is the rightful owner of this estate and all that lies herein."

Magee scowled, her face bunching up like discarded paper. "We'll see about that!" She stormed out, catching her skirt on the corner of the door. Yanking it free, she stomped down the hall and outside.

Brianna blinked wide and released a shocked puff of air. "It was all Magee. I can't believe this is all because of her."

Blackman went behind Magee's desk and started rummaging through the drawers. Michael sat in the vacated seat while his parents huddled around Brianna. "I'm so sorry. Such a senseless loss of life and legacy." Michael took Brianna's hand. "Are you alright?"

Brianna let her gaze fall, freeing her mind to replay Magee's words over and over. She stared at her and Michael's fingers intertwined, pulling strength and comfort from the connection. Grief washed over her anew for the loss of her parents. For the first time, she mourned knowing more the depth of the void they left behind. When they were just nameless, faceless parents—mere theories rather than real people—Brianna keened for all that remained unknown. But now, the reality of all that had been ripped from her hit in a horrifically painful way. And yet beneath all the pain and even anger, gratitude flickered.

Her lifetime prayer had been answered. She knew who she was. She knew whose she was. And it was more wonderful and terrible than she could have ever imagined. The swell and ebb of her emotions tugged her in a dizzying merry-go-round that left her breathless. A single tear slid down her cheek. Michael's thumb reached up and wiped it away. Brianna met his gaze and such kindness reflected back in his eyes, she crumpled into a racking spate of sobs.

Instantly, Michael's strong, tender arms embraced her in safety and warmth. He slid to his knees by her side and bent his head over hers. He held her, letting her weeping cleanse her from all she'd carried with her for twenty years. Time seemed to stand still until, at last, no more tears would come. Behind her, sniffling pulled her attention away from herself. Lifting her head, she turned toward the sound, amazed to see Mrs. Wray wiping her own red, puffy eyes.

Michael released his embrace and Brianna stood and stepped over to the woman.

"Brianna." Mrs. Wray sniffled, shaking her head. "I'm so terribly sorry."

Nodding, Brianna pulled her close and wrapped her arms around her.

"You'll never be without a family again," Mrs. Wray said. "No matter what happens."

"Hear, hear," Michael said, his voice thick.

Brianna clutched at her heart. Michael's own cheeks were streaked with tears.

Mister Blackman cleared his throat. Brianna had forgotten he was there. "If you'll excuse me, I'm going to go check Mistress Magee's chambers."

"Is that prudent?" Mister Wray asked. "I mean to say, can you do that?"

Blackman nodded, slipping some folded papers into his breast pocket. "I can. While I was researching, I secured the authorization to find whatever evidence necessary to execute the conditions of the agreement." He tapped the file.

"Very good," Mister Wray said. "Perhaps it's best if you don't go alone?"

"Ah, quite right. Good idea." He stepped round the desk and made for the hallway with Michael's father close behind.

"I'll join you," Mrs. Wray said, then turned to Michael and Brianna. "Where can we find you after?"

Brianna looked to Michael, and they regarded each other for a moment. Brianna was torn between collapsing in her bed for a nap or visiting her beloved woods, which she'd been away from for far too long.

"Walk with me?" Michael asked and she nodded. He turned to his mother. "We'll be back at the cottage after a while."

Mrs. Wray placed a kiss on his cheek. Then she gave Brianna's hand a squeeze and hurried after her husband and Mister Blackman.

Michael stretched his hand to the door. "After you, Miss Boyd."

Brianna offered him a watery smile and slipped into the hallway. Outside, the bracing November air was a welcome relief to her face. She tilted it skyward, letting the sun kiss her cheeks. Michael's hand slipped into hers, lacing their fingers together.

"Is your ankle alright to walk?" Michael asked.

Her ankle had been the last thing on her mind. She'd forgotten it was even injured, so all-encompassing the news over the last hour had been. She glanced down at her feet, then looked up at him and nodded. "As long as we don't go too quickly."

His eyes searched hers, the golden flecks in them gleaming in the afternoon light. "I'm in no hurry." He winked and Brianna melted a bit inside.

They set off down the path at a nice, easy pace. When the tree line came into view, Brianna gasped. A gust of wind picked up, setting the branches swaying, the evergreens almost sparkling as they danced in the breeze. "I think they missed ya," Michael said with a smile.

"I know I missed them." She sighed and then started to take off toward the forest.

Michael tugged her hand gently. "Whoa now, lass. I won't have ya hurtin' yourself." He stopped and waited for her to face him. "I never want ya to hurt again." He brushed his hand along her cheek, and she leaned into it, wrapping her fingers around his forearm. Standing here, lost in his gaze, she almost believed he could keep her from any pain.

His hands slid around her waist. "I mean it."

She looked up into his face, her gaze tracing, memorizing every inch, trying to reconcile all she felt for this man with the warning that sounded in her heart. The thought of surrendering to all that it meant to love someone terrified her. She'd already endured so much betrayal and death at the hands of those who were meant to protect her. It just seemed so much easier—safer—to be on her own.

"I always want ya to feel safe, loved. Forever." He tucked a stray shock of hair behind her ear. "And I'm sure your faith has been shaken. Why wouldn't it be? But I want to spend my life proving it to ya."

He must have read the question in her eyes, because he added, "Proving that I love ya, Brianna."

Her heart lurched and she longed to reach for him. But how could she let go? Her gaze fluttered to the ground.

"C'mon," he said, his voice low and beckoning as he gestured to the path before them. They strolled along under the archway of trees leading into the forest. They didn't speak for a long time, both just taking in the scene unfolding before them. The evergreens spread a rich, emerald canopy overhead, while the autumn leaves laid a jewel-tone carpet below. Bare branches joined with rich, thriving foliage—as if nature itself had painted a portrait of Brianna's heart. So much death and pain, but mingled throughout a rich, lasting beauty. To try to remove one would destroy the other. Instead, she was learning to thrive through each, weather the seasons as they came.

Stopping their stroll, she reached up and took Michael's face in her hands, giggling at the shock that registered in his eyes. Her touch skimmed down his neck, over his shoulders and arms, until it reached his hands. Gripping them in her own, she searched his gaze once more, finding the courage there she needed to take the leap of faith she knew was right. "I love ya, too, Michael." Her voice caught and she blinked away tears. "With all my heart."

A slow smile spread on his lips, and he squeezed her hands.

Brianna's heart raced as his gaze dipped from her eyes to her mouth. He held it there for a long beat before ever so slowly lowering his head until his lips met hers. The kiss was tender and slow, yet chaste. Neither one rushing for it to end.

When they broke apart at last, Michael rested his forehead on hers. "We stopped walking."

Brianna laughed. "Yes, I believe we did." She turned her head to look deeper into the forest. "Shall we continue on? Or would you rather . . . stay here?"

A low, guttural chuckle rumbled in Michael's chest. Then he pecked her lips briefly. "I think we'd better move on."

They laced their fingers once more and carried on their journey. They rounded a bend and Brianna's heart leapt. She drew Michael forward.

"Your tree," he said.

She smiled, her eyes fixed on its sturdy trunk. "You remembered."

Michael stepped closer. "How could I forget?" Brianna turned to find him gazing at her, and somehow, she thought perhaps he wasn't talking about the tree.

33

As they emerged from the woods, Brianna already felt lighter. Despite the shocking turn of events and devastating revelations made by Mistress Magee, she seemed to have been freed by it all somehow. Liberated not only by the news that she was now the owner of Ballymacool Estate, but also freed within herself. She took in a cleansing breath, then released it, a strange sort of guarded contentment settling over her as she did. Michael smiled down at her and squeezed her hand.

They approached the cottage to find his parents and Mister Blackman enjoying a cup of tea on the courtyard lawn. Blackman stood when he saw them. His face solemn, he set down his cup and stepped toward them.

"I'm glad you're here," he said.

Brianna tightened her grip on Michael's hand, and he pulled her in closer to his side. "What is it?"

"We've found several items among the headmistress's things that will be of some interest." He handed Brianna a tattered book. "This was hidden in a carved-out space at the back of her bookshelf."

Brianna looked over the well-worn cover. Several thin papers stuck out around the edges. She looked to Blackman, questioning.

"I've marked the pages I believe will be most, eh, useful," he said.

Sliding her finger behind the first mark, she opened to a page dated March 1914. As her eyes skimmed the page, Brianna nearly faltered. "Magee and . . . my father?"

Michael hissed. "*Dáiríre?*"

"Really." Blackman nodded. "According to her journal entries, she and Richard carried on a sordid affair for nearly two years. And then, suddenly, they stopped."

"I can't believe it," Brianna said, making her way to one of the empty chairs on the lawn. She lowered herself onto it.

"It's really quite something," Blackman said. "She also makes mention several times of some sort of arrangement for her to continue on in some capacity in the household. From what I gather, she was going to start as the nanny and then work up to be in charge of running the day-to-day operations of the house as head housekeeper." He shrugged. "And that suddenly went away, too, when the Boyds let her go and brought in a new nanny shortly before you were born."

"Finnuala," Brianna whispered.

"At the time, Magee was within her legal rights—as far as reporting the Boyds' alleged rebellious sympathies. But with our current independent status now, she can be held accountable by the courts for her actions."

Brianna wagged her head. "I-I don't know."

"But the ownership agreement is clear—you are the rightful heiress to Ballymacool Estate. By the terms laid out there, nothing else needs to be done." He stretched out his hand. "Congratulations, Brianna Boyd of Ballymacool."

Mouth agape, Brianna shook Blackman's hand, shock numbing her, and then she turned her face to Michael. Blackman shook each of the Wrays' hands in turn before gathering his papers. "I'm afraid I must be off. Do be in touch and let me know how you'd like to proceed."

Brianna nodded. Mister and Mrs. Wray shuffled into the cottage and slid the door shut.

Michael closed the distance between them and took her hands in his. "How do ya feel?"

"I don't know. Like an imposter?" she said on a laugh.

"Hmm, let me just see." He lifted her plait and bent close to her ear. He traced his finger down her neck. "Still there." Wrapping his arms around her waist, he pulled her closer and brushed his lips against the mark that declared her to be, once and for all, a Boyd.

Brianna's eyes fluttered closed, and she leaned in to his kiss. When he straightened, he said, "I love you, and I don't care if yer last name is Kelly, Boyd, or Queen of Scots. I will love ya with all my heart for the whole of my life." He searched her face. "Do ya think you can live with that?"

Reaching up, she stopped his mouth with a kiss. "I do."

Epilogue

MARCH 1939

Brianna stepped onto the front porch, watering can in hand, and showered the pots of tulips flanking the door to Ballymacool House. She smiled at the cheery shades of pink and yellow as they danced in the makeshift rain. Footsteps ran around the corner and up the steps.

"Mrs. Wray! Mrs. Wray!"

Brianna looked up to see twelve-year-old Maeve grinning at her breathlessly.

"What is it, my dear?"

Maeve took her hand and tugged. "Come and see!"

Setting the can on the porch, Brianna hurriedly descended the steps after the girl. Bright curtains hung in the windows, looking down on them from the house, the colors popping against the freshly whitewashed exterior. Flowers lined the perimeter of the building, and lilting tin whistle music floated on the air.

Rounding the corner to the courtyard, Brianna stopped.

317

Colorful bunting crisscrossed overhead, keeping watch over a gaggle of squealing girls in a rousing game of tip, led by Adeline, who now served as the head teaching assistant in Ballymacool's youngest class. Along the back edge stretched a table piled with sweets, sausage rolls, and a large cake.

Maeve clapped loudly twice and everyone stilled. A pregnant pause ballooned until they cried, "*Breithlá sona, a Bhean Uí Rhiabhaigh!*" The mob ran over, and all tried to hug Brianna at once.

"Oh my goodness, go *raibh mile maith agaibh!*"

One by one, each girl filtered past, expressing their well-wishes. When they'd all said their piece, Brianna gathered them all back together.

As she surveyed the faces before her, her heart swelled. "I don't know what to say." Her voice hitched. "Ya needn't have gone to so much trouble."

"Yes, we did!" said Siobhán, Brianna's youngest boarding student, at ten years of age.

"Ya did?" Brianna replied.

"Yep." She revealed a mostly toothless grin.

"And why's that?"

"Because," Maeve said, "you do so much for us every day. And ya always make everyone feel so loved and special on their birthdays—especially if they can't spend them at home. We wanted you to feel special too."

Brianna blinked away the tears that filled her eyes. Four years ago, she never could have imagined she would be here, leading Ballymacool.

Her mind drifted back to all those lonely days in the kitchen. She could almost hear Magee's screeching voice eking out the next command. Maureen Magee had sailed off to America in an attempt to escape any legal ramifications of her deeds. Never mind that Brianna had chosen not to press charges. She just wanted to move forward, not delve further into the past. Now, all these years later, the pall of Maureen Magee seemed to be clearing, and Ballymacool was finally the place of love and belonging Brianna had never had as a child.

"Mrs. Wray? Are you alright?" Adeline's voice broke through Brianna's thoughts.

Suddenly realizing all the girls were staring at her, Brianna nodded. Then she turned to the group and said, "Just tell me one thing." She planted her fists on her hips playfully and gave Maeve a look of mock scolding. "How did ya know it was my birthday?"

Maeve grinned, clearly pleased with herself for helping pull off such a surprise. "Oh, a little birdie told me."

Pressing her lips together, Brianna shook her head. Movement in the corner of her eye caught her attention. She looked up to see Michael emerging from the cottage where he'd stayed when he first visited Ballymacool. A bouquet of flowers burgeoned from his hand and even from this distance, his dimples shone through his beard.

"Well, what're ya waitin' for? G'on!" Maeve shooed her toward Michael.

As she neared, he held out his hand. She took it and he pulled her into an embrace. He kissed her neck behind her left ear and whispered, "May I have this dance?"

Brianna pulled back, grinned, and curtsied. "Ya may, indeed."

Michael looked past Brianna and nodded. She turned to see Finnuala, Batty, Pádhraig, and Mary sitting in a group, instruments in hand. Batty counted them off, and they erupted into a lively reel. Michael wrapped Brianna in his arms and whisked her off, bouncing and twirling around the dance floor. Song after song they danced, surrounded by their charges.

"So," Brianna asked, "was it worth it?"

Michael's steps slowed and his brow creased. "Was what worth it?"

"Leaving Castle Wray, settling here at Ballymacool?"

Michael grinned and gently brushed a stray lock of hair from Brianna's face. "I could think of no better way to manage my inheritance than to support Ireland's finest boarding school." He winked and added, "Besides, I think the headmistress kinda likes me."

Brianna giggled and swatted his arm just as two of the girls came up and asked them each to dance.

After several rounds of Michael and Brianna partnering with different girls, or leading a set of group dances, Michael sidled up to his wife. Pulling her in tight, he looked deep into her eyes. Without breaking their gaze, he called to the musicians, "Play us a waltz."

Author's Note

Thank you for joining me back here in Donegal. I hope you enjoyed your time at Ballymacool. While fictional, this story was inspired by many true events. For example, Ballymacool House and Wood are real and are still there today. In fact, the inspiration for this setting was an Instagram reel of drone footage all around Ballymacool House, which is now abandoned, roofless, and covered in vines. It had such a haunting feel to it, it seemed the perfect backdrop for the story already brewing in my heart about a young woman searching for identity.

The Boyds really did occupy Ballymacool and were ousted due to the Irish War of Independence, but I did take some creative license with the timeline and some of the details. According to the Letterkenny Historical Society, during that time,

> there arose a ruling class of aristocrats, landlords and prosperous lawyers, commonly referred to as "The Protestant Ascendancy". Estates that were characterised by stately

mansions and large tended gardens arose around the ever growing town of Letterkenny with several privileged families such as the Wrays of Castlewray . . . and the Boyds of Ballymacool creating Letterkenny's very own Ascendancy class between the 17th and 20th Centuries.[1]

The house was taken over in 1921 by a band of antitreaty IRA forces—not British forces—who kicked the Boyd family out and ordered them never to return. To my knowledge, none of the Boyd family members were harmed in the process, and Richard, Margaret, and their baby, as well as Richard's affair with Maureen, are completely fictional. Any similarities to actual occupants of the house are purely coincidental. Also, Ballymacool never served as a boarding school. That part of the story was inspired by my research of Kylemore Abbey in County Galway, and it was fun to imagine what it might have been like were Ballymacool to host students.

As you can see above, Castlewray Estate and the Wray family also really existed, though Michael, Edward, and Johanna are figments of my imagination. One thing that was not made up by me, though, and is quite possibly one of my favorite details of the story, is the platter that Brianna uncovers. When the IRA forces occupied Ballymacool, they looted many precious items and heirlooms. One of those items was "a priceless salver (plate) . . . which had been in the family since 1467, when Thomas Boyd was married to Mary Stewart, daughter of King James II of Scotland."[2] According

1. Kieran Kelly, "The Wrays of Castlewray," Letterkenny Historical Society, October 30, 2018, https://www.letterkennyhistory.com/the-wrays-of-castlewray/.
2. Kieran Kelly, "The Boyds of Ballymacool," Letterkenny Historical Society, October 9, 2018, https://www.letterkennyhistory.com/the-boyds-of-ballymacool/.

to the Letterkenny Historical Society, the Boyds purportedly received letters claiming to know the whereabouts of the platter, but it was never found.

I had already decided to set this story at Ballymacool, and when I learned of the platter, it was like a priceless treasure to this story. It also holds special significance to me, because just after I learned of its existence, I also learned that my husband's family traces back to Mary, Queen of Scots!

I couldn't set another story in Donegal within the proper timeframe and not include a cameo from a few of the dear characters from my debut novel, *A Dance in Donegal*. Don't worry, I didn't spoil any details of that story, so if you haven't read it yet, you're in the clear.

This story is near and dear to my heart, as over the years I've done my own soul searching as to my purpose in this world. Granted, I'm not an orphan, nor have I been mistreated anywhere near as severely as Brianna, but I feel that search for significance and true identity is one that resonates with most of us. I wanted to explore what it would look like to learn to trust again when every ounce of trust had been broken at some point throughout life.

I pray that if you are struggling to see how you matter in this world—to your friends, family, or even to God—that this story will beckon you closer to your Father and whisper echoes of your true worth to your soul.

If you'd like to see more about Ballymacool, including photos of the area, check out my Pinterest board dedicated to all things *The Maid of Ballymacool*: https://www.pinterest.com/mrsdeibel/the-maid-of-ballymacool/.

Acknowledgments

First and foremost, I need to thank my heavenly Father for the opportunity to share the stories He puts on my heart. Thank You, Lord, for the privilege of telling these stories. May every word bring honor and glory to Your Name and Your Name alone.

To my amazing husband, Seth, thank you for being my partner. You remind me of who I really am and help me see my purpose with fresh eyes when I get discouraged and want to hide away from the world. Thank you for being my champion and biggest cheerleader.

To Hannah, Cailyn, and Isaac, thank you three for being the joys of my life. Thank you for walking alongside me as I live out this dream, and for believing more in me than I often do myself.

I can't thank my parents, Bonnie and Jerry Martin, enough for their continued support and encouragement. Your enthusiasm has not waned three books into this crazy ride. If anything, it's grown. Thank you.

To my amazing mother-in-law, Cheryl Deibel, thank you

for always being a willing ear and for your wisdom and encouragement. I'm so grateful for the unexpected time we got to spend together while I was editing this story. Thank you for being a sounding board and a patient listener when I needed to talk through an issue. I'm so grateful for you and thankful that I get to be part of your family.

To my wonderful new friend and coteacher, Elisha Colson, I am so glad God allowed our paths to cross. You have been such an encouragement and blessing to me in the short time we've been working together. Thank you for jumping in with both feet and being a great partner, and uber-fan.

Brittany Verlei, Matt Verlei, Mark Anderson, and Danielle Ware, thank you for continuing to support my author journey, and for being just as excited about book three as you were book one. I can't imagine my teaching life without you all. And to the rest of my Highland Lakes family, thank you for being the answers to my prayers for so many years. Getting to work alongside such wonderful people every day is such a blessing. The way you continue to ask about my books, share them with your friends, and more blesses my heart beyond words.

To Cynthia Ruchti, my incredible agent and friend. Thank you for your unending support, prayers, and wisdom. Thank you for patiently answering my myriad questions, then letting me brainstorm and speculate. Thank you for always bringing me back to the one thing, and one Person who truly matters in all of this.

My incredible Panera Girls—Liz Johnson, Lindsay Harrel, Sara Ella, Ruth Douthitt, Breana Johnson, Sarah Popovich, Tari Faris, and Erin McFarland. The sisterhood I have found in you all is one of my greatest treasures. I'm so grateful for our little community to share joys and sorrows with, to lift one another up in prayer, and encourage, support, and laugh together. Thank you for being my people.

To my incomparable friend community—Donna Carlson, Sara Walton, Lori Palmer, Charity Verlander, Tiffany Kilcoyne, Nancy Patton, Cathy Brooks, Cathy Sparks, Stacy Dyck, and Terri Logelin—thank you all for always being there for coffees, chats, and encouragement.

To my dear amazing, wonderful, incredible team at Revell. Rachel McRae, your kindness, encouragement, prayers, and guidance are such a blessing. There's no way I could put these stories out into the world without your help and expertise—and when it comes to your critique, I will always ask for it. Brianne Dekker, thank you for your wonderful management, support, and continued excitement for these little Irish tales. I'm so grateful to continue to get to work with you! To Robin Turici, my eagle-eyed line editor. You keep my story lines straight and find all my crazy, weird errors. You love my characters like I do and treat their stories with respect and dignity. Thank you. Karen Steele, thank you for your endless work in spreading the word about my books, and for being gracious with my insane schedule and less-than-stellar memory for details. And to the rest of the design team and fiction team—thank you, thank you, thank you!

And, of course, to you, dear reader. I know you have a million demands on your time, so the fact that you have chosen to spend your precious moments in these pages with these characters is such an honor. Thank you for trusting me with your time and being trustworthy with these stories. I certainly couldn't do what I do without you, and I'm so very grateful for each and every one of you.

Glossary of Terms

a chailín—[UH HAH-leen]—girl/young lady, when addressing her directly

a haon, a dó, a trí—[UH HAYN, UH DOE, UH TREE]—
one, two, three

a mhac—[UH WAHK]—son, addressing directly

a mhantach—[UH WAHN-tahck]—toothless old hag, addressing directly

a stoir—[UH STORE]—my dear/darling, when addressing
directly

a thaisce—[uh HASH-kee]—a term of endearment, used
when speaking to someone (not about them)

amach—[uh-MAHCK]—away, leave, out

amadán—[AH-muh-dahn]—idiot

an bhfuil tú ceart go leor—[AHN WILL TOO KART GUH
YORE]—are you all right?

an cailín rua—[AHN KAH-leen ROO-uh]—the red girl/the
red-haired girl

329

an mhaith, ar fad—[AHN WAH AIR FAHD]—very good, indeed

anois—[UH-nish]—now

babaí—[BAH-bee]—baby; young one

Bhean Uí Rhiabhaigh—[VAN EE RAY-vee]—Mrs. Wray

breithlá shona—[BREH-lah HAHN-uh]—happy birthday

bricfeasta—[BRICK-fast-uh]—breakfast

bróg/bróga—[BROEG/uh]—shoe/s

buíochas le Dia—[BWEE-huss leh JEE-uh]—thank God/thanks be to God

cá bhfuil sí—[KAW WILL SHEE]—where is she?

cá bhfuil tú—[KAW WILL TOO]—where are you?

cáca millis—[KAH-kuh MILL-ish]—sweet cake

cad a tharla—[CAD uh HARR-luh]—what happened?

cailín—[KAH-leen]—girl

céad mile fáilte—[KADE MEE-luh FALL-chuh]—a hundred thousand welcomes

Ceard? An ceann ó do mhamaí?—[KYARD? UHN KEE-yan oh doe WAH-mee?]—What? The one from your mom?

céard sa diabhal—[suh JAW-uhl]—what in the world?

céilí—[KAY-lee]—a party with music, dancing, and often storytelling

cheap mé—[HYAP may]—I thought . . .

cinnte—[KINN-chuh]—certainly/indeed/of course

craic—[CRACK]—fun, good times; often, but not always, involving music

craiceáilte—[CRACK-ahl-chuh]—crazy

créatúr—[KRAY-turr]—creature/poor little thing

cuppa ouiche—[CUH-puh EE-huh]—nightly cup of tea

dáiríre—[dah-REE-ruh]—really? seriously?

Dia cuidiú liom!—[JEE-uh KOOD-ju LUM]—God, help me!

dean deifir—[JEHN JEH-furr]—hurry up

deas bualadh leat—[JASS BOO-loo LATT]—it's nice to meet you

fan—[FAHN]—wait

gardaí—[garr-DEE]—police

go dtí sin—[GUH JEE SHINN]—until then

go maith—[GUH MAH]—good

go raibh maith agat—[GUH ROW MAH uh-GUT]—thank you

go raibh mile maith agaibh—[GUH ROW MEE-luh MAH uh-GEE]—thanks a million, plural

grúpa—[GROO-puh]—group

haigh—[HI]—hi

i gcónaí—[ih GO-nee]—always

iontach—[EEN-tock]—excellent

is bhi sceimh mhna na finne le mo chailín rua—[ISS VEE SHKAYV MNAW NAH FIN-uh LEH MOE HAH-leen ROO-uh]—and she resembles the women of beauty

is sea—[SHA]—yes/it is

le do thoil—[LEH duh hull]—please

m'aintín—[MAHN-cheen]—my aunt

mo chailín—[MUH HAH-leen]—my girl/little girl

mo chara—[MUH HARR-uh]—my friend

mo chistin—[MUCH HISH-chin]—my kitchen

mo chroí—[MUH CREE]—my heart/my love

muise—[MIH-shuh]—oh my/dear, dear

níl—[NEEL]—no

níl a fhios agam—[NEEL a ISS uh-GUM]—I don't know

níl aon rud—[NEEL AYN RUDD]—not a thing/not one thing

Och! Go luath?—[OCK GO LOO-uh]—Ack! So soon?

oíche mhaith—[EE-huh WAH]—good night

páistí—[PAHSH-tee]—children

peata—[PA-the]—pet; a term of endearment

pláta—[PLAH-tuh]—plate

praiseach—[PRAH-shuck]—mess

seafóid—[SHA-foij]—nonsense

sláinte—[SLAHN-chuh]—an Irish toast of blessings and health

slán—[SLAHN]—bye/health

slán abhaile—[SLAHN uh-WAH-leh]—safe home/get home safely

slán leat—[SLAHN LAHT]—goodbye to you/health to you

tá—[TAH]—yes

tá fáilte romhat—[taw FALL-chuh WROTE]—you're welcome/welcome

tá mé i ngrá leat—[TAH MAY ih NGRAH LATT]—I'm in love with you

táe—[TAY]—tea

Tiarna Dia—[TEER-nuh JEE-uh]—Heavenly Lord

Can't wait to return to Ireland?

Turn the page for the first chapter of *The Lady of Galway Manor*, another dazzling romance from Jennifer Deibel!

CHAPTER

1

No one ever tells the truth about love.

The stories and fables paint a glowing portrait of valiant acts and enduring romance. Love, it is said, is the most powerful force in the world.

Stephen Jennings knew better.

He watched the pair from behind the polished-glass case as they huddled together, giggling and fawning over one another. Stifling a groan, Stephen slid his hands into his pockets and leaned on the stool behind him. His fingers curled around the worn paper in his right pocket, its presence both a comfort and an annoyance.

"This one here, lad." The gangly man gestured to the top shelf of the glass case. "We'll take it."

The rusty-haired lass swooned. "Oh, Charlie, do ya mean it? In earnest? Oh!" She squealed and threw her arms around her beau's neck.

"Very good, sir." Stephen removed the silver ring from the case and buffed it carefully with a polishing cloth. He started with the hands that encircled a heart, then moved to the crown that topped it. How many times had he recounted the tale of the Claddagh? More than he cared to tally. With any luck, the lovebirds wouldn't ask him to regale them with the legend today. When the ring was sufficiently shined, he handed it to the gentleman.

Fingers trembling, the man took the ring. A foolish school-boy grin spread across his face. His lass clapped incessantly, still giggling. The man glanced at Stephen out of the corner of his eye, the all-too-familiar twinkle of delight mixed with mischief gleaming in it.

Oh no. No. Not here.

The man sank to one knee. "Maggie, you know I love you."

Maggie erupted into hysterics. Stephen gritted his teeth, jaw aching from the movement, and pasted on his best smile—though he feared it came across more as a grimace.

"You know I love you," Charlie repeated. "And I couldn't wait another second before askin' ye . . . will you marry me?"

Unintelligible sounds gurgled from Maggie's lips as she yanked him off the floor and kissed him hard, then held out a trembling hand.

"Is that . . . is that a yes?" The man's puppy dog expression rivaled that of any canine begging in the alleys.

Good heavens, man, are ye daft? Stephen fought the urge to roll his eyes, while ignoring his own painful memory that surfaced unbidden. *Not now.*

"Oh, aye, Charles! Yes! Yes! A thousand times, yes!"

"I love you!" they declared in unison.

Stephen had seen what "love" could do. Not even a mother's love—which is said to be the most powerful—could protect his own beloved mammy from leaving this world while bringing Stephen into it. And the glassy-eyed, giddy type of love the couple before him now displayed had certainly not served any grander purpose than deluded self-fulfillment. How could they be so blind?

Charles slipped the ring on Maggie's finger and presented her hand to Stephen. "Is it on properly?"

Stephen cleared his throat. "Aye, that's right. The tip of the heart points in, toward her own heart, if she's spoken for." He looked between the two, who only had eyes for one another. "And it seems she is most certainly spoken for." Though he tried to avoid it, his voice sounded flatter than it should have. After all, the store needed this sale. He pasted another smile on his face. "*Comhghairdeas.*"

Charles looked at him now. "*Go raibh míle maith agat.* A million thanks." He handed the payment to Stephen and guided his bride-to-be out of the shop.

Stephen watched them leave, resisting the urge to rush and slam the door behind them. Bolt it. *Fools.*

"I can't do this anymore." He dropped his head. His knuckles were white, and the edges of the case dug into the heels of his hands. He slapped his palm onto the wood beam acting as the side of the case, anchoring it to the wall.

It was bad enough he was the only one who seemed to understand the truth of this ruse the world called love. But his family made their living peddling the idea and legend of it. It was salt in an ever-open wound. How could no one else see? Love was a myth. A crutch. And he couldn't be part of flogging the lie any longer. He rubbed his hand over his head, down his face, then pulled the worn piece of paper from his trouser pocket, unfolding it.

He read the words he already knew by heart.

Dear Mr. Jennings,

We are delighted to accept you as an apprentice at Sánchez Iron and Masonry Works. Your family's skill with design and craftsmanship is well known. We look forward to adding your expertise to our repertoire. Once you have acquired the necessary funds to relocate, please let us know and we will make your lodgings ready.

Sincerely,
Roman Sánchez

Eyeing the door to the shop, Stephen could no longer deny the inevitable. *It's time.* His father would be devastated. But the thought of staying here, hocking jewelry, and reliving his family's legacy day in and day out was enough to bolster his courage to tell his father of his plans to leave. Any shards of regret that remained melted away like the wax in their jewelry molds, leaving only white-hot frustration to solidify in his heart.

Replacing the letter in his pocket, he turned to search for Seamus Jennings. But before he could take a step, his father entered from the back door of the showroom, the faint scent of lavender wafting in his wake. And he wasn't alone.

"Ah, Stephen, there's a good lad. I've someone I want you to meet." Seamus's eyes carried more spark than usual, and there was a bounce in his step Stephen hadn't seen in ages.

Stephen turned his attention to his father's guest. Standing arm in arm with his father was a strikingly beautiful woman. Her golden hair twisted on top of her head in an intricate weave of braids and coils before falling around her shoulders in soft curls. Blue eyes pinned Stephen where he stood, and soft dimples accented her rosy cheeks as she smiled at him. She was beautiful, aye, but something about her seemed . . . amiss. Her dress, too fine. Her posture, too straight. He'd been around long enough to know a beautiful face and beguiling smile meant nothing. The most striking face can hide the blackest heart. What was this lass's secret? Still, Stephen's heart thudded unnaturally against his chest. He told himself it was due to the uncertainty of her presence in the shop and not her allure.

"Stephen, my boy, this is Lady Annabeth De Lacy." Seamus beamed.

Stephen shook himself from his thoughts and turned his eyes sharply to his father. "Lady? De Lacy?" Stephen's voice rose an octave. "As in—"

"How do you do?" Annabeth interrupted him and extended her left hand, fingers daintily dangling down.

Stephen looked from Annabeth to his father and back. "De Lacy?" He practically spat the name out.

"That's right," she continued, hand still extended, and lifted her chin. "My father, Lord De Lacy, is the new landlord for this parish." She cleared her throat and gave her hand a slight twitch, her unblinking eyes boring into Stephen's with expectation. Nae, demand.

Seamus continued to beam. When Stephen failed to respond, Seamus frowned and jerked his head slightly in the direction of the woman. "Where're your manners, lad?"

Making no attempt to mask his irritation at his father bringing a British courtier into the shop, Stephen stepped forward, grasped her fingertips, and waggled her hand briefly before dropping his arm back to his side. "Miss." He nodded curtly. "Father? A word?"

"*Lady* Annabeth is to be your apprentice," Seamus announced, so proud the buttons practically popped off his waistcoat.

"Appren— My what?"

"Just what I said, lad. Lady Annabeth here is to be your apprentice. You're to teach her the way of things. Ensure she knows the legend of the Claddagh, show her how to make the rings. She's quite an accomplished artist." He winked at Annabeth, and she rewarded him with a pearly white grin.

Nodding at Seamus, the woman said, "Please, call me Anna."

Oh, now *she wants to be informal? Not likely.* Stephen glanced at her from the corner of his eye but kept his attention fixed on his father.

An apprentice? What was the old man thinking? Sure, it could work to Stephen's advantage if there were someone capable of staying on when he left. But a woman? And a *British* woman no less? Had his father forgotten they were in Galway? Having a woman like this in the shop could only serve to hurt business, not help it. Unless they wished to cater only to the blow-ins and invaders from across the Channel. Despite his own frustrations, Stephen would sooner die than see that happen. He crossed his arms over his chest, cleared his throat, and repeated himself, this time through gritted teeth. "Father. A word!"

"Och!" Seamus waved a dismissive hand then patted Annabeth's arm. "I'll only be a wee minute, lass. Take a look around the shop, so."

She offered him a polite but tight-lipped smile and took a half step back.

Father and son stepped to the front of the shop, as out of earshot of their new guest as possible. "What's the meaning of this?" Stephen hissed.

"Now, now. It's not as bad as all that." A hint of resignation flickered in the old man's eye.

"Is that so?" Stephen's jaw ached.

Seamus pressed his lips into a thin line and shrugged.

Stephen scoffed. "And what about Tommy, huh? After what they—"

Seamus lifted a silent hand. He stared hard into his son's eyes for a long moment before answering. "No matter what has happened in the past, this is our present right now. You're going to do this." He paused. "I need you to do this."

Stephen's heart hitched at the look in his auld man's eye. But then he glanced back at the woman invading their shop and ire burned anew in his chest. "A British lady?" He ran his hand down his face. "The landlord's *daughter*? Father, have you gone mad?"

"Mad? Have you seen the lass?" He chuckled and winked at Stephen.

Oh, no you don't. Stephen wasn't going to let his father use humor to defuse this situation. Not this time. Not with this. "Be serious, man!"

Seamus's smile faded again, and he closed the small distance between them. Lowering his voice further, he said,

"Serious, ye say? How's this for serious? The British government has sent us lowly Irishmen a new landlord." Seamus glanced over his shoulder then continued, "I don't know if ye'd noticed, but the last one they sent us was a real saint." Sarcasm laced the old man's voice.

Stephen released a puffed laugh. He couldn't deny the previous landlord had been a tyrant. "True."

"Well, that shiny new landlord—who we have no idea whether he will be benevolent or worse than the last fella—has requested we apprentice his daughter. It's a mite out of the ordinary, I'll grant you, but I'm not quite in the mood to cross the Brits at this stage." Footsteps punctuated his point as a unit of soldiers marched past the shop. Whether Irish or British troops was impossible to tell.

Stephen sighed as an unwelcome shiver traversed his spine. He crossed his arms over his chest to stave it. The auld codger had a point, much as he hated to admit it. "Fine, I'll grant you, we need to stay in their good graces, if they even have any. But why me? The pair of ye seem to get on just fine. Why can't ya teach her yerself?"

"In case ya haven't noticed, lad, I'm no spring chicken." He stretched his arms out to accentuate his point. "I'm gettin' too auld to even be running the shop, let alone teachin' another wee one. I was going to talk to ya about it anyway, but when Lord De Lacy approached me last week, it was mere confirmation. It's time."

"Time?" Stephen's brow furrowed. "For what?"

Seamus's hand worked the back of his neck, and he stared at the ground for an uncomfortable stretch of minutes. Finally, he cleared his throat and said, "For you to take over. You're a better jewelry smith than I ever was, and you've a smart head for business on yer shoulders. That last bout with the fever I had over the winter is what clinched it. The shop . . . she's yours." Seamus pulled a handkerchief from his waistcoat pocket and swiped at his eyes. "Come now, lad, and properly meet your apprentice."

Jennifer Deibel is the bestselling and award-winning author of *A Dance in Donegal* and *The Lady of Galway Manor*. She's also a middle school teacher whose work has appeared on (in)courage, on The Better Mom, in *Missions Mosaic* magazine, and others. With firsthand immersive experience abroad, Jennifer writes stories that help redefine home through the lens of culture, history, and family. After nearly a decade of living in Ireland and Austria, she now lives in Arizona with her husband and their three children. You can find her online at www.jenniferdeibel.com.

Explore the Emerald Isle in

The Lady of Galway Manor

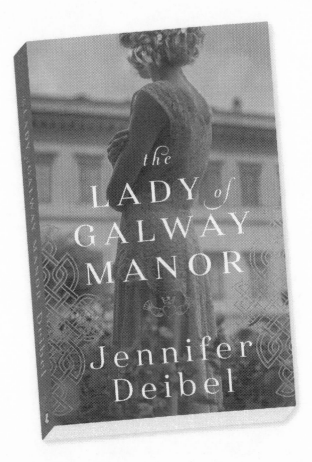

"An immersive read that left me feeling as though I had actually traveled to Ireland. Deibel is proving herself a master at taking readers from all over the world and throwing them into the culture and time of her stories. Pick up this book and be transported to 1920s Ireland, where folklore abounds, conflict is brimming, and love is in the air."

—RACHEL FORDHAM, author of *A Lady in Attendance*

She seeks to navigate
a life she'd never dreamed of . . .
but perhaps was meant to live.

"The misty air of Donegal will seep into your soul just as swiftly and surely as the characters do in Jennifer Deibel's debut novel. Jennifer clearly knows and loves Ireland, and she fills every scene with vivid description and lilting dialogue. *A Dance in Donegal* is a romance, to be sure, yet there are secrets to uncover and a tender spiritual journey at its heart. Pour a cuppa and curl up with this gem of a story."

—LIZ CURTIS HIGGS, *New York Times* bestselling author of *Mine Is the Night*

Revell
a division of Baker Publishing Group
www.RevellBooks.com

Available wherever books and ebooks are sold.

Meet *Jennifer*

Find Jennifer online at
JENNIFERDEIBEL.COM

and sign up for her newsletter to get the latest news
and special updates delivered directly to your inbox.

Follow Jennifer on social media!

JenniferDeibelAuthor   ThisGalsJourney   JenniferDeibel_Author

Printed in the United States
by Baker & Taylor Publisher Services